I0684880

Hunted

Mark Sekela

Hunted

ISBN: 978-0-9879059-3-2

First Addition 2012

Printed in the United States of America

Please visit www.MarkSekela.com for details about the other
books in the Convergence Series.

For Michel, Michael, Marianne and Matthew –
Thank you!

ACKNOWLEDGMENTS

I am grateful for the outstanding professional editing and formatting skills of Mark Hooper and the team at Angel Editing, who once again transformed my manuscript into a novel and my graphics into a cover. Chris Eckley and Melissa Gledhill provided endless feedback and constructive changes for which I cannot possibly thank them enough. I continue to be blessed with Melissa's professional and meticulous proof reading. Finally, I continue to get my inspiration from Matteo and Luca. Their continuous encouragement sustained me during the countless late nights in front of my computer.

Hunted

By

Mark Sekela

CHAPTER 1

JUMP

The last amber rays of sunlight slipped beneath the surface of the ocean, giving birth to a warm Hawaiian evening. Heat continued to radiate from the ink-black lava rocks like the embers of a fading fire. No breeze could be felt; the air was void of the familiar musky scent of the ocean, replaced with the sweet fragrance of frangipani. An unprecedented calm held the water in its grip, thwarting even the smallest of waves from reaching the shore. Darkness gathered as Christine stood on the edge of the cliff, peering into the tranquil water.

"What are you waiting for?" said the voice inside her head.

"What?" she replied and snapped her head around, expecting to see someone.

"Do it!" said the voice.

"I can't."

"You want to, don't you?"

"I do but..."

"Jump!" commanded the voice.

"I can't," she repeated, the tears racing down her cheeks.

"You must."

"Jasper... I'm afraid."

"Don't be."

Christine closed her eyes and stepped off the cliff, leaving her anxiety embedded in the rock. A smile filled her lips as a childlike laugh rushed from deep inside her, fueled by the euphoria of the fall. All sensation of time vanished. Christine was certain the Hand of God carried her to the water, for it felt like hours before she reached the surface. No cool wind poured over her skin, and there was no sound of air filling her ears. She cut through the surface of the water like an Olympic diver, sliding effortlessly into the ocean.

Christine opened her eyes when the warm salty water enveloped her. The swarm of bubbles streaming past her face dissipated like a curtain opening in a theatre, allowing the last remnants of the surface to fade from view. Complete darkness surrounded her. Absent was the urge to breathe, and she remained motionless, her senses held a prisoner of the vacuum she had entered.

"Jasper, where are you?" she asked, but only silence remained. "Where are you?" she repeated, anger evident in her thoughts. The silence was absolute.

Suddenly, the darkness was punctured by a pinhole of bluish-white light. A sharp pain accompanied the appearance of the light. Christine lowered her hands towards her waist in an effort to quell the ache originating from below her ribcage.

The diffuse light continued to expand towards her like an approaching subway train. The pain grew in unison with the light, radiating out from her stomach and growing more intense. The underwater silence was broken by a faint rhythmic pounding. It too began slowly like the beat of a drum but increased in intensity with the light. She was convinced it was her heart about to explode.

Christine focused on the light as it approached in an effort to distract herself from the growing pain. Her incredible physical condition was no match for the burning agony ripping through every nerve in her body. Her mind begged for an end of the torture, and her body curled into a fetal position. Then she noticed it, the once single point of light had become two; like the eyes of a cat reflected in the headlights of a car. Christine grabbed the top of her knees, sinking her fingernails deep into her flesh as the lights came closer in the darkness.

***

"Christine... Chris..." said the soft voice of her mother, Sandra Anderson.

Christine's eyes remained closed when she put her hand on Christine's head. Sandra slid the sheet off, uncovering her daughter's sweat-soaked body still clenching her knees.

"Honey, you need to get up," said Sandra while she pulled back Christine's sun-bleached hair off her face. Like surfacing from a dive, Christine's eyes and mouth opened simultaneously as she inhaled a deep breath.

"Mom?" she said with panic in her voice.

"Yes."

"I had the same dream, but it was worse."

"How so?"

"The light wasn't really a light—it was a pair of eyes. And this time the pain was terrible, like some kind of monster eating me from the inside."

"Don't worry, it's only a dream."

"But it's so real," she said, fighting back her tears. Christine drew upon her faith for support and rarely cried. The twenty-plus years surfing the waves off Kona had carved Christine physically, but her faith in God remained steadfast—the foundation of her strength.

"You need to eat something," said Sandra, not able to hide the concern spilling from her crystal-blue eyes, the very same eyes as her daughter's. "You haven't had a thing since yesterday."

"I'm not hungry."

"Christine S. Anderson, you listen to me, you will eat something this morning even if I have to spoon-feed you myself," raged Sandra in an effort to get Christine to eat.

"Okay, I hate it when you call me that. I'll get something after I shower," she replied, knowing she was going to lose the battle based on the tone of her mother's voice.

"Fine, I'll get it ready. What do you want?"

"Just some fruit, a piece of toast and…"

Christine's request was interrupted by a knock on the front door.

"I'll get it, you go get cleaned up," said Sandra as she walked to the door. When she opened it, a plain-clothes police officer stood on the porch.

"Hello, Officer," Sandra said, spotting the officer's police badge hanging from her breast pocket.

"Good morning, ma'am."

"Can I help you?" asked Sandra in a surprisingly relaxed voice.

"I'm Officer Sorren. Is your daughter Christine at home?"

"Is there a problem?

"No. Is she home?" the officer repeated.

"Yes, but she's in the shower. Can I help?"

The office looked at Sandra and decided to begin her questioning with her.

"Do you know a Jesse Struger?"

"Yes. Why?"

"Have you seen him recently?"

"No, he hasn't been around in weeks. Is everything okay?"

"His family is looking for him. They haven't been able to contact him for the past two weeks and…" continued the officer, but she stopped mid-sentence to answer her radio.

"Excuse me, Mrs. Anderson, I have to leave. Please have your daughter call us if she has any contact with Mr. Struger."

"Of course, immediately."

"Thank you," said the officer as she swiftly made her way to her car.

***

Christine entered the bathroom and walked directly to the shower, avoiding her reflection in the mirror, as she had been doing for the last two weeks. She turned on the hot water and waited patiently for the steam to fill the room, rendering the mirror useless. The past two weeks had left Christine emotionally and physically debilitated. Each morning the sight of herself in the mirror sent her racing to the toilet, nauseated to the point of throwing up. Her naked body unleashed a flood of memories beginning with the image of Jesse holding a bloodied piece of wood and ending with the morning her mother had found her naked and shivering on the sands of Kua Bay.

Time offered Christine no relief from the anguish and confusion of that horrible night. Her uncontrollable attraction to Jasper, a guy she had known for less than an hour, remained steeped in confusion. *Why did I covet him? How could I kiss him?* Their naked bodies were entangled and on the brink of consummating their carnal attraction when Jesse had delivered the fatal blow. *How could he do it?* she thought, and the image of Jasper played over in her mind.

Christine's thoughts focused on Jesse as she left the shower feeling lightheaded. *Where is he now?* Suddenly, another thought concerned her more, and her mind overflowed with anger toward her mother.

Why won't she talk about it?

CHAPTER 2

DR. BROOME

"Chris, breakfast is ready!" Sandra called from the kitchen of their small home.

"Okay, I'll be there in a sec. Who was at the door?"

"Wrong address. Someone looking for the neighbor," Sandra lied.

Christine dressed in her usual shorts and t-shirt and searched through the mess in her room for her ball cap, which she used to control her shoulder-length hair. She spotted its bright red brim sticking out from below her bed and picked it up. When she returned to a standing position, the room began to sway and a thousand points of light filled her vision. Unable to keep her balance, Christine fell forward, landing on her bed.

She rolled onto her back and stared at the ceiling fan, which was spinning even though it wasn't on. Christine regained control of herself and sat up on the edge of her bed. Like the nausea, the loss of balance had become a regular morning occurrence over the past two weeks.

"What's the hold up?" Sandra asked, now standing in the bedroom doorway. She saw Christine's disorientation and quickly took a seat on the bed next to her daughter. "You okay?"

The strength of Christine's faith forbade her from lying, so she scrambled to find an answer. She knew if she told her mother about her dizziness, they would be driving to the doctor's office that instant. That was something neither could afford, as Christine only made minimum wage at the Surf and Dive shop, and Sandra worked at the local Wal-Mart as a cashier. The cost of a visit to the doctor would put a financial strain on them both, so Christine knew she had to avoid the question. Her response was immediate and truthful.

"Fine, I got a little lightheaded from getting out of the hot shower too quickly."

"You're sure?"

"Yes, Sandy, now go to work," replied Christine, knowing this would agitate her mother and quell any further questions.

"All right, that's enough," Sandra said through a smile. "It's Monday, and I want to leave a bit early so I can stop by the shop and tell Marco you won't be in for the rest of this week."

Christine's face immediately formed a scowl as she leaped from the bed.

"What, you're joking! The only surfing I've done is on the Web. I'm tired of just reading emails all day. Kerri and Ty keep emailing me photos of the waves they've been riding. I can't spend another week stuck in here, I need to get out this place. Besides, it's the beginning of October and the start of the tourist season. I'll lose my job."

"Don't worry. I'll speak to Marco and let him know you're still sick. It'll be fine. Now get some rest."

"I don't need any more rest, I'm sick all right—sick of this place."

"Listen, Chris, you've got to relax; you've been through a lot."

"What do you know of what I've been through? You weren't there. You won't even talk to me about it!"

"We've been through this. We'll talk, but right now the best thing for you is rest. Let things settle. Please, just stay home and rest. I promise we'll talk."

"Fine. Next weekend I'm out of here," snapped Christine,

her stubbornness and independence unwillingly giving way to her mother's request.

As the week progressed, things didn't improve for Christine; her bouts of nausea and dizziness increased, making mornings unbearable. She could handle the sickness, but it was nighttime she hated most. The nightmares grew worse and continued to unsettle her even when she was awake.

***

The sunlight lifted the darkness from Christine's room as a flock of Asian Myna birds cackled outside her bedroom window. Their six-o'clock chatter was deafening and woke her like an alarm clock.

Sandra worked the early shift on Fridays, and the smell of coffee brewing indicated she was already up and getting ready for work. The fragrant aroma was usually pleasing to Christine, but not this morning.

Her throat tightened as her empty stomach convulsed. She leaped out of bed, tripping over the pile of dirty clothes lying on the floor, and raced to the bathroom, only to find it occupied. Cupping her mouth with her hand, she turned for the kitchen. The acid filled her mouth before pouring out onto her hand. Christine grabbed the edge of the counter and leaned over the sink, heaving twice more.

Not wanting her mother to see her state, Christine quickly turned the water on and rinsed her hands and the sink.

The bathroom door opened, and her mother popped her head out, peering down the hall towards the kitchen.

"Wow, you're up early this morning, everything okay?"

"Fine, just getting a glass of water," Christine said as she reached into the cupboard above the sink and removed a glass without facing her mother.

With her legs still shaking from the power of the stomach contractions, Christine scooted back to her bed the second she heard the bathroom door close again. She knew this would keep her mother from asking any more questions before leaving for work.

Thursday night had been the worst yet. The reoccurring nightmare had finally taken its toll. Christine was emotionally exhausted, and the constant nausea was leaving her physically weak. She knew something was wrong— something serious. It had to be more than stress, which her mother insisted was the problem.

The steady clicking of the clock resonated inside her head as Christine lay patiently waiting for her mother to leave. Anxiety grew in her mind and quickly blossomed into fear. *What if I have cancer? Maybe I'm dying. Why is God doing this to me?* Her remaining nausea evaporated, to be replaced by determination. Not willing to suffer any longer, she decided to see a doctor.

Christine lay in bed with her back to the open door, concealing the conviction from her mother. Desperate to begin her day away from her mother's prison sentence, she began counting the clicks of the clock. Her impatience was both a blessing and a curse. Once she had decided to do something, nothing could stop her, and she considered waiting a form of torture.

Christine heard Sandra wash her coffee cup and listened for the sound of her mother's car driving over the crushed lava rock driveway. She then got out of bed. The anticipation of leaving the house for the first time in three weeks filled her with happiness—a feeling noticeably absent from her life at the moment.

Christine threw on some clothes and her ball cap, grabbed her wallet and phone and tossed them on the passenger seat as she jumped into her Jeep.

The drive down the island highway rejuvenated her. The morning sunlight filtered through the clouds surrounding the summit of Mauna Kea, coloring the ocean a deep turquoise blue. The breaking waves soared fifty feet above the shoreline, causing snow-white wash to crash over the lava-rock cliffs.

The view prompted an explosion of memories: surfing with Jesse at their private beach, hammering the spikes in the surfboard sign... Jasper's lifeless body floating in the water. Her thoughts were interrupted by the rocking of the Jeep as the passenger side wheels left the pavement, knocking Christine back to the present. She regained control and focused her attention back on the road.

After a quick stop at an ATM, Christine realized she didn't have enough money to pay a doctor. *How am I going to pay?* she thought as she returned to her Jeep. The last time she had needed money and couldn't ask her mom for it was when she was sixteen. It was for a new surfboard—the same one she had used to make the sign at the private beach. Father Shannon lent her the money that time, and he never told her mom. Christine knew she could trust him to do it again.

She parked her Jeep in front of the rectory but sat glued to her seat, tormented by what she was about to do. Not since she was seven and had her first confession heard by Father Shannon had so much trepidation pumped through her veins. To get help she would either have to tell Father Shannon what had happened or lie to him. But there was no way she could tell him, and lying simply wasn't an option.

The sun intensified as it rose above the clouds, and her ball cap offered little protection from the heat. The conundrum grew tiresome, wearing on her already fragile mental state. Still with no solution, Christine followed through with her decision and knocked on the rectory door, not knowing what to say.

Father Shannon took a few minutes to arrive at the door, not expecting anyone so early in the morning. A warm smile filled his face when he opened the door.

"Chris, it's so nice to see you. What a pleasant surprise. How you feeling?"

"Hi, Father. Not so great. That's kind of why I'm here."

"What is it? Come in, come in. What can I do for you?"

Chris entered the rectory and took a position leaning on the wall just inside the door. Her heart sank as she gathered up the courage to ask.

"Father, I hate to ask..." she started but was interrupted before finishing.

"What is it, dear?"

"I need to see a doctor, and I don't have enough money to cover the visit right now. I haven't been able to work lately, so I'm a bit short. I don't want to put mom out," she explained while staring at the floor, unable to look into Father Shannon's eyes.

"What's wrong? Are you okay?"

"I don't know; I'm just not myself."

"Do you want me to take you to the hospital?" he asked, unable to hide his concern.

"No, I'm going to the clinic."

"You're certain?"

Christine nodded.

"Okay, hang on. I'll get it," said the priest walking away. He returned a minute later and handed Christine two hundred dollars.

"Thanks so much, Father," Christine said, the relief unmistakable in her voice.

"You sure I can't take you?" Father Shannon asked once more.

"No thanks. I'll go to the doctor, and I promise to let you know what happens, but I don't want mom to worry."

"I understand. It'll be our little secret," he said while throwing Christine a wink.

"Thanks, Father," Christine said as she wrapped her arms around his chest, giving him an extra long bear hug. This was her way of thanking him for not asking more questions, even though she knew that's what the wink really meant.

She returned to her Jeep and headed toward the medical clinic.

Christine pulled off her hat and tossed it on the passenger seat, covering her cell phone, and then adjusted her hair in the rearview mirror. She took a deep breath as she got out of the Jeep.

Just past eight o'clock in the morning, she entered the clinic to find the waiting area already filled with people, leaving only a single chair unoccupied.

"Good morning. How can I help you?" asked the woman sitting behind the counter.

"I'd like to see a doctor," Christine replied.

"Is it an emergency?"

"No, why?" asked Christine, surprised by the question.

"Emergency medical care is provided by the hospital; we only administer routine medical services here."

"Oh, I just need a check-up."

"Have you been here before?"

"No, this is my first visit."

"Please fill out these forms and give them back to me when you're done," the woman explained and handed Christine a clipboard with the forms attached.

The forms consisted mostly of checking a 'Yes' or 'No' box, and the process went smoothly until the final section: 'Reason for today's visit.'

Christine paused for a moment before writing in the box 'Trouble sleeping' and returned the clipboard to the woman.

"Please have a seat. The doctor will see you shortly," said the woman as she smiled, knowing what 'shortly' really meant.

Christine returned to her seat and stared absently at the TV hanging from the wall in the corner of the waiting room. An hour and a half passed, but Christine never noticed; she was too distracted by her thoughts of what to tell the doctor. She didn't hear the woman call her name the first time from behind the counter.

"Christine Anderson," repeated the woman, this time standing up.

"Yes, that's me!" Christine leaped out of her seat.

"The doctor will see you now. This way please," said the woman, and Christine followed her to a small examination room.

Christine took a seat in a vinyl and chrome chair positioned across from the examination table as the woman closed the door on the way out. The cold chair sent a shiver up her spine, leaving her arms covered in goose bumps. A moment later, a middle-aged man entered the room dressed in Bermuda shorts and a navy blue shirt covered with bright yellow hibiscus blossoms.

"Hi, I'm Dr. Broome," he said through a gaping smile.

"I'm Chris." She instinctively lifting her hand to shake his, but his remained attached to the clipboard.

"So, what can I do for you today, Chris?" he asked without lifting his eyes from the information Christine had filled out in the waiting room.

Before Christine could reply, he said, "I see you're having trouble sleeping. How long has this been going on?"

"But it's not the lack of sleep as much as the nightmares."

"Did these nightmares start at the same time?" asked the doctor, finally looking directly at her.

"Yes."

"Has something traumatic happened to you lately; a car accident or a death in the family for example?"

"I broke up with my boyfriend," she said, hoping to stop any further questioning.

"Sorry to hear that. Was it a long-term relationship?"

"Ten years."

"Wow, that's longer than I've been married." The doctor laughed. "I suspect you're stressed and slightly depressed from the breakup."

Christine shifted her eyes away from the doctor's, attempting to hide her anger and frustration. *Mom was right,* she thought as her cheeks flushed. *I just blew a hundred bucks on advice my mother's already given me.*

19

"I'm going to give you a prescription for some sleeping pills. You can take them an hour before you go to bed until your sleep returns to normal. If your sleeping doesn't improve over the next two weeks, come back, and we'll try an antidepressant," he said as he removed a small prescription pad from his shorts pocket. He scribbled the prescription on the pad and ripped the sheet off, handing it to Christine before opening the door.

"Will these pills help with the nausea too?"

The doctor stopped and turned to face her.

"Nausea? How frequent?" he asked, raising an eyebrow.

"I've been having dizzy spells and vomiting almost every day."

"How long has this been going on?"

"It started the same time as the nightmares."

"I'd like to run a couple quick tests if that's okay with you."

"What kind of tests?" Christine asked, the anger rapidly dissipating to be replaced with concern.

"Some simple urine tests—they'll only take a minute. We do them right here in the office. Are you in a hurry?"

"No."

"Great. The nurse will get you a sample bottle, and you can use the bathroom around the corner. When you're done, come back and we can go over the results."

Christine heard the doctor speak to someone out of her view, and a minute later, a nurse came in, handing Christine a small orange-capped plastic bottle.

Returning from the bathroom, Christine placed the half-full bottle on the nurse's cart and returned to the examination room. She sat on the chair reading the medical posters on the opposite wall feeling her heart begin to race.

The pounding in her chest accelerated with each passing moment; it was so hard Christine was certain she could hear it. The anxiety rendered rational thoughts useless, and her mind filled with visions of cancer and other terminal illnesses. Only once before had such strong feelings overpowered her body—the moment she met Jasper.

The door suddenly opened, interrupting Christine's train of thought, and Dr. Broome entered the room carrying what appeared to be a couple of pens in his left hand. Not having a poker face, Christine's near panic attack was clearly evident.

Dr. Broome, aware of her condition, kept his expression professional.

"Chris, I need to ask you a few personal questions. Is that okay?"

"Sure… What's wrong?"

"When you completed the forms, did you understand everything?"

"Yes, why?" she asked, looking for some indication of what was wrong from Dr. Broome's eyes.

"When was the last time you were intimate with someone?"

"Why? What is it? Is it herpes or something?" she asked, then held her breath in anticipation of the answer.

"You understand anything you say to me is kept in strictest confidence?" the doctor said in an effort to reassure her.

"I have nothing to hide," Christine replied.

Dr. Broome handed her the two test strips.

CHAPTER 3

POSITIVE

C hristine stared at the two white strips in his hand, completely unaware of what they were. Confusion filled her face as she looked up at the doctor for guidance.

His expressionless face began to warm when he realized she didn't know what she was looking at. His facial transformation did nothing to reduce her accelerating anxiety, however.

"Do you know what these are?" he asked.

"No."

"Well, Chris, these are pregnancy test strips," he stated in a slow and clear tone. "They are used..."

"I know what they're used for," interrupted Christine. "Why are you giving them to me?"

"I'm not. I'm showing you the results. It's quite clear on both of them if you look right here," said Dr. Broome as he rolled one of the sticks and pointed so Christine could see the tiny blue '+' sign displayed in the small plastic window at the top of the strip.

"You're pregnant."

"I don't think so," she said with a nervous laugh.

"Well, I'm quite certain. These tests are very accurate, and we always use two different brands to be certain we don't make a mistake."

"Well, I'm positive you have. I've never even had intercourse. I'm Catholic; my faith is everything to me."

"The nightmares, poor sleep, dizziness, nausea. These all point clearly to pregnancy."

Christine thought about the last couple of weeks and the sickness that welcomed her every morning, but she refused to accept the reason.

He's wrong. It's impossible, she thought.

"I'm telling you, it's not possible. I'm still a virgin," she protested emphatically without the slightest hint of hesitation.

"You're absolutely sure?" asked Dr. Broome, now staring directly into Christine's ice-blue eyes in search of the slightest hint of doubt.

None surfaced as she responded, "Yes, one hundred percent," she said as she slid to the very edge of her chair.

"And you've no recollection of any recent sexual activity of any kind?"

"No! I'm telling you, I'm not pregnant," Christine said. The insistence in her voice was enough to convince the doctor to perform a third test.

"When was your last period?"

The question hit her like a kick in the stomach, knocking the wind out of her. Confused and dazed by the last few weeks, she found herself unable to recall.

"What's the date?"

"Friday, October 8th."

The answer was the final crippling blow. She was over a week late, and she had never missed a period in her life.

"I'm late," she said, feeling embarrassed for not realizing it until that moment.

"Okay, we'll do it once more just to be thorough. Do you think you'll be able to fill another bottle, or do you want to administer the test yourself?"

"I'll do it."

"I'll be right back."

Dr. Broome left the examination room and returned a few seconds later with an unopened test strip, handing it to Christine.

"Place it in your urine stream."

"Okay," she said and walked to the bathroom.

Christine subdued the shock and imprisoned her emotions with denial. She followed the doctor's instructions and returned to the examination room to wait for the test strip to display a result. She leaned against the examination table, holding the test strip so she could watch the results window.

Dr. Broome entered the room just as the faint outline of a '+' sign appeared in the window. Christine slid back in the chair, unable to speak, and tried in vain to make some sense of what was happening. A stunned look on her face replaced the need to speak, and her continuous disbelief materialized as an unconscious back and forth shaking of her head.

"Chris, I can see this is unplanned."

Christine didn't acknowledge him and continued to block out her surroundings, oblivious to his presence. She snapped out of her shock when he placed his hand on her shoulder.

"Chris, are you okay to answer a few more questions?"

She used sheer determination to force herself to nod a 'yes' and focus her attention towards Dr. Broome.

"You have no idea how you got pregnant, correct?"

Christine could only shake her head, still incapable of acknowledging that she was pregnant.

"Have you been to a nightclub, rave or party where there were a lot of people and maybe drugs and alcohol? Have you any unexplained bruises or injuries—particularly in the genital area?"

"No. Why?"

"Is it possible you were drugged and raped?"

"No, that didn't happen. Nothing happened. That's what I'm trying to tell you. I can't be... I just can't be."

"I'm going to call a colleague; she can help you. I'll make

sure she'll see you immediately. You do have a number of options at your disposal, and I think you need to discuss them with a professional."

Dr. Broome pulled his prescription pad from his pocket and wrote 'Dr. Roberta Wilson, Kona County Mental Health Clinic, Unit 43-50, Old Island Highway' then handed the paper to Christine.

"I want you to see her today. Do you feel well enough to drive?"

"Yes, I'll be fine. Thank you, Dr. Broome."

"Please, take your time. You can stay here as long as you need to collect yourself."

"Thanks."

Christine remained in the room for only a moment before the urge to leave overwhelmed her. She walked to the front desk, paid her bill and left the office.

She sat in her Jeep, holding on to the steering wheel for support. *A number of options,* she thought as she pulled her hair through the back of her cap. *He meant abortion.* The meaning of Dr. Broome's last statement finally took hold in her mind, and she was angry. The thought was so vile she nearly vomited; it went against every moral fiber in her body.

The suggestion of an abortion was sacrilegious. The need to pray returned to her for the first time in weeks, and she began to crave the strength her faith brought her. *That's it,* she thought. *Father Shannon.* Faith coursed through her body like an injection; it was the perfect antidote to the venom left by Dr. Broome. *Father Shannon will know what to do.*

Christine couldn't recall the drive back to the church, her mind consumed with the morning's events.

She drove into the church parking lot, and her spirits lifted when she spotted Father Shannon's car.

After three unanswered knocks on the rectory door, Christine walked to the front of the church. The sight of the large wooden doors pierced her heart like a dagger, triggering the memory of when she first met Jasper. She mustered the strength to pull the heavy door open and stepped inside.

Father Shannon was changing the linens on the altar with the help of one of his deacons, Richard Whyte. They didn't notice Christine until she approached the foot of the three steps elevating the altar from the church floor.

"Chris, how nice to see you again," said Father Shannon as she walked up the steps.

The priest at once recognized the look on her face and put down his end of the tablecloth. Richard released his end and followed Father Shannon towards Christine, reaching her before him.

"Hello, Christine," the deacon said, his unforgiving face unable to crack a smile, and his eyes shifting to the bright red ball cap on her head.

"Hi, Mr. Whyte," Christine replied, cognizant of the meaning of his icy stare.

"Oh, I forgot," Christine apologized.

She then turned to face Father Shannon as she went for her cap. She reached behind her head and lifted her ponytail in order to pull it through the back of the cap. In doing so, she exposed the fish-shaped birthmark on the back of her neck.

Chapter 4

Run

Richard's face, no longer an apathetic monolith, transformed at the sight of the birthmark. The image shown to him and Father Shannon three weeks before by Father Derksen and the other Vatican staff was still fresh in his mind. Christine's birthmark was identical to that image—the one they were searching for.

Father Shannon's eyes never left Christine's face as she approached him, the distress in her eyes signaled her need to talk to him, but Richard spoke first.

"That's an interesting tattoo, Christine. When did you get it."

Surprised by Richard's question, Christine turned and faced him without attempting to hide her confusion.

"What?"

"The Sign of the Fish, the Christian tattoo on the back of your neck. When did you get it?"

"That's not a tattoo; it's a birthmark. Why?"

"Really? It looks just like a fish. I'd swear it was a tattoo," Richard said, looking at Father Shannon with intent.

Father Shannon interrupted their discussion with his own question. "What brings you here, dear? Is there something I can do for you?" he asked with his eyes as much as his words.

Richard, unhappy at the interruption, locked his eyes on Father Shannon, wanting to gain his attention.

"Father, might I have a word with you?" he asked.

"Of course, but first let me find out why Chris has made a special visit here today."

"But, Father..." interjected Richard.

"Richard, I'm certain it can wait. Let's go to my office, Chris," Father Shannon said, putting an end to Richard's attempt to speak to him.

Richard couldn't prevent his frustration from overwhelming him. *She has to be the one they're looking for,* he thought. *And Shannon doesn't know it.* Richard returned to the altar to finish his work, anxious to meet with Father Shannon alone. He watched as the priest and Christine disappeared at the back of the church.

***

Father Shannon opened the door for Christine to enter his small office, closing it behind him. The room was filled with beams of multicolored light coming from the small stained-glass windows crowning the two windows at opposite ends of the room. The one to the right of the desk depicted a praying Virgin Mary while the other the crucifixion. Half the room was filled with an oversized wooden desk so covered with paperwork that the surface was invisible. Like the top of his desk, the wall behind it was also covered, not with artwork or religious paraphernalia but with hundreds of photographs. Each contained an image of Father Shannon holding a child. Christine had never been in his office before, and for a moment, she forgot the urgency of her visit. It didn't take long for the forbidding reason for her visit to return. The hundreds of baby photos served as a perfect reminder.

"Chris, what's the matter?" Father Shannon asked.

Christine sat staring at the wall of photos, unable to speak. There was no place for her to begin. Shock and disbelief coursed through her veins, quelling the fear that attempted to escape. Confident her faith would rescue her from the train wreck of confusion the morning had delivered, she awakened her inner strength and smiled at the priest.

"Father, I don't know where to begin… it's unbelievable."

"Chris, I've known you since birth. Just like the rest of my flock," he said while lifting his hand towards the wall of photos. "But you've always been special to me. Please, tell me."

"I'm pregnant." She blurted the words out like admitting guilt at a trial.

"Oh, I see," said Father Shannon, and he paused for a moment. "Well, this isn't as bad as I… It's much better than what I was imagining," he said in an effort to comfort her. "I was worried that you might be seriously ill."

Christine's hands shook in preparation of what she was about to say. The words spun around her mind like a roulette wheel, the final outcome unknown to the last second. She glanced at the stained-glass window and the courage came. She spoke, but the words didn't flow freely from her mind.

"Father, that's not it."

"What is it?"

"I'm… I'm a virgin,'" she coaxed from her lips as her crystal-blue eyes strained to hold contact with his.

"I don't understand."

"That's just it, I don't either. I just can't be pregnant," she said, struggling to hold back tears.

"Are you sure? How do you know?"

"The doctor tested me this morning—three times!"

"Could it be a mistake? It happens."

"I thought the same thing, but I've had other signs. You know… morning sickness and stuff."

Father Shannon sat quietly, collecting his thoughts while Christine tried to hide her emotional turmoil in the silence. Father Shannon was as close to an actual father as Christine had ever known. Their closeness allowed a tidal wave of emotions to fill her thoughts, cumulating into a single, intense feeling—shame. Other than her mother, no one knew the conviction of her faith more than Father Shannon.

"Did you and Jesse...?"

"No!" she shouted. "It never happened, not with him or anyone. Like I said, I'm a virgin!"

Father Shannon left his seat and walked over to the window on the right, pausing in front of it before looking up.

"I only know of one other miraculous..."

A knock on the door interrupted him midsentence and drew a sigh of annoyance.

"Yes?" he asked without hiding his displeasure at the interruption.

The door opened slowly and Richard entered the office.

"Sorry for the interruption, Father, but I must have a word with you now—it's urgent," said Richard without taking his eyes off Christine.

She remained seated, watching Father Shannon's face become angrier.

He walked to the open door and cast Christine an apologetic glance for the disruption. Christine smiled back.

"What is it, Richard?" the priest snapped.

"Can we speak in private, Father? I only need a moment?"

Upon hearing his request, Christine started to rise from her seat when Father Shannon placed his hand on her shoulder, indicating she should remain seated.

"Certainly, let's go outside," he said, and the two men left the office, closing the door behind them.

Christine had gained a little reassurance from her conversation with Father Shannon. Her spirits were lifting when the sound of an argument in the hall captured her attention. The voices grew louder, and she strained to hear their conversation.

"I'm telling you what I saw, she has the mark. The one they're looking for," said Richard, his voice in decrescendo, concerned Christine may be able to hear their discussion.

"I don't care if she hears. Christine has far more pressing issues to deal with. I'm not going to ask her," replied Father Shannon, equally as loud.

"But they requested we…"

"I told you, I don't care what the Vatican wants. Right now, I have a young lady who desperately needs my help. I promise we'll deal with this later. Thank you, Richard, I must go now," Father Shannon said, the finality unmistakable in his tone.

When the office door opened, Christine turned in her seat and looked out at Richard. He was texting on his phone and raised his head to meet her eyes. Stone faced, her eyes cut through Richard, forcing him to look away before she turned back and looked at Father Shannon.

***

Darkness filled the small Vatican flat as Father Derksen entered his home. It was late on a Friday night even for him to be getting home. As the official head of the Vatican Secret Service, the dreaded VSS, there was no time of day he was not expected to work.

Father Derksen undid the crimson rope around his waist and removed his jet-black robe in preparation for sleep. His phone chirped twice, indicating the arrival of an email, so he walked over to his nightstand and retrieved it. He glanced at the time on the screen. *It's nearly one in the morning. This better be important,* he thought. Not recognizing the sender's name, 'HawaiianWhyte,' and because it was so late, Father Derksen assumed it was spam and decided to delete it. He had scrolled the cursor through the menu to 'delete' when a thought entered his mind. *Could it be?* He opened the email.

Dear Father Derksen, I recognized the symbol you inquired about a few weeks back. A woman who attends our parish has the identical shape on the back of her neck. Her name is Christine Anderson, and she claims it's a birthmark, but I think it's a tattoo. I've never seen such a perfectly shaped birthmark like that before. I can put

her in touch with you if you'd like to speak with her.
Sincerely, God's Servant, Richard.

Father Derksen was so taken aback that he fumbled with his phone before he could hit the speed dial. He waited for the line to pick up.

"You have important news?" said a man's voice on the other end of the line, seemingly unaffected by the late call.

"Sir, you were right. I think we've found her," said Father Derksen, trying to contain the exuberance in his voice.

"Where?"

"She's still in Hawaii. St. Michael's—remember that's Shannon's parish?"

"I want that island shut down. Nobody gets on a flight without us knowing who it is. Do you understand?" the voice demanded.

"I'll see to it at once."

"Give me Shannon's number."

"I'll send it to you."

"Call Gino, have him ready the Vatican jet and meet me at the airport. I have some calls to make," the voice said before the phone was hung up.

***

Father Shannon stood quietly facing his wall of photographs, his attention focused on the children's images. He found what he was looking for, and his eyes settled on a twenty-five-year-old photo of him holding an infant. He leaned closer to the wall, straining to examine every detail of the photograph. It was one of the first he had put on the wall. Printed on the bottom right of the photo was 'C.S. Anderson 1985.'

"Is everything all right, Father?" Christine asked.

"Fine. It's you I'm worried about," he said, still staring at the photo.

Rational thought continued to evade Christine; the hallway conversation further exasperated her, and she remained confused. The uncontrollable urge to leave saturated her entire body, rendering all her other thoughts secondary. Barely able to contain herself, she leaped from her chair when Father Shannon turned to face her.

"What's wrong, Chris?"

"Nothing. I have to go."

"But we haven't finished."

"Thanks so much, Father. You're so kind, but I really need to go."

"Where are you...?"

Father Shannon's words were interrupted by the ringing of the telephone on his desk.

"Home. I just want to go home," she said and turned to leave.

"Wait, Chris, please wait," the priest begged.

Christine didn't turn and raced toward the door.

As she left the office, she heard Father Shannon pick up the phone and say, "Hello. Yes, I remember you, nice to speak to you again. How can I help you?"

When Christine left the church, her eyes began to tear from the bright sunlight and the confusion filling her thoughts.

Christine drove down the Island Highway completely on instinct until she saw the green and white Henry Street road sign. Seemingly under a spell, she turned into parking lot of the shopping mall where her mother worked. Sandra wouldn't get off work for another half-hour, but Christine had to see her.

The sliding glass door opened, allowing the cool air from inside the store to cover her body, releasing a shiver. The cold was short lived, and the anticipation of seeing her mother caused her heart to race, in turn chasing the goose bumps from her arms.

Sandra was working the cash register farthest from the

entrance. Busy with a line of customers, she didn't notice her daughter come in.

Christine walked halfway to her mother's lane when Sandra caught sight of her. Surprised that Christine wasn't at home, Sandra greeted her with a forced smile. The instant their eyes met, Sandra knew something was wrong. She knew her daughter well, and Christine was terrible at disguising her emotions.

"Excuse me," said the next woman in line as she waited to pay for her articles.

Sandra turned back to face the woman. "I'm sorry. I'll only be a moment," she said, and turned to talk to Christine, but she was gone.

Still functioning on impulse, and aided by the sick feeling in her stomach, Christine decided this wasn't the best place to tell her mother of the day's events. She ran back to her Jeep and had just left the parking lot when her phone rang. She turned it over so she could see the call display. 'Mom' scrolled across the screen. A rare moment of complete uncertainty glued Christine's hands to the steering wheel and prevented her from answering. The phone rang three more times before she made the decision to answer it.

"Hi, Mom."

"What's wrong, Chris?"

"Can we talk when you get home?" asked Christine, not wanting to explain on the phone.

"Christine S. Anderson, what's wrong?" Sandra demanded.

Christine searched her mind for an answer that would satisfy her mother for now. The only thought she could conjure up was the topic of the hallway conversation between Father Shannon and Richard Whyte.

"It's nothing really. I was coming to see you when I began to feel a little nauseous, and you were really busy. How did you get away?"

"I took a washroom break. What did you want to see me about?"

"I was sick of staying in the house, so I decided to visit Father Shannon. I overheard him arguing with Richard Whyte in the hall about me."

"Arguing? About you? What on earth about?"

"That's the weird thing; it had something to do with my birthmark."

"What!" Sandra nearly shouted.

"Mom, relax," Christine said through a nervous laugh.

"Christine, what exactly did they say?" Sandra demanded, attempting to hold her concern at bay.

"It was hard to tell. It was really strange because they were talking about my birthmark and the Vatican," explained Christine, not hiding any of the confusion in her voice.

There was no reply from Sandra, only silence for twenty seconds.

"Mom, Mom, what's wrong? What's the big deal?" asked Christine, beginning to detect the concern on her mother's end of the phone.

"Christine, where are you?"

"I'm almost home, why?"

"Stop! Don't go home! Turn around at once. Do you understand? Chris? Chris?" Sandra insisted.

Christine heard her mother's words but couldn't process them fast enough. She continued her course, making the turn into their driveway.

"What's going on?" Christine asked, growing impatient with her mother's nonsensical orders.

"Just listen to me. Turn around and get out of there. Meet me at Honokohau Marina. I'll explain everything there."

"Okay. I'll turn around."

Christine had just pulled the Jeep over to the side of the driveway when she saw the flash of police lights in the rearview mirror. The police were waiting for the traffic to stop so they could turn into the Anderson driveway.

"Mom, did you call the police?"

"Chris! Run, run, get out of there now! Don't let them find

you!" Sandra yelled into the phone.

Christine had never been in trouble with the law, so obeying her mother's command went against everything she had been taught. However, confused, she scrambled out of the Jeep as the noise of the police car's tires racing down the crushed-rock driveway became louder.

It had been years since she had raced through the lush green vegetation surrounding their home. The trail was overgrown, and the path faded, making it difficult for her to navigate the twists and turns in the shade of the tropical canopy.

The sound of the police car sliding to a stop in the gravel jolted her into action. The route through the forest unfolded in front of her as if she was fifteen again. Like a deer hunted by a cougar, Christine navigated the bush flawlessly. The pounding in her chest grew stronger with every step. Afraid to look back, Christine continued her escape, her long legs moving her effortlessly through the tangle of vines and roots.

"Stop!" shouted a police officer, but Christine never missed a step.

The Hawaiian sun was relentless; its mid-afternoon heat penetrated the forest and pressed hard on her chest. Her body performed like a machine, gulping in the air laden with humidity. The heavy footfalls of the officers resonated through the foliage but faded slightly as she gained a lead.

The tropical canopy acted like a steam room, offering no relief for the fully uniformed officers, and this gave Christine the advantage.

Adrenaline rushed through her veins, putting her mind on autopilot. She glided through the trees, skipping over roots and ducking below branches. The reason for the familiarity of her escape route became apparent; she was following a childhood route. Jesse and Christine had raced down this trail a hundred times before.

Her adrenaline high collapsed when she emerged from the greenery that shielded her. Her running waned to a few quick steps, and horror overtook her flight response. The unlimited expanse of the Pacific Ocean stretched before her—she arrived at a dead end.

Christine approached the pinnacle of the lava cliffs where Jesse had taught her to dive. The jagged ebony cliffs remained unchanged, towering four stories above the azure water below, the surging waves swirling a lighter shade of blue.

Christine's speed put her on the edge of the cliff ten seconds before her pursuers. With her bravado left behind in her childhood, she gazed over the edge.

The officers emerged from the bush completely out of breath. She heard the larger male officer's voice first as he spoke into his radio.

"Stop!" he shouted as he clipped the microphone to his collar and walked toward her.

"Don't do it!" yelled his female partner.

Christine's body held motionless as if fused to the rock. Christine continued to stare out over the ocean when a single white tern floated in front of her just a few feet from her face.

Warm droplets of water carried by the sea breeze covered her face as the waves met the rocks below. She resigned to give herself to the police, never knowing the reason for fleeing in the first place.

The sound of the officers' labored breathing grew louder over the breaking surf. Christine slowly turned to face her pursuers, who stood just out of reach. Christine cast her eyes toward the woman.

"Don't do it," repeated the female officer, but this time she used a more motherly voice as she lifted her hand toward Christine. Their eyes never broke contact.

A few seconds of silence followed until it was interrupted by a call over the police radio.

"Bravo 212 and 310 have located the murder suspect," said the dispatcher.

"Murder suspect?" Christine repeated in horror.

Her face filled with anguish upon hearing the announcement. She looked down toward the officer's hand, but Christine's eyes ignored it, focusing instead on the ground beneath her feet. A faded etching remained barely discernible on the black lava rock. It was heart shaped with the letters 'CA + JS' scraped in its center. The memory struck like a bolt of lightning, galvanizing her strength. Christine's eyes reconnected with the officer's for an instant.

Then, she stepped backwards.

CHAPTER 5

GUARDIAN ANGEL

I t was a backwards step in time. Each passing second of the fall seemed to erase a year from Christine's life until she felt fifteen again. Until now, the exhilaration of weightlessness was long forgotten, preserved only as a memory of childhood days playing with Jesse. She pointed her toes, enabling her to cut through the surface of the water. The plunge was welcome relief from the heat of the chase. The water swallowed her body, leaving her red cap swirling on the surface.

The male officer stepped to the edge of the cliff and peered down to see the cap moving violently in the current. He turned to look at his partner.

"I'll call it in," he said, and they both headed back to their vehicle.

Christine moved below the surface like a dolphin. She reached the base of the cliff and grabbed a familiar rock. Moving on autopilot, again she waited for the water to rise, timing her exit perfectly with the surging wave. She clung on to the ledge and quickly pulled herself higher to avoid the next wave. It was then an easy scramble up the rocks to the large lava tube cave.

Her first steps inside instantly unleashed a flood of emotions. Sparked by the chase and made worse by the pebbles of white coral scattered on the floor of the cave, a lump grew inside her throat. Christine tried to catch her breath while her heart ripped open. The stones once formed an 'I Love You' message from Jesse, but now nothing remained except the broken pieces of coral scattered by a decade of winter storms.

Time progressed unnoticed by Christine as a flood of childhood memories consumed her thoughts. It may have been the first rays of the setting sun warming her face or the arrival of the small white tern at the mouth of the cave, but something prompted her into action. The voice inside her head told her to move... *before they come looking for me.*

It was easier than she remembered to cling to the rocks along the base of the cliff; her running shoes taking the brunt of the sharp rocks. *Why didn't we wear shoes?* she thought, pulling herself to the top of the cliff. She scanned the area for the police before running for cover under the lush tropical growth. Christine knew it was hopeless to go back to her Jeep or the house—her only choice was on foot.

Progress was slow and painful without the luxury of a trail. Her clothes were still soaked, and her running shoes dug into the back of her ankle. She struggled a few hundred yards farther, reaching a small opening in the canopy where the last remaining rays of sunlight covered a fallen tree.

Christine stripped naked and rung out her clothes as tightly as she could, placing them on the tips of the leafless branches near the end of the fallen tree. She squeezed her shoes and placed them on the log to dry in the last minutes of direct sunlight.

Christine sat on the log next to her clothes listening to the forest come alive. The distant crash of waves was muffled by the thick foliage, allowing the songbirds to be heard. The faint breeze carried a sweet scent, one she instantly knew. It didn't take her long to find the papaya tree and the welcome fruit it provided. She shook the small tree, causing the largest and most ripe fruit to fall at her feet.

The fruit worked magically, satisfying her hunger and quenching her thirst. Then the solitude sank in, and her thoughts focused on her situation.

Why is this happening to me?

She searched for answers, but nothing came to her. Christine used this time to pray. She realized that God was watching over her, and it was He who had guided her to the cliff. Her prayer was cut short by a low, rhythmic rumble emanating from the sky. She glanced up, only to see the white tern circling high above the small clearing. *My guardian angel*, she thought, but the sound interrupted her thoughts as it grew louder.

Realization exploded in her mind, and she leaped off the log, tossing the papaya in the process. She collected her clothes as fast as possible.

The helicopter passed directly overhead, barely skimming the treetops as Christine dove for cover under an enormous palm leaf. Shaken, she lay motionless on the forest floor. It was another minute before she gathered the strength to investigate the burning sensation in her left elbow and both knees. The leap for cover had scraped her body while the pile of clothes in her arms had protected her face. She lifted herself from the forest floor, threw her clothes to the ground and brushed the debris from her body. Christine looked at the blood dripping down her legs and arm.

"That's it!" she shouted, angered by her predicament.

She grabbed her shorts and wiped the trail of blood from her legs before it reached her feet and repeated the procedure on her arms. Anger grew strong inside her, overtaking her faith.

Christine donned her partially dried clothes and resumed her trek through the forest. With each step, the evening light grew dimmer, slowing her progress to a crawl. Frustration had replaced her anger when she succumbed to nightfall. Walking was impossible, so she used the last bit of twilight to find a place to spend the night.

Ripping a half dozen large leaves from a palm tree, she laid them between the roots of an enormous fig tree. Shiny speckles of starlight dotted the otherwise complete darkness that surrounded her. Their light moved like fireflies between the tips of the forest trees. The warmth of the day quickly disappeared as a chill ran the course of her body, worsened by her damp clothes. The throbbing in her knees was synchronized with the beat of her heart, but it soon fell behind as her heart raced. Fear radiated through her body, sending adrenalin rushing through her chest. It wasn't the darkness or her capture in the middle of the night she feared—it was sleep.

***

Sandra was startled by the ring of her phone on the passenger seat next to her. She recognized the number at once and answered.

"Hello, Andrew."

"Sandra, I'm sorry to call so late but I'm worried about Chris," said Father Shannon.

"I haven't heard from her," Sandra replied.

"What do mean? Didn't she come home?" he asked, his voice filled with concern.

"I'm sorry, Andrew, I can't talk right now. I'll call you later," she said and hung up.

"No... wait, Sandra," he pleaded, but she had gone.

Father Shannon put his phone back on the nightstand and lay in bed for hours, struggling to get to sleep. Frustrated and exhausted, he gave up trying and went down stairs to watch TV. He eventually dozed off while sitting on the wicker couch.

He was woken up the next morning by the ring of the doorbell.

"Come in!" he shouted, rushing up the stairs to get dressed.

"Good morning, Father," Richard said, walking into the empty living room holding his favorite coffee mug.

Father Shannon came down the stairs and walked into the

living room while Richard searched for him in the kitchen.

"Richard, I won't be able to..." began Father Shannon, but he stopped speaking when his eyes caught the story on the morning news.

He glared at the TV. There was a live video of the Anderson home from a news helicopter showing it sectioned off with yellow tape and police officers entering the house. He turned up the volume so he could hear the story but missed the commentary, only reading the captioned, 'Police Search for Murder Suspect.'

The priest walked with purpose toward the door as Richard stepped out of the kitchen in front of him, nearly spilling his coffee.

"Wow, what's your hurry?" Richard asked.

Father Shannon cast his crystal-blue eyes away and maneuvered around him so he could leave without the deacon noticing them.

"Father Shannon, what's wrong?" Richard insisted, clearly confused by his sudden departure.

"A family emergency," Father Shannon said, refusing to look at Richard.

"What? Is there something I...?" Richard started from the front door of the rectory, but Father Shannon had already closed his car door and was driving away.

Richard returned to the kitchen, dumped his coffee in the sink and left.

***

The night delivered none of the foreboding nightmares, but the morning sickness remained. Christine was rattled awake by the thunder of a helicopter passing overhead. The reprieve from the constant pounding in her chest the night brought was far too short. The helicopter's unexpected wake-up call brought her back to reality.

She resumed her fight through the undergrowth,

determined to get to Honokohau Marina, where her mother said to meet her. The hours of walking slowly chipped away at her conviction and planted a seed of doubt in her head.

It's already been a day. What if she's not there? How long will she wait? she thought as she walked.

Her disbelief ran rampant, gaining momentum with every step forward. Aware of her weakening, Christine sat on a large lava rock, closed her eyes and prayed. Still seated, she felt the warm ocean breeze caress her face. She opened her eyes to find brilliant sunlight had penetrated the forest a few hundred yards to her right. In less than a minute, Christine covered the distance and emerged from the shadows of the forest.

Like an endless black ocean, the massive lava flow stretched in front of her as far as she could see. A river of black originating high above the clouds, it flowed uninterrupted to the Island Highway more than a mile away. The late afternoon heat baked the rock, casting heat waves to dance above the lava.

Exhilarated to be free of the darkness, Christine had just stepped onto the rock when her guardian angel appeared, its snow-white feathers glistening against the cyan sky. The bird landed a few feet in front of her.

"Of course," Christine said.

She reluctantly headed back to the cover of the forest to sit and wait, knowing it would be suicide to try and walk across the lava in the middle of the day. If the heat didn't kill her, the police would spot her in a second.

Accustomed to getting her own way, she removed her shoes and tossed them at a large chunk of lava where the sunlight made its way through the dense forest cover. Neither shoe landed in the sunlight, which further angered her. Forced to pick them up, she placed them on a rock to dry. Christine always lost the waiting game, but this time she knew the stakes were much higher and wallowed in her disappointment.

The hours of sitting with nothing to do but think aggravated her. She tossed stones at the flies attempting to land on her shoes to pass the time, all the while straining to understand what was going on. *They don't think I killed Jasper, do they? Could Jesse be blaming me? How did Mom know?* None of this made any sense to her.

Hunger and thirst arrived, shifting her thoughts away from her unanswered questions. There was only thirty minutes of light left, so she decided to search for another fruit tree before heading out onto the lava flow. Christine found another papaya and finished it before darkness arrived. She resolved to complete the eight-mile hike to the marina that night and headed off on the lava.

An uncomfortable feeling hovered over her, like the first time Father Shannon had asked her to read a passage to the congregation. Standing alone in the pulpit, she could feel every eye in the church watching her. That same feeling lingered as she walked. She longed for the forest she had hated a few moments ago and the security it provided. The blackness of the night elevated the demand on her senses, which struggled to keep up. The sound of the lava crushing under foot was all she could hear, and she had underestimated the difficulty of walking over lava at night.

With the ocean breeze diminished, the heat radiating from the rock drew sweat from her body. She knew this would be her last day before dehydration overwhelmed her.

Guided solely by the glow of Kona over the horizon, she stumbled in the darkness in an effort to maintain a steady pace.

Her first break that night came with the arrival of the three-quarter moon as it rose slowly above the horizon. The dull moonlight was sufficient to illuminate the ground and double her pace, but it wasn't enough. Even with the increased pace, the faint glow of dawn arrived all too soon.

Christine was still half a mile north of the airport when she first saw the blue and green runway lights sparkle in the distance.

Stifled by exhaustion and dehydrated, an unwanted feeling lingered in her mind. It was one she hated more than any other, and one she never accepted—failure. Broken by the elements and weakened by her thoughts, Christine was ready to give up when the white tern arrived in front of her. Dejected, Christine sat on the rock holding her head in her hands. Even the return of her guardian angel couldn't lift her from the hole of despair she had fallen into.

The bird released a loud call as if it were injured, then took flight. Startled by the noise, Christine lifted her head and saw the bird land at the top of a small rise in the lava a hundred feet up the hillside.

"I can't," she said, speaking to the bird as if it were a human. The bird continued its chatter, beckoning her to follow.

Driven by her hatred of failure and her determination to see her mother, Christine pulled herself to her feet and climbed the rise to where the bird had landed. Her mouth formed a smile, which was quickly followed by a stinging pain from the split that appeared in her lips. The smile was the result of the small gravel road used to access the radar tower for the airport.

Christine found a large shelf of lava on the side of the road and took a seat on the edge. She made the sign of the cross and thanked God out loud.

"Thank you, God, for sending me this guardian angel, and for giving me the strength to continue. Thank you for…"

A small private jet flew overhead on its final approach, drowning the words of her prayer.

Chapter 6

Nice Fish

Silver rays of sunlight rose above the surface of the ocean as the sleek jet made its final approach into Kona Airport. The morning breeze had yet to rise, leaving the coconut palms lining the airport road lifeless. The terminal was vacant except for the lace-neck doves scavenging crumbs under the empty benches. None of the Sunday morning charter flights stuffed with tourists had arrived as the private jet powered down in front of Terminal One.

Three men dressed in business suits, each carrying a briefcase, stepped out of the aircraft and proceeded though the terminal to the US Immigration desk. After clearing customs, they made their way curbside where a large white SUV arrived, stopping at their feet. The driver left the vehicle and handed the keys to Father Derksen. Gino got in the back passenger seat and Tonino entered the front. Gino immediately opened his briefcase and removed his tablet.

"Make a right when you get to the highway. It's not far from here," said Gino, reading the map on the screen.

"How long?" barked Tonino with a strong Italian accent.

"Ten minutes."

"You don't expect her to return?" asked Father Derksen.

"Of course not. We need information, and if we're fortunate, a photo," replied Tonino, not hiding the insult in his tone.

They turned off the highway onto the Anderson driveway

only to find it blocked by a police car and bright yellow tape. At first glance, the car appeared empty, but the sound of Father Derksen shutting his door caused a single head to pop up from behind the steering wheel. Their unannounced and extremely early arrival had awoken the lone officer. He scrambled to find his hat and exit the car as Father Derksen approached.

"Can I help you?" asked the officer, stepping out of the car.

"We're here to see the Andersons," said Father Derksen, intentionally sounding surprised.

"Are you family?"

"Yes. What's going on?"

"I'm sorry, I can't say, but if you can call this number," said the officer as he handed over a business card.

"Thank you." He put the card in his pocket and returned to the vehicle.

"Have they found her?" asked Tonino.

"He said nothing; just handed me this," replied Father Derksen, and he gave the card to Tonino.

"Let's pay a visit to Father Shannon," Tonino said, signaling for them to leave.

Father Derksen turned the vehicle around and drove to St. Michael's Church. It was ten minutes to eight when they arrived. The SUV had difficulty getting in the parking lot, as the line of vehicles trying to leave stretched a dozen long. Finally making their way into the lot, Father Derksen parked alongside the old church. The three men left the vehicle and walked to the entrance, Gino carrying his briefcase, not wanting to leave it unattended. They looked more like Wall Street bankers than parishioners as they approached the front doors.

"Mass is canceled," said a large Hawaiian woman as she left the church.

"Canceled?" inquired Tonino, for once not faking the surprise in his question.

"Father Weston isn't back from the mainland," said the

woman.

"Oh that's too bad," Tonino said with a return to his normal disingenuous tone. "Do you know why Mass is canceled?"

"Father Weston is away, and Father Shannon had a family emergency."

"Really... that's too bad. Do you know when Father Shannon will return?"

"I'm not sure; you can ask Richard—he's the Deacon. He may be able to help you. Ask anyone inside, they can point you to him," she said as she got in a waiting car.

"Thank you."

The men entered the church and walked down the aisle toward a group of people talking near the altar. Tonino's lack of height exaggerated Father Derksen's massive size. Tonino's grey hair glowed against his black suit as they marched down the aisle side by side, followed by Gino.

Richard Whyte noticed the men at once but didn't recognize them until he saw Gino. Gino's short round body and briefcase triggered Richard's recollection. Astonishment flashed across his face when he realized they had returned. He and Father Shannon had met these men in the very same spot nearly a month before, and he knew it was no coincidence they were back, especially since it had been less than two days since he had sent the email to Father Derksen.

"Father Derksen, I must say I'm surprised," said Richard as he extended his hand.

Father Derksen didn't immediately recognize the deacon but greeted him as if he did.

"Hello, Richard. Do you remember Tonino and Gino?"

"Yes, nice to see you again," he said as he shook their hands enthusiastically.

"Do you know why we're here?" asked Tonino.

"Yes, of course. I emailed you about Christine and the mark on her neck."

"Yes, that's correct. Do you...?" Tonino started, but before he could finish, Richard interrupted.

"I've got to ask why it's so important that you'd come back so quickly?"

"Christine has something the Vatican is very interested in," replied Tonino. "Do you know where she is?"

"No, I haven't seen her since I emailed Father Derksen," he said, turning to look at the tall priest.

"Father Shannon?" Tonino asked.

"He left yesterday morning."

"Did he say why or where he was going?"

"No. All he said to me was that he had a family emergency. Then he left in a big hurry. He wouldn't even look at me or say good-bye—just drove off. It was rather strange."

"Any idea where he went?"

"If I had to guess, I'd say Europe. I know he has family there. But that's just a guess," Richard said, looking at the three men for some explanation for their interest in Christine.

"Thank you, Richard. You've been very helpful."

"No problem... Is there anything else I can do for you while you're here?" Richard asked, still trying to gain any indication of their business.

"Actually there is. If Father Shannon or the girl contacts you, let us know at once. You still have our email?" asked Tonino.

Richard nodded, and the three men made the sign of the cross and left the church.

The sun had lifted well above the horizon by the time the men walked back to their SUV. Father Derksen started the engine and turned the air-conditioning on to lessen the impact of the morning heat. Tonino removed the cell phone from his jacket and made a call.

"Detective Payne?"

"Who's calling?" asked the woman's voice on the other end of the line.

"Tonino Fabro."

"Just a moment," she said.

"Hello, Mr. Fabro, we haven't located her yet," said the detective.

"There's another. Father Andrew Shannon."

"My men will find them."

"You said that about the girl and her mother," snapped Tonino.

"We'll find the mother, but that girl's shark bait; we've searched every inch of that coast."

"I want the body," Tonino snarled back.

"We're still searching."

"The airports?" asked Tonino.

"Nobody's flying off this island without us knowing," said Detective Payne.

"Keep me informed," Tonino stated as he hung up. "I'm going to the rectory," he said without facing the others.

Tonino walked to the rectory and rang the doorbell. The faint sound of talking could be heard coming through the door. He rang the bell again, followed by three stern raps on the door. He waited for a moment then turned the door handle.

"Hello!" he called, but there was no reply. He walked into the small living room and found the source of the voices—the TV had been left on. Sunlight filtered through the blinds, casting a pleasant ambiance into the room. The ceiling fan moved the pages of the Saturday morning paper as it lay open on the coffee table, held in place by a half-empty coffee mug.

The walls were covered with photographs of Father Shannon and his extensive world travels. There were images of him riding an elephant in Thailand, standing in front of the pyramids in Egypt and hiking to Machu Picchu, but none appeared recent.

Tonino went upstairs to search for information. He found what he was looking for in the bedroom. Sitting atop Father Shannon's dresser were five photographs, each sealed in an ornate self-standing frame. All had a small description and the date when the photo was taken written on the back. They were aligned chronologically, with the oldest on the left.

Tonino picked up the first photo, which displayed an image of a young Father Shannon and a woman who appeared to be no older than eighteen. She was holding a newborn and was standing in front of the wooden doors of St. Michael's. The description read 'Sandra and Christine, 1985.' Tonino placed the picture back on the dresser and picked up the one farthest to the right. It was the most recent looking photo with an image of a woman in her mid-thirties and Father Shannon shaking hands with a teenage girl. The girl was wearing a high-school graduation gown and hat, and the back of the photo had 'Christine's Graduation, 2003.' Tonino was holding the frame in his hand when his phone rang. He looked at the caller ID and took the call.

"You have news?"

"We found Shannon," said Detective Payne.

"Where?"

"He's driving north on the highway, towards the airport."

"Follow him, nothing else. Make sure he doesn't know. Understand?"

"Yes."

"We're on our way there now," said Tonino and hung up.

Tonino took the photo with him and ran back to the vehicle. A moment later, they raced out of the parking lot and drove straight for the airport with Father Derksen at the wheel.

***

Father Shannon continued driving on the Island Highway unaware of the unmarked police car following him. Still headed north, he drove past the marina and didn't slow down until he reached the radar tower service road. He turned onto the unmarked dirt road and followed the tire ruts carved into the lava as they twisted and turned toward the tower. He navigated the small silver car around a large lava outcrop, where he found Christine still sitting on the edge.

Disbelief paralyzed Christine. *This is a hallucination*, she thought as the car came to a stop. Her breathing was shallow and rapid. She dare not move, afraid the vision would disappear. No explanation could account for his arrival. Suddenly, she understood, and Christine's mind raced with jubilation. *God answered my prayers.*

Father Shannon stopped the car in front of Christine and raced over to meet her. The moment he placed his hand on her shoulder, the vision suddenly became a reality. Christine stood up and hugged him, refusing to let go. The last two days had weakened her physically, but at that moment, her faith ignited inside her, giving her strength.

"How's my mom?"

"Worried. She's waiting for us."

"God sent you, didn't he?" asked Christine, but Father Shannon didn't answer.

"We really need to get going. Get in the car, Chris. There's some water and food on the front seat."

"I want to call her. Can I use your phone?" Christine asked.

"It's between the seats."

The priest walked Christine to the front of the car and helped her into the passenger seat, closing the door as she started on the water. A large silver jet flew overhead as Father Shannon walked to the back of the car, the thunder from the jet engines shaking it. He paused as the white tern landed on the roof of the car, and an intense bluish-white light reflected off the inside of the car windshield.

Christine turned to see the source of the light, but it had disappeared.

"What was that?" she asked when Father Shannon got in the car.

"What?"

"That light."

"It must have been the sun reflecting off the jet," he said dismissively as he started the car.

"Oh," she said, distracted while dialing her mother's number.

Sandra answered her phone on the first ring.

"Chris, are you all right?"

"How'd you know it was me?"

"Are you okay?" Sandra repeated, ignoring Christine's question.

"I'm exhausted. What's going on?"

"We'll talk soon, dear. I'll see you in a bit."

"Love you, Mom," she said and closed the phone.

"What's going on, Father?"

"Like your mom said, we'll talk soon. Right now, we've got to keep you safe."

"From what? The police? What's going on?" Christine repeated, noticeably frustrated that no one was answering her.

"Be patient, Chris. It won't be long, I promise," he said, glancing at her.

"What happened to your eyes?"

"No more questions. Relax, we're almost there," he said, as they drove past Keahole Airport road.

***

Tonino, Father Derksen and Gino were waiting in their SUV out front of the airport for Father Shannon to arrive when Tonino's phone rang.

"You have an update?"

"My men are following them, but they're not going to the airport," Detective Payne explained.

"Them?"

"You won't believe this, but he picked up the girl just north of the airport."

"What? Where are they now?" Tonino shouted.

"Headed south, just past you."

"Drive, drive!" commanded Tonino, waving his phone at the windshield. The SUV squealed away from the curb, leaving a cloud of blue smoke. "He's got the girl."

Tonino put the phone back to his ear.

"What are they driving?"

"A small silver Toyota..." Detective Payne started, but the rest of his description was interrupted by a call over the police radio.

"They turned on to Kealakehe Parkway. They're not going to the airport—they're headed for the marina."

"Listen to me, Detective. You are to use whatever force is necessary to stop them. Have I made myself clear? These people are murders," said Tonino in a calm but authoritative tone so as not to be misunderstood. "Understand?"

"Yes," the detective replied with slight apprehension.

***

Father Shannon saw the dark blue police sedan pass a line of cars just before he turned on to Kealakehe Parkway, its small blue flashing light forcing the oncoming traffic to pull over.

"Matteo, Simone, they're coming."

"Was that you? Who's Matteo and Simone?" asked Christine, staring at Father Shannon while her heart raced with uncertainty. *I'm hearing things*, she thought, trying to convince herself that Father Shannon had spoken.

"I'll explain later. Right now, you've got to trust me. Your life depends on it—promise me."

Father Shannon's lead on the approaching police had diminished quickly. The row of palm trees lining the side of the road passed the window like a picket fence as the priest accelerated, but the blue sedan still grew larger in the rearview mirror.

The horseshoe-shaped harbor came into view. The wharf lined the entire shoreline, each slip identified by a large wooden banner indicating the name of the vessel tied to the berth. Father Shannon slowed as they approached the wharf.

"Chris, listen to me carefully. We have to run. Promise me you'll do exactly what I say. When I stop the car, we have to sprint to the wharf. Get on the boat called '*Nice Fish.*' Promise me you won't stop—no matter what happens."

"What?" she said, looking out the back of the car at the police cruiser.

"Just do it!" implored Father Shannon.

"Okay," Christine agreed reluctantly.

"Chris, you understand—you can't stop until you're on the boat."

Father Shannon stopped the car directly in front of the gangplank leading down to the wharf. The *Nice Fish* was berthed in the fifth slip down, meaning a two-hundred-foot sprint.

Christine hesitated before opening the door.

"Go!" Father Shannon yelled, and they opened their doors simultaneously.

Christine leaped out of the car, the adrenalin rush wiping all thoughts from her mind but one—getting to the boat. Like a sprinter focusing on the finish line, she would stop for nothing until she reached the boat.

She approached the top of the gangplank and prepared to launch herself down the ramp when she saw her mother. Christine's focus was broken, the sight of her mother trumping her need to reach the boat.

"Run, Chris, run!" shouted Sandra as she followed Father Shannon and Christine toward the boat.

The blue sedan slid to a stop in the gravel, sending a cloud of dust into the air, and the two police officers sprang out of their car with their guns drawn.

"Stop!" yelled the first officer as he chased the three fleeing suspects.

The second officer ran along the shoreline, gaining an advantage over the time it would have taken to get down onto the wharf. He was nearly parallel with Sandra when he fired a shot.

It missed Christine by inches and exploded the surface of the water beside the wharf. The sound of the gunfire rang in her ears, triggering her to duck instinctively.

"Keep going, Chris!" Sandra and Father Shannon yelled simultaneously.

The gunfire snapped Christine back into action, and the three of them sprinted down the wharf. Father Shannon now led the way, followed by Christine and Sandra.

The first officer leaped off the gangplank and fired two rounds toward them, but the movement of the floating wharf disturbed his aim.

The captain of the *Nice Fish*, sitting in the pilot seat high above the boat's cabin, shouted at them to run. His voice was muffled by the noise of the boat's idling engines. He had already removed the lines and held the boat in place using the engines.

The white SUV drove past the gangplank and skidded to a halt on the harbor wall opposite the stern of the boat. Both passenger side doors opened at once, and Tonino and Gino drew their guns from their shoulder holsters, taking aim at Christine.

The morning air ruptured from the gunfire like the grand finale of a fireworks display, their pursuers unleashing a firestorm of bullets. Shards of the boat hull landed in the water as splinters dropped like snow onto the deck.

The captain revved the twin engines to the redline as the three runners neared the stern. A cloud of thick black diesel fumes billowed from the exhaust, obscuring the vessel a little, and the moving targets slipped into the curtain of exhaust, disappearing from view.

Bullets came from every direction as the boat's deck shook under the strain of the engines. Father Shannon landed on the fiberglass boat deck first and turned to locate Christine.

The blinding curtain of soot made tears well in Christine's eyes, but she forced them to remain open.

The deck appeared beneath her feet just as she felt a blow to her shoulders. A dull pain spread across her back, sending her flying forward. She landed hard and face first on the rough deck. The ache spread from her shoulders and her face until it painted her entire body with pain. Still lying on the deck, she blocked the burn and turned back to see who had pushed her.

The vibration of the deck lessened and the roar of the engines subsided. Sandra suddenly appeared through the rapidly dissipating fumes.

The boat moved from the wharf as Sandra crouched down in preparation to leap. Her body flew into the air, propelled by a spray of bullets hitting her back. Her chest exploded as her torso turned crimson. Blood showered the deck and hit Christine's face like droplets of warm salt water.

Sandra's body bounced off the stern and disappeared from view.

CHAPTER 7

MS VOLENDAM

Shock incapacitated Christine and numbness flooded every part of her body. She fought to inhale with every breath, but the massive weight upon her chest prevented air from entering her lungs. No sound left her lips as the dull emptiness paralyzed her mind. Her senses rejected reality. The sound of gunfire was gone, and the pungent smell of diesel fumes slowly dissipated. Finally, the three men in dark business suits, made conspicuous by the white SUV, faded to black.

Father Shannon remained on top of Christine, a human shield protecting her from the gunfire. Unable to determine if seconds or hours had passed, Christine was frozen in time. The grip of terror was relentless in her mind, strangling her will to live. Finally, her need to breathe overpowered her.

Christine struggled under the weight of Father Shannon's body. She pushed hard against his chest and forced a breath into her burning lungs. He put his hands on the deck and lifted his body off hers in a push-up-style movement. Relief was immediate; Christine inhaled rapidly like a child after a breath-holding contest. She turned to the priest, grabbed his shirt and began shaking him violently.

"We've got to go back! She can't be dead!" Christine screamed.

Father Shannon didn't speak and tried to put his arms around but her without success.

"Why, why is this happening to me? What did I do?" Christine cried.

She let go of his shirt and fell back to the deck, sobbing uncontrollably. Father Shannon made a second attempt to console her, but she pushed him away. He left her crying and stood up to see if they were free of immediate danger.

Christine continued to cry as she lifted her body to a sitting position and leaned against the cabin wall.

Father Shannon knelt next to her and offered her a hand. "Chris, we need to get inside, come," he said gently.

She looked into his crystal-blue eyes, much bluer than her own, and took his hand. They moved slowly down the three small steps into the cabin, but Christine froze when she heard a voice inside her head.

"Let me know if they're following us."

Christine's tear-laden eyes, far more red now than blue, connected with Father Shannon's.

"Did you hear someone? It's the second time I've heard it," she asked.

"Hear what?"

"A voice, it sounded like…" she stopped talking, knowing it was impossible.

"Sounded like what?" Father Shannon asked.

"Someone who's dead. I'm hearing things."

Father Shannon didn't answer but walked over to the small sink and wetted a towel.

The droplets of her mother's blood had dried to Christine's skin and looked like freckles covering her face. He was concerned she would see them, knowing the pain they would resurrect.

"Hold still," he said as he wiped her face of blood and tears, ensuring she couldn't see the streaks of red forming on the bright white cloth.

"Why are they trying to kill us?" Christine asked, her need for answers growing stronger.

"I'll explain everything, but you need to rest now," he told her.

"I can't," she said as a new round of tears welled up in her eyes.

"You must, you've been walking all night."

In a knee-jerk reaction, she pushed Father Shannon away from her. Christine locked her eyes with his before she spoke.

"How do you know I was…" started Christine, but Father Shannon cut her off.

"Get some rest. There's a bed and some clean clothes up front," he said pointing to a small cabin door at the front of the boat.

"But…" she protested.

"We'll talk later. I promise."

Christine reluctantly crawled into the bed, deciding to change her clothes later and pushed the pillows into a mound. She lay facing the ceiling of the small cabin, unable to stop the tears from forming in the corners of her eyes. The rhythmic motion of the vessel cutting through the waves combined with the complete exhaustion gripping her body. She drifted in and out of sleep for more than an hour, reliving the real-life nightmare until she finally fell asleep.

Father Shannon waited on the deck for her to fall asleep. Once he was certain she was sleeping, he removed the fresh water hose from its hanger and washed the blood off the deck. He then pulled himself up the silver ladder to talk with the captain, a native Hawaiian no more than twenty years old. His long sandy-brown dreadlocks tied with rainbow-colored beads hung over his face like a sheep dog, covering his unusually blue eyes. The *Nice Fish* had been his home and place of work since he was twelve.

"Matteo was right; she's progressed further than I expected. She can hear me, so we need to use our voices unless it's an emergency or until I can explain things to her," Father Shannon said.

"Everything's ready; we'll be there by five."

"Good," Father Shannon replied as he returned to the

lower deck.

***

Gino and Father Derksen sat inside the SUV waiting for Tonino to return. Tonino walked along the harbor and dialed his phone. Anger raged in his voice as he spoke.

"I don't care!" he yelled into the phone.

"There's nothing available; this isn't Honolulu," replied Detective Payne.

"Where's the nearest vessel?"

"Up island—at least six hours away."

"Get me a helicopter."

"I'm trying, but it'll be an hour."

"Can they make Maui?" asked Tonino.

"Absolutely. It's about thirty miles, but in that boat, they could make any of the islands."

"Have their photo sent to all of them—I want them found!" Tonino shouted, further enraged by the information he was hearing.

"But the odds…"

"Just do it!" Tonino nearly screamed and slapped the phone shut.

Tonino got in the SUV and slammed the door.

"Sir, do you…?" started Father Derksen, but his question was halted midsentence by Tonino's raised hand. Silence filled the vehicle. Tonino turned and faced Derksen, the daylight disappearing into the vacuum of his coal-black eyes. With his anger at bay, the right side of Tonino's mouth raised to fashion an intimidating smile.

"Things have changed," he said, still facing Father Derksen.

The priest was too afraid to say anything other than, "Sir?"

"She must be pregnant," Tonino snarled.

"Pregnant," repeated Gino.

"This changes everything. We must find her soon," Tonino said, staring out the windshield. "To the airport. I must return to the Vatican at once. We have no time to waste."

***

The sun settled below the horizon, leaving a light purple trail over the ocean. The steady rocking of the boat as it cut through the turquoise swells cradled Christine as she slept. The constant low rumbling sound of the engine slowed as the boat approached Kailua Bay. She continued to sleep when the boat pulled alongside the pier.

Father Shannon tossed the bumpers over the side and tied the lines to the large rusted cleats on the wharf.

"Chris, you need to get up," Father Shannon said, shaking her gently.

"Mom!" Christine shouted, wishing it was all only a nightmare.

"Chris, it's time to go."

"Where?"

"We're leaving the island."

"What? I can't. What about my mom? I can't just leave her..." Christine said and her voice trailed off to a sob.

"Listen, Chris, this is what she wanted. Your mother wanted you safe, and right now, we need to focus on that. Those men who killed your mother, they're hunting for you as we speak. They won't stop until you're dead. You've got to trust me. I promise, it'll all make sense soon. We have to focus on getting away from here, and to do that, I need you to do something you're not very good at."

"What?"

"Lie."

"About what?" she asked, confused by the request.

"We need to use someone else's ID to leave the island," he said, hoping she would understand.

"I've never left the island; I've never even flown before.

What happens if I can't and airport security figures it out?"

"Don't worry. We're not flying," said Father Shannon, trying to sound reassuring.

"Not flying?"

"Let's go up top, and you'll see."

They left the cabin and climbed the steps to the back deck of the boat. The fresh air felt cool on Christine's face. The Kailua-Kona skyline was spectacular, with Tiki torches burning along the beachfront of the largest hotels. The lights from the Alii Drive businesses reflected off the water, and the sound of people mulling caught her ear. The pier was crammed with tourists covered with flowered shirts and straw hats. It was then that she realized how they were leaving the Island.

"We're going by cruise ship?" she asked with a hint of excitement.

The idea of boarding a cruise ship provided a momentary distraction from the day's horror. Ever since she could remember, it had been her childhood dream to take a cruise, and her anxiety subsided for a few moments. She stepped onto the pier and faced the ocean; the gigantic ship looked like an island anchored in the bay.

Father Shannon scanned the crowd of tourists. The few poorly spaced streetlamps provided little light, making it impossible to see anything more than a crowd of people. A loud roar of a boat engine attracted Christine's attention. It came from a deep orange tender docking next to the pier behind the *Nice Fish*. Dockhands secured the lines to the wharf and began helping the hoards of people into the boat. The crowd thinned considerably as the tender filled. Christine noticed that Father Shannon continued to search the pier with his eyes.

"What's wrong?" she asked, concerned by the intensity of his search.

"Nothing."

"What are you looking for?"

"I'm looking for an acquaintance."

"You look worried."

"We've got to make the next tender—it's the last one," said Father Shannon, unable to hide the urgency in his voice.

Christine wandered down the wharf, the faint sound of the last tender growing louder as it approached the pier. Father Shannon looked back to the *Nice Fish*; the captain sat on the pilot seat shaking his head in an obvious 'no.' The tender was tied up and was loading the last of the cruise ship passengers when Christine heard it.

"Simone, they're loading," said the words inside Christine's mind. She ran back the short distance to Father Shannon, frantically trying to get his attention.

"Did you hear it, that voice? I'm not going crazy. I heard it again, and this time it was even clearer!" she shouted at him.

"Please, Chris, I'll explain later…"

"Explain what?" she demanded.

"Meet us at the tender," said the voice inside Christine's head.

"Meet who at the tender? What's happening to me?" The confusion was taking its toll on her.

The voice she heard was Jasper's, and it disturbed her. The memory of him dying in her arms was still fresh in her mind, and it reminded her of her mother's death. The excitement of the cruise vanished as the two most horrific events in her life appeared simultaneously in her thoughts.

"Chris!" shouted Father Shannon, but she couldn't hear him as she relived her nightmares.

"Chris, let's go!" he shouted a second time, much louder than the first.

"What?"

"We need to go, right now!"

They sprinted the fifty yards to the gangplank in front of the tender. The dockhands had already removed the bowline, and the security officer gave the order to remove the gangplank.

"Wait!" yelled Father Shannon.

The security officer raised his hand to the dockhand, indicating him to stop.

"We left our passports at the shop; they're bringing them to us right now," Father Shannon pleaded, pointing to a figure running up the pier.

The security officer instructed the dockhand to leave the gangplank in place. The woman ran out of the darkness straight to Father Shannon and handed him a large brown envelope. Unable to catch her breath, she couldn't speak but only looked at Christine.

Christine formed a nervous smile, and through the dim light of the tender, she saw a faint sparkle of blue in the woman's eyes.

Father Shannon pulled three red lanyards from the envelope and handed them to the security officer, who was now waiting at the bottom of the gangplank. The officer looked at the cards and handed one back to Father Shannon and another to Christine.

Christine looked at the card and saw her photo and the name 'Christine Yandel.' She instantly recognized her driver's license photo—she always hated the way her hair looked in it. She hung the lanyard over her head. The security officer held the third card in his hand and looked at Father Shannon.

"Where's your wife, Mr. Yandel?"

"She had a family emergency and flew back to Canada," Father Shannon explained.

"That's too bad. Be sure to tell your purser, and I'll inform the bridge," the security officer said.

"Thanks, may I keep her ID? She wanted it as a souvenir," asked Father Shannon as the security guard turned to walk away.

"Sure," he said as he handed the lanyard over.

The tender left the pier and motored through the darkness toward the floating city. The enormity of the vessel captivated Christine, and butterflies filled her stomach when the ship began to dwarf the tender. Excitement returned, temporarily dissolving the anxiety of pretending to be someone else. Christine was lost in her thoughts, having never known luxury; up until now, the idea of a cruise had only been a dream.

The tender slowed as it approached the side of the vessel, and the large white lettering on the navy blue bow of the *MS Volendam* was now visible through the darkness.

Father Shannon led the way up the gangplank, followed closely by Christine. They entered a small holding area packed with people waiting to clear security. The crowd funneled through the metal detector like bottles on a filling line, each person scanning their ID card and putting their bags on the conveyor belt.

Father Shannon placed the envelope on the conveyor belt, stepped through the metal detector and handed the security guard his ID. The guard swiped the card in the reader, and it instantly beeped twice. Father Shannon then walked past the guard and waited for Christine.

She walked through the metal detector and handed the guard her card. The officer swiped the card and a single long continuous beep occurred. He swiped the card again, but with the same result. The line of people waiting behind Christine grew impatient, and her face glowed crimson from the rise in blood pressure. She fought to control the panic running berserk inside her body.

"Miss, please step over here," said the guard as he pointed to a small open area to the side.

"Is there a problem?" asked Father Shannon.

"Are you family?" asked the guard.

"My daughter."

"We're having trouble reading your daughter's card. It'll only take a second," said the guard, and a white uniformed ship's officer arrived, taking Christine's card.

Christine's eyes, already swollen from crying, begged for help from Father Shannon, and he welded his eyes to hers.

"Don't panic," said the voice inside her head.

"Oh my God. It's you! How?" she asked, stupefied by the realization.

"Pardon me?" asked the officer, clearly confused by her sudden outburst.

"Stay calm," said the voice.

"I'm sorry, I thought I recognized you," she said, struggling to lie.

Christine didn't need to be calm, the shock had left her catatonic.

"Miss Yandel, do you recall if you put your card near a strong magnet?" asked the officer.

Unaware of her surroundings and the officer's question, Christine never took her eyes off Father Shannon's.

"Miss Yandel?" the officer asked as he walked over to the security desk computer to type in her ID information.

"Maybe I put them too close to my cell phone case; it has a pretty strong magnet on the flap," interjected Father Shannon, hoping to snap Christine back to reality.

"What?" she said, returning from her mental hiatus.

"Your card has been damaged; I'll need to reprogram it. It'll only take a moment," said the officer from behind the desk.

The officer returned with a new card and handed it to the security guard processing the last few people returning from the island. The guard swiped the card and instantly two short beeps sounded. He handed the lanyard to Christine.

"Thank you for your patience, Miss Yandel," the officer said.

Father Shannon and Christine left the security area and began the long walk to their cabin. Desperate to understand, Christine relied solely on willpower to keep from talking. She followed Father Shannon up countless elevators and down endless hallways. Completely impervious to what was happening around her, Christine remained overwhelmed by the revelation in the security area. Questions stacked up in her mind like a tower of blocks, each new thought bringing the tower to the brink of collapse.

Father Shannon opened the door, and Christine walked into the cabin. For an instant, her mind filled with visions of Cinderella entering the grand ballroom. She was awestruck by the living room, which was twice the size of the one in her house. The two-bedroom suite was filled with the scent of tangerine and hibiscus, and fresh-cut flowers erupted from a vase on the living room table. The sliding glass door at the opposite end of the cabin framed the Kailua-Kona shoreline, the city lights twinkling through the glass like a night sky filled with stars.

The opulence of the cabin distracted Christine from the burning desire to know why she was there. She was unaware the ship was underway until the city lights faded from view. The window went black, and the movement of the ship restored her determination to get some answers.

She didn't know how or where to begin, so she blurted out the first ridiculous thought that entered her mind.

"Are you an angel?"

CHAPTER 8

OUR FUTURE DEPENDS ON YOU

Father Shannon smiled at Christine as she stood in front of the sliding glass door looking for answers. His blue eyes sparkled like jewels under the bright cabin lights. The moment their eyes met, he knew her question wasn't a joke and he relaxed his expression. He paused for a moment and assessed Christine's condition. Father Shannon searched for some indication that she was capable of understanding what he was about to tell her. The death of her mother was too much to process in a single day, so he hesitated. He knew it was unwise to expect Christine to handle anything more, especially what he needed to tell her.

"Well, are you?" she asked.

"What?" he replied, purposefully being evasive to avoid the discussion she was desperately trying to initiate.

"An angel."

"Look, Chris, you've had a very difficult day, and I think you need to get some rest. We'll talk in the morning—I promise to..."

"Not a chance!" she snapped, making certain he knew she wasn't going to bed without answers.

"My mother is dead, and people are hunting me like some kind of animal. I need some answers."

"It's complicated. I don't think now is the right time. I'm concerned it'll be too much for you after everything you've been through today."

"I don't care; I want to know what's going on."

Father Shannon walked over to the window where Christine was standing and stopped three feet in front of her so he could look her straight in the eye. He spoke without using his voice.

"Chris, have a seat," he said as he pointed to the couch.

Christine stepped backward when the voice entered her mind. Her back pressed against the window, and a burning sensation, like sitting too close to a campfire, filled her face. A blank stare accompanied the shock of hearing another voice inside her mind. Father Shannon shook his head, turned and walked toward the couch.

"It's complicated," he said aloud, not wanting to upset her further.

"I don't understand. How...?"

"If we're going to do this, then you need to sit." He pointed to the couch again.

She walked over and sat down, never taking her eyes off the priest. Anticipation traveled to every nerve in her body, leaving her anxious and apprehensive. Unable to find a comfortable position, she crossed her arms and waited for him to begin.

Father Shannon pulled a chair from the writing desk across from the couch and sat facing her.

"Chris, what do you remember about Jasper?"

"How do you know about him? Did my mother tell you?"

Just saying the word 'mother' scorched her heart. The ache was so great she was certain it was a heart attack unleashing the fire in her chest. *Why her? Why did she have to die?* Confusion settled on her face.

"Do you recall where we first met?" asked Jasper, using his own voice so she could hear it inside her mind.

"No," she said, with a nervous laugh. "Is this a trick question?"

"I'm sorry, Chris, I don't mean Father Shannon, I mean

Jasper."

The words filled Christine's mind, blocking every other thought. She jumped off the couch and stood up to meet Father Shannon. Standing with her nose less than an inch from his, her eyes bored into his.

"I don't know how you're doing this little trick, but stop it. It's not funny!"

"Please, Chris, sit down. It's not a trick."

"How do you know about Jasper?" she said through clenched teeth.

Christine backed her way onto the couch, unable to control her emotions. Countless images appeared in her mind like flashcards, each a memory of her short time with Jasper: the moment they met at the church door, the constant unbridled urge to be with him, how he subdued it with his touch, the weight of his body as he collapsed in her arms. Their only kiss.

"I... am... Jasper."

He waited for her to process his unspoken words, but Christine appeared on the verge of shattering like a Christmas ornament fallen from a tree. A small frown curled her lips.

"Jasper's dead. I saw it myself," she said, trying to refute the nonsense.

"His body is gone, but his existence continues here inside," he said and rubbed his chest with his hand.

"No!" she shouted.

"Whose voice do you hear inside your mind?"

Christine paused before she answered, "Jasper's."

"My voice."

"How can you be Jasper? You're Father Shannon."

"This is Father Shannon's body, but you hear Jasper. We are the same; we share consciousness. Father Shannon's mind rests deep inside his subconscious while I share his conscious mind."

"I don't understand. He died in my arms; I don't believe

you."

"Jasper's body is gone, but he still exists."

"This doesn't make sense."

"The first time you met Jasper was at the front door of St. Michael's."

Christine paused; she thought of the moment when she pushed the church door open and saw Jasper's face, and the incredible urge she felt to be with him.

"You could've seen us; you were conducting mass," said Christine, clinging to her denial.

"That night on the beach, you heard my voice in your mind. And the last word I spoke to you was 'Sanctuary.'"

Christine's pulse pounded in her forehead. Her eyes widened with the memory of the old surfboard she had painted with the word 'Sanctuary,' the name she had given to her favorite beach. *How could he know? Jasper whispered that to me just before he died.*

"I kissed you, and then my body died in your arms. But you heard another voice that night, didn't you?"

"This isn't possible," she protested, pushing herself to the back of the couch.

Christine was unable to blink; rainbow rings formed around the cabin lights and the room began to dim from the edges like someone was drawing a curtain. The low rhythmic humming of the ship was replaced by the sound of her short shallow breaths. Her breathing was made more difficult by the knot building in her stomach. Christine's vision blurred and she sunk her nails into the arm of the couch, trying to keep the room from spinning. A chill ripped through her body, and the color in her face turned to chalk.

"Chris, you better lay down," Jasper said, as he got up from his chair to help her.

"I'm just a little lightheaded. I'll be okay."

"Do you want some water?" he asked and quickly moved to the small bar fridge under the TV stand. He opened the fridge and took a bottle of water and a candy bar back to

Christine.

"We haven't eaten all day. Have this," he said, handing her the food and water.

"I don't think I can eat right now; my stomach is tied in knots."

"Try."

She opened the bottle of water and drank while contemplating everything she had just heard. Christine recalled the other voice she had heard in her mind that night and she asked again, "So you really are an angel?"

"No," Jasper replied.

"You're right, that night I did hear another voice— it was God, and He told me to swim away. I obeyed, but the current was too strong and it dragged me under. A moment later, I was carried to the surface by a pair of dolphins. They stayed with me the entire night, taking me to shore in the morning. God sent those dolphins; God saved me that night. It was God," she said with conviction, her faith unwavering.

"It wasn't God, it was me."

Christine choked on the words and coughed up some water as she struggled to catch her breath. A blotchy pink color instantly returned to her cheeks from the lack of air.

"Give me a break. Now you're telling me you're God? I don't think so," she said, faith welling to the surface in her voice.

"That depends on what you believe. All that matters is you. You are what's important."

"Whoa, whoa, whoa! What do you mean? You're telling me if I believe you're God, then I'm standing here talking to God?" she stated sarcastically.

"If that's what you believe."

"You're not God!" she shouted.

"What I am is what you will become... what all humans will become. We know it as Primoris."

"Pri... what?"

"Primoris. It is existence."

"Existence. What are you talking about? This is getting crazier by the second."

"Try to understand; it'll all make sense when I finish. But you have to let me finish."

"How can anyone make sense of this? First, you're Father Shannon, then you're Jasper, then you're God, and now existence itself. Who could believe any of this?"

Jasper paused for a moment and made sure his eyes met hers before he continued.

"Every time a human is conceived, something unique occurs. A tiny bit of energy is created within their DNA; it's the sum of this energy that makes Primoris. You and I, we form an infinitely small part, but it's the sum of all this energy throughout the universe that forms the Primoris. Think of the universe as a jigsaw puzzle. The energy within each human's DNA represents the small piece of the image of the completed puzzle. When you connect more pieces together, small parts of the image begin to form; these partial shapes represent an Animus. It is when you finally combine all of the individual pieces together that you form Primoris."

Christine's look changed from disbelief to confusion. The words registered in her mind, but their meaning eluded her. *What do human DNA, energy and the universe have to do with me?* A raised eyebrow and look of bewilderment covered her face.

Jasper paused as he searched for another way of explaining it to her.

"The Father, Son and Holy Spirit form one God?" Jasper asked, knowing Christine's faith was the answer.

"Yes."

"Do you believe in the power of the Holy Spirit?"

"Absolutely."

"Where does the Holy Spirit dwell?"

"Here, inside my heart, inside all of us," Christine said, holding her hand to her chest.

"Yes, imagine you can actually see the Holy Spirit, like a

small flicker of light."

"Okay," she said with hesitation.

"Do you think you would be able to see that light if a person was standing a hundred miles from you?"

"Of course not."

"Now imagine if you combined the power of the Holy Spirit from ten humans. Do you think you could see it then?"

"I'm not sure," she replied, somewhat confused.

"What if we combined the power of the Holy Spirit of all humans on earth?"

"Okay, I get it; I'd be able to see it?"

"Every time a human is conceived, the power of the Holy Spirit is created within them. Combine that power into one, what do you have?

"God," said Christine in sudden realization.

"If that's what you believe," Jasper replied with a smile.

She swallowed hard and formulated her next words, but they couldn't escape the jumbled mess of conflicting ideas in her mind. The strength of her faith remained intact. Christine struggled to connect the random events of the past forty-eight hours but without success. The mere suggestion of the physical presence of God was incomprehensible. A conflict raged between her belief in God and the facts before her. Her mental struggle found no compromise—spirituality and reality left her confounded. Not wanting to think of the implications of what she heard and if it was true, Christine scrambled to change the topic.

"Why me?" she asked, not convinced by Jasper's explanation.

"It has everything to do with you. You hold the key," Jasper said as his eyes dropped to her stomach.

Christine had completely forgotten about her pregnancy, the spark that had ignited the disaster of the last few days. She put her right hand to her stomach and slowly rubbed her belly. *Maybe the knot wasn't just nerves.* She had to know.

"You mean this?" she said and looked down to her

stomach.

"Yes."

"Tell me… How? How'd I get pregnant? It's not possible," she demanded.

"Do you believe in the Virgin Mary?"

"Yes, all Catholics do. Why?"

"Just as we did then, we have done for you."

"What?"

"The kiss," Jasper said.

"What kiss?"

"When I… kissed you on the beach."

"The blood," she said, the magnitude of her realization gripping her thoughts.

"That's why it burned. Growing inside you is someone unique, someone exceptional and unimaginably important. Our future depends on you."

CHAPTER 9

REFLECTION

Christine sat motionless on the edge of her seat as Jasper's words whipped through her mind like the bitter cold of a winter storm. She placed her hands over her stomach while repeating his last words inside her head, *"Our future depends on you."* Fear grew inside her, flooding her body like a rising tide. She looked into the blue eyes staring back at her and searched for something to say. Words escaped her; emotions ruled her actions. She stood up, walked to the balcony door and looked into the darkness. A moment passed until the need to be alone overwhelmed her.

"You okay?" Jasper asked.

His voice inside her head startled her. It instantly banished her confusion and provided the clarity she needed to enable a response.

"Yes, but I'm tired. I'm going to bed."

"You're certain you're all right?" Jasper asked, not convinced by Christine's excuse.

"Yup."

"Okay. I'll see you in the morning."

Christine lay on top of the bed without taking her clothes off—over-exhaustion made sleep impossible. Her thoughts tugged at her mind from every direction, never giving her a moment's peace. The death of her mother was etched into her mind, and she prayed for hours, but no relief arrived. The sound of the waves slamming the hull of the ship was mesmerizing, and the gentle rocking of the vessel lulled her into an incoherent state between sleep and consciousness.

Jasper's voice inside her head accompanied his knock on her bedroom door. Christine looked at the clock on the nightstand and squinted from the daylight flooding her room.

"Chris, you up?"

"Yes," she responded out of instinct, her voice cracking from the dryness in her throat.

"You need to eat."

"I'm not hungry," she replied, hoping to be left alone.

"It's been two days since you had a proper meal. Come and get some breakfast," Jasper demanded.

"I'll meet you there."

"Don't be long," he said, indicating by his tone that he would return for her if she didn't arrive.

Christine heard the cabin door shut and lifted herself to the side of the bed. The room began to spin, so she closed her eyes and grabbed the edge of the mattress in a futile attempt to stop the movement. Certain of what would come next, she raced to the bathroom. She held the sides of the toilet with both hands as the first convulsion rolled through her body like the waves outside. The morning sickness continued for another ten minutes, leaving her legs unable to support her. She quickly filled the plastic cup next to the sink and rinsed her mouth before closing the lid of the toilet. She sat on the lid facing the shower, trying to regain her strength.

Concerned by the time it was taking Christine to join him, Jasper returned. When she heard the cabin door open, Christine cut her rest short and stood up to remove her clothes. Like a slap in the face, disgust stunned her when she saw her reflection in the mirror. Barely visible behind the mass of disheveled hair in front of her face, Christine's blue eyes were floating in a sea of red. Her broad shoulders and athletic physique filled the rest of the image. The honey-oak tan covering her body lightened under the artificial light of the bathroom, contrasting with her sun-bleached brown hair. *I can't go out like this. I don't have any clothes; I don't even have a toothbrush.*

Christine finished her shower and put her clothes back on. She used the hair dryer to shape her hair as best as she could before putting it back on the hook on the wall in an act of surrender. Hunger pains swirled in her stomach, reminding her that Jasper was right. She reached for the bathroom door and let out a large sigh.

"Oh, there you are. I was getting worried," Jasper said, slightly embarrassed for returning to get her.

"You're right; I'm hungry," Christine said, ignoring his embarrassment in an attempt to be polite.

"How you feeling?"

"Okay. Please stop worrying about me."

"Chris, a lot has happened, and all at once. It would be difficult for anyone to handle."

"I just need some time, that's all."

"You'll have plenty of that. We'll be here for the next two weeks."

"Two weeks!" Christine stated, unable to hold back the surprise in her tone.

"Yes, we can't get off until Sydney."

"We're going to Australia?" she asked in disbelief, having never left the Big Island. The news of going to a foreign country stunned her momentarily.

"Is that a problem?" Jasper asked, aware of the concern in her voice.

"No, it's just that I've never left Hawaii before. Why Australia?"

"We can hide there, and they've got excellent medical care."

"We're staying there?"

"Yes."

"How long?"

"You need to get something to eat. Let's get some breakfast, and then show you the rest of the ship," Jasper replied, avoiding her question.

Christine was annoyed by his change of topic but didn't have the strength to pursue the matter any further. She followed him out of the cabin to the breakfast buffet, where they sat on the deck and watched the waves.

***

The days drifted slowly by as the ship made its way to the southern hemisphere. Christine ignored the ports of call and remained on the Lido Deck sunbathing by the pool. Jasper bought her an MP3 player when they were shopping for clothes and other essentials from the onboard boutique. Exhausted by lack of sleep and soothed by the warmth of the sun while lying on a lounge chair, Christine drifted off to sleep. When not dozing off, she passed the time reading a Bible she found in her nightstand drawer.

She read each passage carefully, desperately looking for guidance. *How can he be God?* she thought. Christine read each page slowly, absorbing the words and hoping to find something to support what Jasper had told her. With every mention of the Holy Spirit, she re-read the passage in search of understanding. Nothing appeared in the text, but she couldn't dispute the facts—Jasper's voice inside her mind was real.

Christine avoided contact with him as much as possible.

Jasper could sense Christine's alienation and gave her the space she needed. He left her to herself with only an occasional check to reassure himself that she was doing all right.

The solitude and lack of sleep, however, made Christine's animosity over her mother's death fester and grow inside her.

It was seven nights before she welcomed a full night's

sleep. The morning sickness subsided, but the constant images of her mother haunted her. Although the days were tolerable, she dreaded the nights. Time wasn't her friend; it fueled her anger while doing nothing to heal her pain. She felt like a prisoner on the ship, and the mental torture of replaying her mother's death occurred continuously in her mind. Christine's anger eventually blossomed into hatred.

With each passing day, it became more difficult for her to return to the cabin and face Jasper. Resentment flowed through her veins like the toxin of a rattlesnake bite. With no one to talk to, she began to direct her anger toward him. The complete upheaval in her life had finally taken its toll.

They met early for their dinner at the entrance to the dining room and were escorted to their seats by the maître d'. Navy blue and peach décor filled the room, making it resemble a gala ballroom decorated for a wedding. The sun cast its remaining rays across the ocean, filling the floor to ceiling window next to their table with an amber glow. Their waiter arrived and welcomed them to dinner before taking their order, but Christine struggled to hear him over the crowd of passengers filling the massive dining room. She ordered her food and immediately began asking Jasper the same questions she had asked every night that week.

"Why me?"

"I told you, I'm not discussing anything until we're off this ship."

"Why not? I have a right to know—it's my life," Christine demanded.

"This isn't about life. It's far more important than that."

"Nothing is more important than life… except…" snapped Christine but quickly stopped midsentence.

"Except…?" Jasper repeated with a tone of expectation.

"God," she finished.

CHAPTER 10

FIND HIM

The rain erupted like popcorn on the corrugated steel roof of the building across the parking lot of the Siam Hotel. Clouds of humidity drifted into the open-air lobby as a flash of lightning bounced off the polished marble floor. The subsequent roll of thunder was muted by the crowd of German tourists gathered at the front desk to check in. A bellboy walked across the lobby carrying an unopened umbrella. He approached a middle-aged man seated in a wicker chair reading a British tabloid.

"Mr. Middleton, your taxi has arrived," said the bellboy, his English hindered by a strong Thai accent.

Dan Middleton folded the paper closed and tossed it on his seat as he stood up to follow the bellboy. Unlike most visitors, he didn't tower over the locals, but his sandy blonde hair identified him as a foreigner. His hazel brown eyes and gleaming white smile were alluring. Dan was a regular at the hotel, so the tropical humidity went unnoticed by him. He struggled to catch up to the bellboy walking through the lobby, and the boy opened the umbrella over him as they left the cover of the hotel. It deflected the pelting rain onto the roof of the taxi as Dan entered it.

"*Kob-jai*," Dan said, and he handed the bellboy a bill before closing the door.

"*Sa-wat dee Kraup*, hello, where to please?" said the driver in poor English.

"*Patpong.*"

The taxi left the hotel parking lot, its headlights reflecting off the sheets of rain falling in the darkness as it tried to enter the busy Bangkok street. The traffic was choked to a standstill by the torrents of water rushing down the pavement. Frustrated by the gridlock, the driver maneuvered the taxi off the street. The downpour allowed him to detour through the normally crowded back lanes without hindrance. He stopped the taxi in front of the Red Bird, one of Bangkok's most infamous dance clubs. Dan paid the driver, jumped out and ran for the cover of the awning at the back entrance. He pressed the buzzer while looking into the camera bubble, and the door opened immediately.

"Welcome back, Mr. Middleton," said a well-dressed man holding the door open.

"Good evening, Rak."

"I have a special surprise for you tonight."

"You're too kind," said Dan with a smile.

They left the entrance and stepped into the reception area to the right of the door. A chair positioned behind a short countertop holding a computer video monitor filled half the room. Dan followed Rak past the counter and through a long black curtain at the back of the room. The dim corridor was lined on both sides with dark green doors, each identified with a dull brass number. The hallway vibrated from the music crashing through the walls and the rhythmic thumping of the dance floor below. The pounding disco beat was deafening, like a jet landing on a runway, making it impossible to speak. Dan stopped at door number seven and faced Rak as he opened it. Rak smiled back and continued down the corridor as Dan entered the room.

The moment Dan shut the door, the noise was reduced to a low background hum. The small room was windowless and furnished with a small bed and large leather chair. Amber light filtered from the two small lamps mounted to the wall on both sides of the headboard. The walls were covered with traditional Thai paintings—elephants and tropical vistas dominated the scenes. He sat in the chair and crossed his legs and a young Asian girl, no older than thirteen, entered the room.

"*Sa-wat dee Kraup*," Dan said as he stood up to greet the girl.

She nodded and approached him with hesitation.

"*Sa-wat dee Kah*," she replied and bowed to him.

"Dan," he said, pointing to himself.

"Lamai," she responded.

"Don't be nervous. Is this your first time?" he asked, now realizing she was Rak's surprise.

***

The air filled with the putrid smell of rotting waste left behind from the overflowing storm drains, and as the rain dissipated, tourists returned to the back lanes like rats returning to an alleyway.

A midnight blue sedan parked twenty feet from the back entrance of the Red Bird, and the driver walked to the door, ringing the buzzer.

"Yes?" asked Rak through the intercom.

"I'm here to see Dan," said the driver.

"Is he expecting you?"

"Yes, we have a special night planned."

Rak moved from behind the counter and walked over to the door to let him in.

"He didn't tell me he was expecting a guest," Rak said, clearly surprised by the unexpected guest.

"How could he tell you anything with that music blaring?" said the driver in a failed attempt at humor.

"They're in seven," Rak replied, and he pointed to the curtain before returning to his seat behind the counter.

The driver turned toward the curtain, reached into his suit and removed a gun. In a single swift motion, he aimed the weapon and fired a single bullet through the side of Rak's temple. The gunfire went unnoticed over the raging music. Blood splattered onto the video monitor and formed a circular pattern of small droplets that slid down the screen like water on a shower door. Rak's head fell forward and hit the counter before his body slipped out of the chair to the floor.

The driver walked methodically down the dark corridor, inspecting each door until he arrived at door number seven. He used a lull in the music to listen for movement from the other side of the door, but he heard nothing so he waited patiently for the noise to begin again before he tried the handle. Lamai had left the door unlocked, so he entered the room undetected. Dan stood to the right of the bed naked, his backside to the door, and Lamai was crouched on her knees in front of him.

"Those British children not enough for you, Father?" the driver asked, intentionally startling Dan as the pounding of the disco returned.

"How did you get...?" Dan said, and he pushed Lamai's head away from his body as he turned to face the man.

The driver reached for his gun and pointed it at Dan.

"Stop! Please, I've got money!" Dan pleaded.

"Money?" laughed the driver. "I don't want money. It's my job to send priests like you to hell."

"No, wait..."

"I'll see you there."

The driver put two bullets into Father Middleton's chest as the priest lunged toward him, and Dan's body crumpled to the floor at the foot of the bed.

Lamai grabbed her face and screamed in horror before the bullet pierced her forehead. The crack of the gunfire was camouflaged completely by the music.

"I'm sorry, dear, but it had to be immaculate," said the driver, looking down at the young girl's body.

He calmly left the room, closing the door as if he were

leaving his office for the evening, and removed the surveillance video computer from the counter before he left.

***

Warm yellow light flooded through the window of the small Vatican office where Tonino stood like a statue staring at the moon, his grey hair appearing luminescent in the moonlight. He was growing agitated waiting for Father Derksen and Gino to arrive.

They entered his office a moment later, accompanied by a young priest dressed in traditional robes. Tonino didn't face the men when they entered; he just continued to gaze into the dark courtyard below. The young priest's tall, stocky physique complimented his early thirties youth, and his short strawberry blonde hair and slightly freckled face gave him the appearance of a university student rather than a priest. It was naivety and arrogance that shielded him from Tonino's presence.

"Did you bring him?" asked Tonino, still unwilling to face the men.

"Yes. He returned from Thailand last week," Father Derksen responded.

Tonino finally turned toward the men, his face featureless in the moon light.

"Ah, Father Black, we finally meet. Father Derksen informed me you had to deal with another who had gone astray from our flock. I had more pressing matters to deal with, and it slipped my mind. I trust it was immaculate?" asked Tonino and looked at Father Derksen before turning to greet the new priest.

Father Derksen nodded in acknowledgment.

"Hello, I'm Father Sean Black," said the young priest with a noticeable Australian accent. "I consider all my work immaculate," he said with a wide smile while he searched the void of Tonino's eyes for a reaction, but none was given.

"I applaud your work and the talent you bring to our organization. That's why I've asked Father Derksen to bring you here tonight."

"Thank you. I love doing the work of God. After all, it's why I was ordained."

"Sit so we can get started. We have much to cover and time is not our friend," said Tonino, speaking directly to Father Black as if they were alone in the room. The men sat in chairs facing Tonino, who sat behind his antique wooden desk.

"We're looking for another priest..." started Tonino, but his sentence was interrupted by Father Black.

"Another one. How many of these perverts...?"

Tonino in turn interrupted Father Black's sentence before he could finish. Casting his coal black eyes into the young priest's, he sent a clear message of his displeasure at the interruption.

Father Black returned a smile and allowed Tonino to continue.

"This one isn't like the others. He's taken something which belongs to the Church, and it is imperative that we get it back."

"What is it?"

"That's not important. You just have to find him," snapped Tonino, and he slapped the desk in front of him.

Father Black sat up in his seat, taken aback by Tonino's forceful show of emotion. He looked left and right to gauge a response from Father Derksen and Gino, but neither man showed any sign of concern at the outburst.

Tonino forced a smile to his lips after realizing his actions had startled Father Black.

"It's imperative you find him as soon as possible. Is that clear?"

"Yes, of course."

"And, Father Black, you have the full extent of the Vatican Secret Service at your disposal," said Tonino, more for Father

Derksen and Gino's benefit than Father Black's.

"Thanks," said Father Black, and he gloated, knowing that the power of the clandestine organization was both highly effective and global.

"When I find him, what do you want me to do?"

"Don't let him out of your sight until I arrive."

"Understood."

The three men stood from their seats and began to leave the office when Tonino stopped them with his words.

"Father Black, it won't be that simple. He knows we're looking for him."

"Yes, that'll present some difficulties but..." said Father Black.

"What is it?" Tonino snapped.

"What's his name?" asked Father Black.

"Andrew Shannon, St. Michael's Parish, Hawaii."

"I'll leave in the morning."

CHAPTER 11

TERMINAL VECTOR

The sun gathered strength as the *MS Volendam* slowly made its way into Sydney Harbor. Joggers and dog-walkers dotted the shoreline, and orange and yellow beams of light reflected off the mirrored windows of the downtown office buildings, announcing the early morning sunrise. The gentle rocking of the ship was gone, and Christine awoke for only the second time with morning sickness. The two weeks aboard the cruise ship had provided countless hours of mental fatigue brought on by continuous mourning.

Confusion lingered in her mind, the whole time crippling all her other thoughts. The sound of Father Shannon's spoken voice conflicted with Jasper's voice in her head. Christine questioned her sanity and wondered if she was becoming schizophrenic. Overwhelmed by the drastic changes thrust upon her, she fought back the anger brewing in her thoughts. *Why is this happening to me? I just want to go home.* And most of all, *Why won't he tell me?* This last thought was directed at Jasper's refusal to explain any more to her since their first night on the ship.

Christine pulled herself from the bed and grabbed the bathrobe hanging on the back of her bedroom door. Uncomfortable walking in front of Father Shannon/Jasper in just her underwear, she made her way to the bathroom to shower and fight back the nausea. Covering up was unnecessary, as Jasper had left the cabin a half-hour earlier for an early breakfast.

Christine had finished adding shampoo to her hair when she heard the main cabin door open. Not sure if it was Jasper or the cleaning staff, she formed the thought in her mind, *Is that you, Jasper?* but she didn't speak the words as soapy water flooded over her face.

"Excellent, Chris, you're able to communicate without speaking," Jasper responded, his voice inside her mind as clear as if he were standing in the shower next to her.

"What?"

"You can communicate with me using only your thoughts," Jasper replied.

Unaware of her new ability, Christine yelled from within the shower.

"What are you talking about?"

"Chris, don't speak, just think your words."

She heard these words inside her mind and responded.

"When are you going to tell me why this has happened to me?"

"Fantastic, but I can't say I'm happy with your choice of questions."

"I want to know what's going on," she yelled through the bathroom door as she pulled on her bathrobe. She opened the door and stepped into the room to find Jasper standing with an exceptionally large smile plastered across his face.

"I'm happy you've progressed this fast. I'll tell you everything you want to know this afternoon."

"Great," she replied, but she was unsure if her tone could have been more sarcastic.

"Go and get some breakfast. I have some calls to make."

Christine returned half an hour later to find Jasper waiting on the couch holding the large brown envelope containing their documents. They left the cabin and entered the long line of passengers waiting to disembark.

Jasper and Christine leaned over the railing of the massive

ship and gazed down at the water below. Jasper pulled his phone from his pocket and dropped it over the side. They watched it freefall to the water and disappear below the surface.

"What are you doing?" Christine asked in disbelief.

"I don't want to make the same mistake twice."

"What do you mean?"

"I'll explain later; it's time to go," he replied as the line began moving again.

They walked with the rest of the crowd down the gangplank and off the ship.

Once disembarked, they took a taxi directly to the MBG Bank in downtown Sydney. A moment of panic flashed through Christine as the driver pulled away from the curb, as the sight of traffic driving on the opposite side of the road was unnerving. It was made worse by the oddity of their driver sitting in the right front seat.

Jasper went in to the bank while Christine waited in the taxi. He returned with a small white envelope that he put inside the large brown one.

"Number 1411 Bronte Marine Drive," Jasper said to the driver.

"Do you have a preference which route, mate?" asked the driver with a slight Indian accent, despite using a very Australian expression.

"Take the scenic route," responded Jasper.

The taxi crawled through the downtown traffic for forty-five minutes before making it to Military Road in North Bondi. Christine's first glimpse of the deep blue Pacific Ocean from the other side of it conjured strong memories of surfing back home. Her eyes tingled as she fought the tears, and she kept staring outwards so Jasper couldn't see her eyes. Sea spray exploded into the air as the waves pounded the light brown sandstone shoreline, and for the first time thoughts of home consumed her. Christine knew she would never see the black lava cliffs again.

Their progress slowed when the taxi turned onto Campbell Parade, impeded by the hordes of beach-goers heading to Bondi Beach. When the driver finally stopped in the driveway, Christine was overcome by the magnificence of the view. She jumped out of the taxi, walked to the back of it and leaned against the trunk as she gazed out over the water. The house was fifty feet above Bronte Beach and had an unobstructed view of the ocean. Her heart raced with excitement when she spotted the surfers floating on the water. Like a powerful magnet, the ocean pulled her toward it, beckoning her into its waves.

"Chris," said Jasper, but she ignored the word in her mind.

"Chris," he repeated, but there was still no response.

"Christine!" he said, and this time the tone of his voice was just below a shout.

She suddenly snapped out of the trance the ocean had cast over her and turned to face Jasper. It wasn't until then that she realized the taxi was trying to leave the driveway. Christine had been so consumed by the view that she was still leaning on the trunk, preventing the car from moving.

"Sorry," she replied, slightly embarrassed as she moved out of the way.

"What do you think? Could you live here?"

"What?" she said, unable to contain the excitement in her voice.

"This is our new home."

"You're joking!"

"You can't be left alone again," Jasper said, not hiding the insistence in his tone.

"I don't need a babysitter, or at least not yet," responded Christine, equally forceful in her tone.

"It's not negotiable."

"Okay. I'm ready to know why."

Jasper removed the small white envelope from the larger one and emptied a set of keys into his hand. He unlocked the front door and held it opened for Christine to enter. She walked straight to the large living room window and pulled open the blinds, allowing the daylight to fill the room.

Jasper inspected the other rooms of the single-level home, leaving Christine in the living room.

"It's two-bedroom, and you have your own bathroom. The kitchen and bathrooms have been updated, but the rest of the place is from the seventies. I hope it'll do."

"It's incredible."

"I'm glad you like it. We're going to be here a while."

"What do you mean?"

"Chris, come sit down. It's time we talked," he said as he took a seat on the couch and waited for Christine to join him.

"You want to know why?"

"Yes, why is this happening to me?"

"Remember what I told you about the Primoris? And how this has everything to do with you?"

"Yah."

"You and I were the last two Vectors the Primoris have been hiding for millennia."

"Vectors? Hiding? From who?"

"From the Vacare."

"The what?" Christine asked, straining to understand.

"Vacare is the exact opposite of Primoris—it's non-existence. The only purpose of the Vacare is to destroy the Primoris."

"What's this have to do with me?" Christine asked, even more frustrated and confused.

"Be patient, and I'll explain. As I told you before, an Animus expands Primoris. They do this throughout the universe by using planets like earth. They do this by creating human DNA—it's like planting seeds and waiting for them to grow. Your mother was a Vector, and her mother before her, and so on. You carry part of a code in your DNA; it was placed there from the first human DNA created on earth. My father did the same for me, and my DNA carried the other half. When the two original DNA are combined, they complete the code and create a Terminal Vector."

Christine's stomach knotted. Breathing escaped her. This was the first moment she realized what Jasper had been explaining to her. Her eyes widened, and her hearing faded as multiple thoughts raged in her mind at once. A crack formed in her faith, weakening the foundation of her inner strength. Questions arrived in her mind that she had never postulated before. The answers scared her and conjured an internal repulsion like nothing she had ever experienced before. Fear tangled her tongue, leaving her mute. *This can't be right. He's not God, he can't be*, she thought.

She sat motionless, staring blankly at Jasper, her crystal-blue eyes glossed over with confusion. Several minutes passed before Christine regained control of herself. Jasper, aware of her consternation, paused, allowing her time to absorb the meaning of his words. Christine's eye indicated that she was about to speak.

"It's not possible. I don't believe it. I can't believe it," she forced from her lips.

Jasper didn't respond. He knew time was the only cure for her.

"Are you God?"

Jasper hesitated before responding. Christine's belief in God couldn't be put into question without completely crushing her faith, and it was her faith that she clung to for guidance when all else failed. Jasper was certain this was one of those times when she needed her faith.

"Chris, I know it's difficult but try and understand. It's only what *you* believe that matters—nothing else."

"I don't know what to believe."

"I think we've talked enough today. You need to get some..."

"Forget it, I want to know everything," she demanded, regaining her resilience when Jasper tried to end the discussion.

"Why do the Vac... whatever they are, want us?"

"It's not *us* or really *you* they are trying to kill; it's the Terminal Vector they care about."

"Why?"

"The struggle between the Primoris and the Vacare begins at human conception. The Vacare are absolute nothingness— a vacuum that will consume all energy. In order for the Vacare to succeed, they require energy; but unlike Primoris, they can't create it.

"The Vacare hunt us across the universe to prevent critical mass. That's the moment in time when enough energy has been created to allow Convergence—the instant when existence expands."

"Vacare, Vectors, critical mass and now Convergence, this is impossible to understand," she said, angered by her inability to follow what Jasper was telling her.

"Let me finish."

"Jasper, just tell me why they're trying to kill me!" she shouted.

"I'm trying to, Chris," replied Jasper, equally frustrated by his lack of progress.

"I'm sorry. You're right; I don't understand any of this."

"Okay, let's try this. When your DNA combined with Jasper's—mine—it formed a special human, we know it as a 'Terminal Vector.' Your unborn child is the key to destroying the Vacare—its destiny was determined millennia ago. It's my job to make certain the Terminal Vector, your child, fulfills that destiny and expands Primoris."

"What if I don't want this? What if he or she doesn't want this?" asked Christine, despising the notion that she didn't have a choice and her unborn child had to play a part of it.

"Chris, there's no second chance; once a Terminal Vector has been created, it must fulfill its destiny or the Vacare will succeed. The Vacare will stop at nothing to prevent Convergence."

"So what, we just disappear?" she snapped, trying to comprehend what absolute nothingness actually meant.

"There are places throughout the universe where Convergence has failed, but the Vacare did not succeed. Nothing remained but a lifeless, vacant planet—a rock floating in space. The Vacare would have this happen to the earth rather than allow Convergence. However, the Vacare's ultimate purpose is to prevent Convergence while at the same time allowing the energy we created to increase unabated. The earth would implode, leaving nothing but a vacuum in space—the essence of the Vacare."

Jasper looked directly into Christine's eyes, hoping she would understand this more simplistic explanation of the importance of her pregnancy.

"So killing me would destroy the earth?"

"Yes, but not just the earth, everything, the entire universe—nothing would remain but a black hole," said Jasper, intending his words to shock her into comprehending the magnitude of Convergence.

Christine raised herself from the couch, walked over to the window and looked down at the beach below. *How can this be happening to me? Why me?* These thoughts drifted in and out of her mind like the waves rolling onto the beach. A cold, dull numbness came over her, triggered by the apathy and powerlessness sweeping through her. With her faith broken, her determination collapsed like a sandcastle meeting the tide. She remained at the window in silence, the uncertainty running rampant in her thoughts.

Suddenly, warmth returned to her body. It started slowly in the pit of her stomach and then spread rapidly to her limbs followed by her fingers and toes. It fired every nerve in her body as it surged up her spine. It tingled the surface of her skin like an electric shock until it finally culminated in her head. The warmth mushroomed into red-hot anger, and it was fueled by her tremendous inner strength.

Christine stared out of the window, her blue eyes sparkling in the daylight. Nothing going to harm her child, and at that moment, she resolved to fight back.

CHAPTER 12

THE PRIZE

T he ocean breeze had yet to rise when Father Black stepped out of the jet and onto the steps leading down to the tarmac. The morning sun filtered through a band of clouds streaming across the Hawaiian sky. A mob of excited tourists happy to exit the six-hour flight from the mainland began funneling their way to the baggage claim area of Kona Airport. Father Black wheeled his carry-on past the crowd to pick up his rental car.

The drive along the Island Highway from the airport to St. Michael's parish was an easy one since it was early on a Saturday morning. His arrival at the rectory was not unexpected; both Father Colin Weston and Richard Whyte were sitting on the front porch. Father Black parked the car next to the rectory and smiled through the driver's side window at the two men awaiting his arrival.

"G'day," said Father Black with no attempt to hide his accent.

"Morning," replied the two men.

Father Weston placed his coffee on the porch railing and stepped down to meet Father Black. Richard remained on the porch as the men exchanged a handshake.

"You must be Father Weston?"

"Yes. I'm Colin and this is Richard Whyte, a deacon with our parish. Can I get you a coffee?" asked Father Weston.

"No, thanks. I had plenty on the flight. I'm Father Sean Black."

"Shall we go in and sit down?" asked Father Weston.

"That would be great."

The three men entered the rectory and sat in the small living room. The morning light filtered through the partially closed blinds, covering the walls in an alternating pattern of light and shadow. The walls were covered with hand-painted images of saints and apostles.

"I understand you're looking for Father Shannon," Father Weston started.

"Yes, that's why I'm here. Has he contacted you?"

"No. I informed the police about a week ago, but they said there's not much they can do since there's no evidence of wrongdoing."

"Do you have any idea why he left so suddenly?" asked Richard, suspecting that it had something to do with the Andersons.

"No idea."

"I know it has to do with the Anderson girl and her mother," said Richard, deciding not to hide his suspicion.

"Who?" asked Father Black, surprised by Richard's comment.

"The Andersons—Christine and her mother Sandra. They live just off the Island Highway near the airport," replied Richard.

"Now, Richard, let's not spread rumors. It's only a coincidence. There's nothing to suggest that," Father Weston put in.

"What's a coincidence?" asked Father Black.

"Just before Father Shannon left, the Anderson girl was here speaking to him and..."

"Tell him what I saw," interrupted Richard, unable to contain his excitement.

"Okay, Richard, if you feel it that important, go ahead," said Father Weston, bowing to Richard's enthusiasm.

A large smile filled Richard's face, and he turned to face Father Black.

"About a month ago, Father Shannon and I received an unexpected visit from Vatican staff. It was a very brief visit. They asked us if we had seen anyone in the parish with a weird fish-like symbol on their body. I thought it was really odd, to tell you the truth. But as it turns out, one of our parishioners did have the symbol on the back of her neck. I saw it the day she came to see Father Shannon."

"Who?"

"Christine Anderson. I told Father Shannon about it, but he didn't seem to care; he was only interested in talking to Chris. Father Derksen left me his card, so I decided to contact him myself. I figured it must have been important if they came to see us directly. We've never had a visit from the Vatican before," said Richard, the pride beaming from his face.

"You called Father Derksen?" asked Father Black, trying to control the surprise in his voice.

"Yes, emailed. Do you know him?" asked Richard.

"I know of him," Father Black replied.

"Not long after that, Father Shannon left on a family emergency and the Andersons disappeared. I don't think it's coincidence at all because..."

"I think that's enough, Richard," interjected Father Weston, silencing Richard with his eyes as well as his words.

"Please, Father Weston, let Richard finish. Any information may prove helpful to locate Father Shannon, no matter how inconsequential you think it is," said Father Black, and then he turned to face Richard again.

"I think Father Shannon's relationship with the Andersons was more than just spiritual."

"Richard, this is nonsense, I've known Andrew for almost twenty years, and I've never had a reason to think that," Father Weston responded, the disturbed look on his face magnified in his voice.

"What makes you think this?"

"He knew Sandra before Chris was born, and they often spent time together outside of church functions like…"

"That's enough, Richard! This is no reason to suspect anything," interrupted Father Weston.

"Father Weston, let him finish!" Father Black said, clearly very annoyed by the interruption.

"From the moment of her birth, Father Shannon attended all of Chris' birthdays and never missed a school function. He attended more of her events than I attended my own daughter's," Richard said, desperately trying to hide the jealousy in his tone.

No longer able to listen to the accusations, Father Weston reached for his coffee mug on the table in front of his seat and carried it to the kitchen. Anger was painted across his face and his stride displayed his displeasure. Father Shannon was not only his co-worker but a good friend, and it pained him to hear Richard's disparaging words.

"Anything else?" asked Father Black.

"Not that I can think of," Richard replied.

"Thank you, this has been extremely helpful."

"Father Black, what's so important about Christine?"

"I have no idea."

Father Weston returned to the room as the two men stood from their seats. His displeasure remained unabated.

"Can you show me to his room?" Father Black inquired.

"Why?" Father Weston asked with surprise.

"I'm looking for anything that might tell me where to look for him. Family photos, letters… anything like that."

"If you think it can help," Father Weston replied, unable to hide the reluctance in his tone.

Father Black was escorted upstairs to Father Shannon's bedroom, which remained exactly how Father Shannon had left it. Father Weston stood in the doorway as Father Black walked to the dresser with the photos on it. He lifted the one of Father Shannon and Sandra Anderson holding the infant

Christine and read the writing.

"I see what Richard means," he stated, casting a glance at Father Weston.

He placed the photo back on the dresser and lifted the last photo to the right. It was a photo of Father Shannon, Christine and Sandra at Christine's sixteenth birthday. Father Black looked hard at the photo before replacing it.

"You don't mind if I look through some of these, do you?" asked Father Black, picking up another much older framed photo of Father Shannon. When he turned the photo over to look for a caption, he found a small newspaper clipping pressed between the frame and the photo. Yellowed by age, the frail slip of paper was folded in half. With the skill of a pickpocket, Father Black removed the paper and placed it in the sleeve of his suit coat unnoticed by Father Weston.

"What are you looking for?"

"I told you, anything that can help me find him," snapped Father Black, his patience running out.

"Why is the Vatican so interested in finding Father Shannon anyway? It seems to me they are unusually concerned with finding someone who we aren't certain is missing."

"I would think you, of all people, would be happy the Vatican is looking for your friend. Or is it possible you weren't as close as you claim?"

"Are you finished? I have an appointment I need to prepare for," Father Weston said with a sigh.

"I'm done," replied Father Black, fully aware of the meaning in Father Weston's question.

Father Weston followed Father Black down the stairs to the front door. Richard stood behind him as he opened the door for Father Black. The warm morning air flooded into the rectory as Father Weston held the door open. Father Black stepped out and stood in the shade of the porch. He then turned and faced the two men.

"Thank you for your time."

"I hope we've been helpful," said Father Weston, offering little sincerity.

"Very helpful," replied Father Black as he looked past Father Weston to Richard.

"Great, now if you can excuse me, I must prepare for my meeting," Father Weston said while looking directly at Richard, signaling it was time for him to leave.

Both men returned to their vehicles and drove out of the church parking lot. Father Black turned his car on to Alii Drive and headed for the Island Highway. Before getting on the highway, he turned into the Kona Coast Shopping Centre parking lot and stopped the car. He shook his right arm back and forth, causing the small slip of paper to fall from his sleeve onto the passenger seat.

He opened the folded paper and read the article published in the Dublin Irish Times on November 8, 1970. The article read:

'*Catholic Orphanage Receives Generous Donation*'

St. Joseph's orphanage received a sizable donation from an anonymous source yesterday following the adoption of a child. Sister Abigail Moyle, the head of the orphanage, refused to comment on the source of the funding, stating, "It was a very generous contribution, and we're all very pleased that the boy is going to a happy loving family." Sister Moyle refused any further comment on the matter.

Father Black refolded the clipping and placed it inside a small notebook he kept in his breast pocket. He removed his phone and searched the Internet for 'Sandra Anderson, Kailua-Kona, Hawaii.' The search returned only five names and addresses. He used the online maps to locate the address nearest to the airport. Father Black placed his phone on hands free, dialed Father Derksen's number and left the parking lot for the Anderson house.

"I hope it's good news," Father Derksen said, his voice a little distorted over the speaker.

"Why didn't you tell me about the girl?"

"It wasn't necessary."

"If you expect results, I need to have all the information."

"He provided you what was necessary—nothing more."

"Who am I looking for, the girl or the priest?"

"Find one and you'll find the other."

"What's so special about her?"

"Don't concern yourself with that, just do your job," Father Derksen said and hung up.

The sedan pulled off the highway and made its way down the crushed lava rock driveway toward the Anderson home. Startled by the grinding sound of the tires, a flock of doves took flight from the middle of the driveway.

Tropical plants had overtaken the flowerbeds at the front of the house as well as the small vegetable garden in the yard. Like a crystal bull's eye, a perfectly formed banana spider web hung between the bottom of the lanai and the papaya tree on the side of the house. A bundle of yellow police tape lay rolled in a ball on the small chair near the front door.

Father Black knocked on the door with his left hand and turned the door handle with his right, certain there was no one home. The handle didn't move, so he returned to the car to retrieve his tools. He wedged the knife in between the door and the jamb, and hit it with a single blow, opening the old door easily.

The entrance was littered with envelopes shoved under the door, and the house smelled of rotting fruit. When he walked through the small living room, his footsteps created the only sound in the unusually silent house. He entered what he presumed to be Sandra Anderson's room first. It was just as she had left it, the queen-sized bed filled half the room with a pair of slippers stationed next to it, and every piece of clothing was hung neatly in the closet. The walls were covered with photos, mostly of Christine at every stage of her childhood, but some contained Sandra and Father Shannon.

Father Black scanned the images as he walked through the room, analyzing each picture with purpose. He stopped near the back of the room, removed a photo from the wall and studied every detail of it. It was exactly the same photo he had held in Father Shannon's bedroom. He turned it over and read the writing on the back: *'To Sandy, Love Andy.'* He hung the photo back on the wall.

He left Sandra's room and entered the other bedroom, obviously Christine's. The room was half the size of Sandra's and appeared even smaller with all the clothing covering the floor. The disheveled condition of the room resembled a teenager's. The walls were covered with posters of famous women surfers.

Father Black pushed the clothing aside with his feet as he moved through the room, making his way to the mirror over the top of the small dresser in the corner. Half a dozen recent photos of Christine and Jesse were taped to the edges of the mirror. Father Black peeled one of the photos off and put it in his pocket. It was on his way back to the door that he found the prize he was searching for—Christine's laptop.

CHAPTER 13

BAD FRIDAY

Autumn arrived in Sydney much the same as it did in Hawaii, with cooler evenings and bigger waves. Christine sat in the shade of the palm trees watching the line of surfers paddle into the horizon. Burdened by self-consciousness and her volleyball sized stomach, Christine kept herself off the water even though she remained physically able to surf. The mental anguish of being pregnant seemed to increase concurrently with her size. Each passing week brought a new experience: foot pain, backache and never-ending hunger; but worst of all was the solitude. Jasper's constant presence didn't fill the void left by her mother.

Christine was happy to see the relentless heat of the Australian summer fade but dreaded the approaching Easter holidays. It would be the last week of April when Good Friday arrived, and she despised the thought of another holiday without her mother. Jasper had barely gotten her through the Christmas holidays, and now Easter was coming. Knowing she couldn't attend Easter Vigil for the first time in her life upset her, but honoring another holiday without her mother left her heartbroken.

"Where are you?" Jasper asked in her head.

"At the beach," she replied.

"Staying out of the sun I hope?"

"Yes."

"How are you feeling?" he asked with genuine concern.

"Fine," she replied, now completely comfortable communicating without speaking. Christine had grown used to her ability to communicate with Jasper over long distances, although at times she felt as though she had no privacy. Jasper never failed to interrupt her long morning walk to The Inbox, her favorite Internet café across from Bondi Beach, for a status report on her condition. She appreciated his concern, but there were times when she was worried that not only could Jasper communicate with her over a great distance, but he could see her too. This uncomfortable intuition was fueled by the guilt she carried for trying to contact Jess. Jasper made it clear she was not to make contact with anyone, and she was happy he hadn't asked her if she had. For the last week, she had been sending him emails from her internet account, but she had received no reply.

***

Hoards of parishioners filed out of the basilica into Saint Peter's Square while cathedral bells resonated off of the ancient stone walls of the Vatican. Good Friday mass ran late into the afternoon, leaving the last rays of sunshine low on the horizon. The sunlight failed to warm the evening air, and a cool breeze entered the partially opened office window.

Gino read the text on his computer screen with anticipation, too focused to notice the cold draft. His heart hammered the inside of his chest, shortening his breath like a face full of snow when the screen changed. Father Black was right; Christine's laptop had proven to be the treasure he knew it would be. Gino's IT skills were unparalleled, and his months of searching had finally paid off. The flashing icon of a person that suddenly appeared was the break he was waiting for. He quickly zoomed in on the icon until the exact location became visible, 'The Inbox Internet Café, 134 Campbell Parade, Bondi Beach, Australia.' He printed the screen and grabbed it from the printer tray on his way to Tonino's office.

"I've found her!" he said, bursting into the office.

"Where is she?" demanded Tonino as he stood up from behind his desk.

"Australia."

"You're certain?"

"Absolutely. I can see she accessed her email account three times over the last week. The username and password are a match."

"Black is on his way to Ireland," said Tonino aloud while he contemplated his options.

"Father Derksen's in Jakarta dealing with the Indonesians, and he's only a couple of hours from there," Gino said.

"Yes, I'll send him while we make our way there," said Tonino, and he picked up the telephone on his desk.

"But, sir..." Gino begun but quickly stopped his protest.

Tonino cast his ice-cold stare on Gino. He didn't say a word. He didn't have to, as his eyes spoke louder than any words.

"I'll inform the pilots to prepare the aircraft, and we'll leave as soon as possible," said Gino as he left the office.

***

"Forgive me," Father Derksen said and put down his fork and knife to answer his phone. The high-ranking government official from the Ministry of Family Development smiled and gestured his approval to take the call and then continued to eat. Their private dinner meeting was cut short.

"We've located her," Tonino said.

"Where?" asked Father Derksen.

"Sydney. Get there as soon as possible. Gino will email you the location. We're leaving now and will contact you when we're in the air."

"I'll leave at once."

"Don't take any chances, I want her taken care of. Do you understand?"

"Of course."

"This may be our only chance. I won't tolerate failure. Is that clear?"

"Understood," Father Derksen replied, and they ended their conversation.

Father Derksen turned back to the table. "Please excuse me, Minister Sukarno, I have a pressing matter that requires my attention, and I must leave at once. Accept my apologies and consider our offer. It remains the Vatican's top priority to assist those nations who support our efforts."

"Thank you, Father Derksen. I'm disappointed you must leave. However, I do look forward to our next meeting. My assistant will show you out," said the minister.

Father Derksen followed the assistant out of the restaurant. The background noise of the traffic was deafening as the limousine arrived at the side of the road. Father Derksen spent the entire forty-five minute drive to Soekarno-Hatta International Airport trying to contact Commissionaire Saputo of the New South Wales police.

***

The jet touched down on the runway as rain began to fall. The flight attendant announced the arrival of the early morning Garuda Airlines flight to Sydney, and Father Derksen's cell phone rang the instant he turned it back on.

"I want every available officer watching that café," stated Father Derksen in such a demanding voice that the flight staff opening the cockpit door turned and looked up at him.

"It's a holiday here, and we're short. I've got one man there now, and others are being called in, but it will take some time," replied Commissionaire Saputo.

"You don't think I'm well aware of what day it is? Get me those men!" Father Derksen shouted.

"I'll do what I can. I have a car out front of the airport waiting for you."

"Make sure they're not spotted," Father Derksen demanded.

"We'll do our job. When will the photo arrive?"

"She's six months pregnant. How many pregnant women would visit a café at this time of day?" snapped Father Derksen.

"Look, you want our help, give us the tools," the commissionaire replied equally tersely.

"I'm having it sent to you as we speak, so you should get the email any moment," said Father Derksen.

"I'll forward it to my men the moment it arrives."

"Do what's necessary. Understand?" said Father Derksen, closing his phone.

"Understood," replied Commissionaire Saputo to a dead phone line.

***

Christine woke up gasping for air. Her reoccurring nightmare was more intense than it had been in months. Darkness surrounded her with only the crimson red glow from her bedside clock lighting the room. She lay on her back shifting from side to side to reduce the pain in her hips from the growing mass they had to support. Anxiety from the nightmare disappeared when she realized it was Good Friday.

Not wanting to walk to The Inbox in the dark, she remained in bed, struggling to fall back to sleep and avoid the sadness consuming her thoughts.

An hour later, she pushed herself to a prone position and placed her feet on the floor. Early morning sunlight snuck into her room between the curtains. Exhaustion lingered from the poor night's sleep and the extra burden she had to carry. She pulled on her favorite board shorts and sports bra and covered her torso with one of Jasper's T-shirts. No longer able to walk in her flip-flops, Christine reluctantly put on a pair of socks and her joggers, knowing the long walk to The Inbox would be far easier with shoes.

Trying not to wake Jasper on her way out, she lifted her hat from the coat hook on the back of the door and closed the door quietly.

The morning was unusually dark as the first autumn storm approached. A pair of dusty, rose-colored Rosellas squawked overhead as they flew for cover from the approaching storm. Battered by the wind, Christine pulled her hat farther down to prevent the sea spray from stinging her eyes.

"Good morning, Chris, you left early this morning."

"Yah, I think the storm woke me," she replied so as not to concern Jasper with the reoccurrence of her nightmare.

"Where you headed?"

"The Inbox, like I always do," Christine replied, not hiding her nasty tone for having to report her whereabouts yet again.

"Will you be back for breakfast?"

"No, I'll get something there."

"Okay, I'm going to stay in bed a bit longer. See you later," Jasper replied, aware of Christine's dislike of his intrusion.

The sound of the waves breaking on Bondi beach muffled the constant call of the gulls riding the wind. The flock held its position a few feet over Christine's head without the need to flap. The Bondi Surf Life Saving Club had already closed the beach, indicating that the water was too dangerous for swimming. She stopped to lean on the metal guardrail that separated the retaining wall from the beach, and the massive surf whisked Christine's thoughts back to Hawaii.

The cold fist of sadness tightened its grip on her as she reminisced about her surfing days with Kerri and Ty.

Solitude swelled inside her like the surf, pushing her dangerously close to breaking point. Unbearable loneliness swallowed her every thought, its insatiable appetite eating every happy memory. Pain and sorrow handicapped her; she was a prisoner of her solitude.

Her depression evaporated when a sharp jolt stung the inside of her ribs. The brief pain brought Christine back to the present. The kick not only ended her despair but triggered her to make a decision: six months of isolation from the only life she knew was enough, it had to end.

Christine turned around swiftly, startling the gulls and dispersing the flock with her movement. She left the sidewalk and crossed the street to The Inbox, unaware of the man sleeping in the front seat of the small white car parked opposite the entrance.

The café was quiet; only three other people were inside. An older, grey-haired couple whom Christine often passed on the seawall sat at a small table sipping their coffee while reading the daily tabloid. The other person was a young-looking teenage boy sleeping in a living-room style lounge chair. His immense size made the chair look like a piece of children's furniture. His long bleached blonde hair rolled over his face down to the waist of his board shorts. His head lay on his folded yellow beach towel, which he was using as a pillow between his head and the arm of the chair. It was clear from his snoring he had gotten up early to catch some of the morning waves but was confined to the shore because of the storm.

"Hi, Chris," said the women behind the coffee bar.

"Morning, Tara," Christine replied.

"The usual?" Tara asked, referring to the de-caffeinated latté Christine ordered most days.

"Yes please, can I have a bagel too? I'm going to check my emails on computer one," Christine said. She preferred this computer since it was right next to the window, and she could watch the surfers while she typed.

"Okay, I'll turn number one on and bring the rest out to you."

Christine looked out the window while she waited for the computer to boot up. She chuckled when she saw a police officer tap on the window of the small white car. The action obviously startled the sleeping driver, who jumped in his seat. Her attention focused back to the computer screen as she keyed in her username and password to log in to her email account.

She stared at the hundreds of unopened emails sitting in her inbox. Most of them were junk mail, but the long list from Kerri tore at her heart. Her determination to follow Jasper's instructions and not to contact her friends began to weaken. She strolled down the list of Kerri's messages, reading the subject line of each, *Hello? Are you there? Where are you? Are you okay?* Christine pushed back the fear holding back her resolve to get some of her old life back and moved the mouse to the most recent email when a voice screamed inside her head.

"Christine, run!"

She looked around the café for the source of the voice. It was so loud inside her mind that it triggered her heart to skip a beat. Nothing had changed, the teenager slept and the old couple read their papers. Tara was walking toward her carrying a plate with a bagel on it and the latté she ordered, but the voice she heard was definitely a man's.

"Did you hear that?" she asked Tara.

"Hear what?" replied Tara, confused by the question, and she placed the plate and cup on the table in front of Christine.

Christine looked out the window and saw the man from the car walking toward the café while the uniformed officer who had woken him drove slowly past the window.

"Animus, they've found her!" said the new voice inside her head.

"Get her out of there!" shouted Jasper. He instantly left Father Shannon and entered one of the gulls circling the shoreline of Bondi Beach while at the same time, Simone replaced Jasper in Father Shannon's consciousness.

"Jasper, what's going on?" Christine asked, now standing up.

"Chris, run! They're coming for you. Run away! Trust no one unless you see their eyes," Jasper demanded.

The man from the car walked briskly toward the café but was delayed by a passing truck.

Christine ignored Tara and ran to the back of the café.

When he saw Christine leaving, the man sprinted for the café door. Christine was trapped. There was no exit at the back, so she went into the women's washroom and locked the door.

Adrenalin coursed through her veins, igniting her senses. The discussion taking place in her mind between Jasper and Luca went unnoticed as the pulsing in her chest intensified. Her flight response consumed all her energy as she scanned the small room for a means of escape. The modern bathroom was equipped with an oversized handicapped toilet stall, a counter and washbasin extending the entire length of the far wall. Hanging above the sink was a large wood-framed antique oval mirror that was held in place by a wire wrapped around a nail in the window frame.

Christine knelt on the counter and managed to open the trough-style window, which was just large enough for her to squeeze through. She pulled it down as hard as she could and snapped the old rusted chains on both ends, leaving the window hanging by its bottom hinge. She jumped off the counter and ripped the mirror off the wall, letting it crash onto the counter before running into the toilet stall.

The second it took to move to the toilet stall filled her mind with fear; the success of her plan hinged on what was on the back of the bathroom stall door. She swung the heavy metal door partially closed, all the while whispering the Holy Mary prayer. She inhaled a deep breath and grabbed the metal coat hook with her right hand, putting her left hand on the rubber doorstop attached to the wall behind her. Fueled by adrenalin, Christine lifted her feet from the floor while ducking her head below the top of the stall.

The bathroom door flew off its frame as the man from the car kicked it open. He slowly made his way into the room, his leather soled boots crackled as he stepped on the pile of broken mirror glass. He glanced up at the open window before moving to his left to check the partially open toilet stall. The man quickly pulled a radio out of his jacket pocket.

"Get to the lane, she went out a window in the back," he said, running out of the bathroom.

Christine simultaneously let go of the hook and put her feet on the floor, allowing the cramping in her hand to disappear. She slowly walked toward the washroom door, the crunching of glass beneath her feet resembling the sound of walking in the snow on a cold winter day.

"Chris, where are you?" asked a frantic voice in her head, the same one that had spoken to her in the café.

"I'm in the café. Who is this?"

"Where exactly?" Luca replied.

"I'm in the washroom," she said as the doorway filled with the body of the young teenage boy, now holding his towel.

Christine looked up, tilting her head all the way back to see the boy's face. She lifted the brim of her hat and saw an unmistakable pair of glimmering blue eyes looking down on her through a thick mane of blonde hair.

"I'm Luca. Stay next to me," came the voice inside her head.

Luca draped the towel around her neck in an attempt to hide her protruding stomach and then put his massive arm around her shoulders.

Tara and the old couple stood near the coffee bar, confused and motionless from the shock of the invasion.

"Chris, what's going on?" Tara asked, watching Christine being escorted out the door.

"Ignore her," Luca demanded.

The first signs of shock began to invade Christine's body when the sound of approaching sirens filled her ears. Luca's steps were twice the length of Christine's, forcing her to skip to keep up with his pace as they crossed Campbell Parade. The rain on the pavement kept the tires from releasing an ear-piercing screech when a squad car came to an abrupt stop in front of the café. The wail of the sirens ceased when they approached the retaining wall separating the beach from the walkway.

The police car doors opened and Father Derksen and the officer leaped from the front of the cruiser.

"Stop!" the priest yelled.

However, his command was rendered mute by the roar of the raging waves.

Luca grabbed Christine by the shoulders and lifted her over the railing as easily as placing a bag of groceries in the back of a car. The moment her feet reached the sand, the crack of gunfire caused her to hesitate for an instant. The pause allowed Christine to feel the ground shake beneath her as the teenage boy's body fell to the ground next to her. Horror ravaged her mind, which was now racing faster than her heart, and neither were under control. The deserted beach offered no cover from her pursuers, so she ran toward the water.

"What do I do?"

"To the water," Jasper answered.

Thirty yards remained between her and the surf line. Running on sand was as natural to Christine as driving a car or riding a bike, so it didn't hinder her speed. The thunder of the waves couldn't mask the series of gunshots piercing her ears. Balls of sand exploded into the air next to her, and a massive wall of blue and white rose in front of her.

"Stop her!" shouted Father Derksen, and his command unleashed another round of rapid gunfire.

Without hesitation, Christine placed her head between her outstretched arms, inhaled deeply and dived into the sea.

The surging water swallowed her without a trace.

Instinctively, she remained parallel to the bottom to keep from tumbling head over heels, but she was no match for the power of the storm surge. She surfaced like a piece of driftwood floating out of control between the waves. Panic counteracted the adrenalin-fueled flight response as the riptide pulled her farther from shore. The agitated water offered little buoyancy, and she struggled to stay afloat.

"Jasper!" she yelled in her mind out of desperation, knowing she only had seconds before she slipped below the surface for the last time.

"I'm here," he replied.

"Help me!" she pleaded while using every last bit of strength to keep from sinking.

"Matteo, are you there?" Jasper asked.

"A few more seconds," someone answered, obviously Matteo, his deep, raspy voice new to Christine.

An enormous sea turtle positioned itself underneath Christine, and like a life raft, it raised her body to the surface.

Relief displaced her panic, and Christine regained control of her senses. She felt the rock-hard shell below her and reached down without looking to find a handgrip. Her fingers located the edge of the shell behind the massive animal's head, which she grasped like a bicycle handlebar. Instinctively, she took breaths between waves.

The turtle immediately began to swim her out of the breaking waves and into the deeper water, freeing her from the relentless surf.

"I've got her, Animus," Matteo said.

"I see you."

The white gull soared effortlessly overhead, diving in the wind as it followed them out to sea.

CHAPTER 14

SOPHOMORES AND SOFT DRINKS

T he complete darkness born from the moonless night was broken by a repetitive silver-white flash that resembled lightning. It originated from the light on the wingtip outside the half-closed window shutter of the Vatican jet. Tonino awoke to the ring of a telephone as the jet cruised thirty-five thousand feet above northern Nepal. He answered the phone, which sat on a small desk next to his seat.

"Sir, sorry to wake you, but there's an urgent call for you. Shall I put it through?" the pilot asked.

"Yes," Tonino responded.

Static filled the earpiece when Tonino placed the phone to his ear.

"Hello," said the faint voice on the other end of the line.

"Good news?" asked Tonino.

"No, sir," Father Derksen replied.

"What happened?" thundered Tonino's voice, waking Gino from a deep sleep in the seat next to him. Tonino sat up in his seat and pressed the light switch on the armrest, illuminating the jet and the anger on his stone-hard face.

"It was out of my control. A couple of rookie police officers went in before we got there."

"Unacceptable. I told you there was no room for failure."

"I know... there was nothing I could do," Father Derksen

pleaded.

"Of course," said Tonino, cracking a small smile, the inky blackness of his eyes turning a shade darker. He lowered the telephone and held it in his hands while he contemplated what to do next. A moment passed before he returned the receiver to his ear and spoke to Father Derksen.

"Get to Canberra and finish it," said Tonino in a surprisingly calm tone.

"At once, sir, I'm sorry I..." said Father Derksen, but his apology was cut short. Tonino replaced the telephone back in its cradle and went to the cockpit to talk to the pilots.

"There's been a change of plans. Take us to Beijing."

"Sir, we don't have the necessary clearance to..." replied the copilot.

"I'll get the clearance, just make the changes," Tonino interrupted as he closed the cockpit door. He returned to his seat, removed the telephone from its cradle and looked over at Gino.

"She's escaped. Derksen has disappointed me for the last time. Let's hope you don't do the same. We're heading to Beijing, so make the necessary arrangements. I want to meet with as many officials as we can."

"Yes, sir. I've got contacts in both the soft drink and tea industries," Gino replied, looking only at the telephone receiver Tonino was handing to him, too frightened to let his eyes meet Tonino's.

"What about the alcohol and pharmaceutical industries?"

"They're much more difficult," Gino replied.

"I want them all," snapped Tonino.

"Yes, sir. I'll do my best, sir."

"I heard that from Derksen and look what happened... You need to do better."

"I will."

"So who's agreed to help us?"

"I've secured individuals within the Hangling Company, which makes soft drinks, and the Fong Tea Company. They're two of the largest in China."

"Excellent. What did it take?"

"The right price," Gino replied, expecting a verbal backlash.

"It always comes down to money," Tonino said with a smirk.

"I've also secured the Clomiphene in China, so we won't have any importation issues," Gino added, looking for some positive feedback.

"Do we have enough?"

"Enough for five years."

"Excellent. Let's get this done as fast as possible. Who are we meeting with?"

"Minister Lau. He's willing to table our proposal, but banning abortions is such a radical change that I don't expect the Chinese to agree."

"Don't underestimate the power of greed. If you've met with the right individuals, it'll pass—trust me."

"But, sir, what if it doesn't?"

"It will," Tonino replied emphatically.

"Of course," said Gino, unconsciously bowing his head to avoid eye contact.

"I want to get to the US as soon as possible. I expect the Americans will be far more difficult to convince than the rest."

**

Dark blue walls of water surrounded Christine as if she were trapped inside a deep blue prison cell. She only caught a glimpse of the Sydney shoreline when the turtle reached the crest of a wave. The pelting rain was unperceivable through the continual surges of warm Pacific water flowing over her body. Christine was unaware of how long she had been holding the turtle's back until her hands began to cramp. She blocked the astonishing situation she found herself in and focused her thoughts on the rapid gunfire, exploding balls of sand and the image of the teenage boy's body. Sickness grew in her stomach, not from the waves but from the realization that someone she didn't even know had died for her. The raging nausea charged through her veins, morphing quickly into anger. *How many more have to die?*

"Are you okay?" Jasper asked.

"Leave me alone," Christine replied, displaying the anger in her thoughts.

Jasper obeyed her wishes and fought the endless wind to stay overhead, following them as they neared the Tamarama Beach shoreline. Christine could see the massive waves breaking long before the safety of the beach and questioned her ability to swim to the shore. Even her swimming abilities were no match for the relentless pounding of the surf.

Matteo held steady, far enough from the beach to keep Christine from rolling over the top of the waves but still close enough to watch the water exploding on the shore. Jasper lifted himself higher into the air to help Matteo with the right moment to head for the shore.

"Christine, are you ready?" Matteo asked.

"Yes, why?" Christine replied.

"Just ready yourself," Matteo demanded.

"For what?"

"Chris, you need to hold your breath," Jasper told her.

"Why?"

"It's the only way to get you to the beach," Jasper explained.

"Animus, I'm ready," said Matteo.

"Chris, when I tell you, you must take a deep breath and hold on as tight as you can. Understand?" Jasper asked.

"Yes," she replied, her anger at the innocent deaths replaced by fear. The sound of the crashing surf roared past her head like a group of fighter jets. Her eyes filled with salt water as she tried in vain to see the shore and judge the distance.

"Now, Matteo!" The words came much sooner than she expected.

With less than a second before the turtle's body was completely submerged, Christine expanded her lungs until they hurt, pulling in as much air as she could. The sound of the crashing waves was muted, replaced with the dull clicking noise of countless bubbles racing past her ears. Incapable of judging how fast she was moving, Christine relied on the sensation of the water passing over her body. Like riding a racehorse in a derby, the back and forth lunging became rhythmic and mesmerizing as they accelerated through the surf.

"Only fifty more yards," Jasper said when he spotted the dark mass below the surface of the frothing waves.

"I can't make it!" Christine shouted in her head.

"Christine, we're going to break through, but don't let go," Matteo demanded.

The moment the words entered her head, Christine felt the cool air slap her face, and she instinctively inhaled. There was no sandy beach or green lawn in front of her; instead, she saw a wall of water. Matteo brought her to the surface inside the tunnel of a wave, the familiar curve of the water she longed for while on her board.

"Breathe!" Matteo yelled inside her head.

With just enough time to take a single short breath, Christine's body returned below the surface. Her feet lifted over her head while the security of the shell disappeared. Her hands held nothing. Weightlessness encompassed her; there was no telling which direction was up or down. Trapped by the surging water and with no idea where the surface was, Christine reached her hands straight in front of her head in preparation for an impact.

"I've lost her!" yelled Matteo.

"I can't see her," Jasper responded, trying to maintain his position in the howling wind.

"Christine... Chris!" Matteo and Jasper shouted in unison.

She didn't answer, so they repeated their call but with the same result.

Christine was incapable of answering, her every thought was focused on survival and never giving up. The wave accelerated as it approached the small sandy beach. Sand filled her eyes, which told her she was nearing the shore. She kicked her legs to gain momentum, but it was impossible to swim in the mixture of foam and water.

Christine waited for any part of her body to make contact with the bottom, but she felt nothing. Suddenly, the water changed direction, and like the hand of a giant, it grabbed her body and began dragging her back out to sea. The draw of the next wave towed her from the shoreline and sucked her to the bottom. Her face scraped along the seabed and ground the sand against her skin. The pain lifted her spirits, for she now knew which way was up and where the air she desperately craved was.

Christine forced her mind to block the urge to breathe as she buried her hands and dug her feet into the sandy bottom. The water rushed backwards over her head, but she refused to loosen her hold on the bottom. The fine white sand ran over her skin like millions of crawling ants.

Instantly the sensation stopped, and the water held motionless for a second, then just as suddenly, a second rush came from behind. Christine pushed forward, mustering every bit of strength she had left, swimming as hard as she could with the flowing water. Her head broke the surface first, and she took a long-awaited breath. She inhaled salt water that was laden with sand that coated her mouth. It seeped down her throat, causing an involuntary cough. Christine continued to swim until her hands hit the bottom with each stroke. Finally, she crawled out of the surf and lay on the beach.

"Matteo, I see her. She's on the beach," Jasper said, his voice filled with relief.

"Okay," Matteo responded.

"When Simone arrives, we'll leave at once," Jasper commanded, knowing the local police would soon be searching the area.

The midsized white car raced down the hill, sliding on the wet pavement as it came to a halt at the edge of the grass. Christine's body lay motionless on the sand twenty yards from the car. Jasper landed on the hood of the car above the driver's side door as Simone opened it. Like a spark from a live wire, a light jumped instantly between the gull and Father Shannon's body before he sprinted across the emerald lawn.

"Chris, are you okay?" Jasper asked, unhappy with her semi-comatose state.

Christine heard the voice inside her head but lacked the mental capacity to communicate. Like someone under a powerful spell, she battled the exhaustion pinning her to the beach. Large raindrops hammered against her, washing away the sand that filled every crevice of her body. The sound inside her head was unbearable, coming from the grit between her teeth. She used her last ounce of strength and spit.

***

Spit flew from Father Derksen's mouth onto his phone as he shouted at Commissionaire Saputo. The squad car arrived at the Kingsford-Smith International Airport and parked directly in front of the entrance, but Father Derksen remained in his seat and continued his shouting.

"I told you there was no room for error! How could you send rookies?" blasted Father Derksen as he opened the car door.

"It's Good Friday. You're lucky I found anyone on such short notice," Commissionaire Saputo retaliated.

"Luck was something one of your incompetent men could have used!" Father Derksen yelled back, slamming the squad car door as he closed his phone.

The airport was crammed with holiday travelers, which made it difficult to walk through the terminal. Father Derksen checked the departures screen and located the first available flight for Canberra. While he waited, Father Derksen arranged for Minister MacDonald, the Australian Federal Attorney General, and an industry contact to meet him.

It never ceases to amaze me how money motivates individuals, Father Derksen thought.

***

Several hours later, Minister MacDonald and Father Derksen met inside the executive lounge in Canberra Airport. The two men ordered their lunch and discussed how the Vatican could assist the federal government in making abortion illegal while at the same time promoting increased family size.

"I think with the right amount of support from the Vatican, it could pass," the minister stated.

"We look after those who share our beliefs," Father Derksen replied with a smile.

Minister MacDonald's face glowed when the priest informed him that Vatican support would arrive on Tuesday after the long weekend.

"You can count..." started Minister MacDonald when his phone rang. He promptly cut his lunch short, excused himself from the table and left to deal with the urgent call.

Father Derksen remained seated at the table eating his food and waiting for his industry contact to arrive.

A short, slender, balding man entered the lounge and stood in the entranceway scanning the room. Father Derksen pushed himself from the table and walked over to the man.

"Peter?" Father Derksen asked.

"Yes," replied the man, clearly nervous about meeting the

priest for the first time.

"I'm Father Helmut Derksen," he said while offering his hand.

"Nice to meet you, Father. Peter Olson." The reply came with a strong Australian accent resembling Father Black's.

"Let's sit. We have much to discuss," said Father Derksen, and he led the way back to his table.

"What can I do for you, Father?" Olson asked as they pulled the chairs from the table.

"No, no, not for me, Peter. The work I ask isn't for me. This is for God. Millions of Catholics from around the world entrust us do the Lord's work and put families first. Your effort will extend the Hand of God to millions of young Australians and others, Catholic and non-Catholic alike. What better way can you offer your services to the Lord?" said Father Derksen, brandishing a smile.

"Will it hurt anyone?" Olson asked with trepidation.

"Peter, would that be God's will? Of course not. It's harmless. No one will even know. It only increases the likelihood of conception. No one will notice a thing," Father Derksen assured.

"So all I need to do is to make sure it's added to every recipe, that's it?"

"Yes, it has to be added to every product."

"Where do I get it?"

"It'll be sent to you. Include it as a hidden ingredient."

"How long do I have to do this?"

"How long do you plan on working as the Master Brewer?" Father Derksen responded, well aware that Olson was in financial trouble.

"I see..."

"Of course, the Vatican will always take care of those who help us," interrupted Father Derksen.

Olson's face filled with anxiety at this. A devoted Catholic his entire life, the mere thought of financial reward coming from the Church riddled him with guilt. Persuaded by faith and desperate for additional funds, Olson nodded in agreement.

"I'll do it."

"Excellent," Father Derksen responded.

"When do I start?"

"The first package will arrive next week. Make sure it is distributed to all your facilities."

"I will," Olson replied, looking dejected and feeling reprehensible.

"Peter, why such a long face? You should be rejoicing and filled with the Holy Spirit. You are part of a growing army dedicated to doing the work of the Lord. For instance, tomorrow I shall meet with your counterparts in the soft drink industry, as well as the two largest bottled water companies. They too see the benefit in doing God's work."

***

It was a warm Easter Sunday morning when the Vatican jet arrived in New York. Sunlight filtered through the steel and concrete mountains as it made its way to street level. The normally congested streets were spotted with only a handful of mustard-colored taxis as the holiday rendered the roads quiet by New York standards.

Tonino and Gino left the limousine and checked into their hotel, agreeing to meet for an early working dinner in the hotel restaurant.

Their meal began with the ringing of Tonino's phone. He glanced at the call display before answering.

"I sincerely hope you're calling with good news."

"Yes, I've got everything in place with the Australians," Father Derksen answered.

"Including the water companies?" asked Tonino, not hiding the surprise in his tone.

"Yes, everyone."

"What about the government?"

"I spoke with the minister, and it looks promising," Father Derksen answered, desperately seeking affirmation.

"Good. Now make your way to India and get it done there."

"On my way," Father Derksen replied, not surprised by the terse conversation.

Tonino had just placed the phone back in his jacket pocket when it rang again. He answered it at once.

"Have you made any progress?"

"No, he was adopted in the sixties," said Father Black, clearly annoyed with his failure. "I just received your voice mail. Did Father Derksen get them?" he asked, now displaying a tinge of jealousy in his tone for not being a part of the capture.

"No, and he's failed me for the last time. I'll deal with him later," Tonino stated with malice.

"I can fly to Australia and take care of your problem, and pick up their trail," Father Black suggested.

"No, finish what you've started. The more information we have about Shannon the better."

"You think it wise? The sooner I get to Sydney, the better the chance I can find their trail."

"By the time you get there, they'll have left the country. I'm sure of it," Tonino snapped, angered by talking about their escape.

"Fine," Father Black snapped back. "I'll finish here."

"Keep me informed," Tonino said as he hung up.

Knowing better than to ask, Gino waited for Tonino to speak first.

"That was Black. He's almost done in Ireland, and then he'll leave for Sydney."

"Has he found anything?"

"He's still working on it. Let's start. We need to get this right, time is running out." Tonino cast his cold dark eyes into Gino's.

Gino took his tablet from its case and opened the file he

and Tonino had been working on. It contained the names and contact information of the most influential US congressional lobbyists. It also identified key staff within the largest soft drink, alcohol and water bottling companies, as well as the largest pharmaceutical manufacturers in the United States. He handed the tablet to Tonino.

"Good. Tomorrow I want you to deal with the bottling companies, and I'll deal with the lobbyists and the pharmaceuticals," Tonino commanded.

"How do you know they'll help?" asked Gino, nervous about questioning Tonino.

"I've canvassed them for their allegiance; you'll find them all devout Catholics willing to support our efforts," Tonino replied, holding in a smirk on his face.

"Isn't security at these pharmaceutical companies tighter than the Pentagon?" Gino asked, surprised by Tonino's confidence.

"Everything is automated and controlled by computers. We'll reduce the potency and at the same time add the Clomiphene. Every birth control pill made in the US and around the world will have it."

"Of course," Gino said, his face turning rose colored from the rush of embarrassment filling his body.

"You of all people should appreciate the power a simple click of a mouse can unleash. If things go as planned, this time next year, there won't be a soft drink, can of beer or bottle of water sold in America without Clomiphene in it. And that will go a long way to getting every sophomore from here to Los Angeles pregnant."

CHAPTER 15

PREGNANT NUN

Sunshine flooded the small room where Christine lay. The distant sound of waves pounding the shore filtered through the open window of the motel room. Her head hurt more than the morning after her nineteenth birthday party, when she had experienced her first hangover. Confusion clouded her mind as the surroundings rapidly came into focus. A dull ache radiated from her shoulders, and the slightest movement caused her skin to sting as if she were being dragged along a gravel road.

She lifted her head from the pillow and kicked the sheets off the end of the bed, the movement causing her muscles to burn. Christine ignored the nagging aches and ran her hands through her hair. Her fingers filled with grit. *I need a shower,* she thought, but a second later, her stomach overruled the shower with a powerful hunger pang. The internal unrest was made worse by the constant kicking inside her ribs.

Memories started to flash through her mind, the images causing her heart to race. She recalled running across the empty beach, clinging to the turtle and nearly drowning in the surf. But her most vivid memory was the disgusting taste of salt water mixed with sand in her mouth. *Sand, that's what it is,* she thought as she rolled onto her side to prepare to sit up, *I'm lying in sand.* Her bed was covered with sand, and the sheets were damp.

"Jasper!" she called in her mind.

"Good, you're awake," he replied.

"What time is it?"

"Just after seven. Can I come in?"

"Sure," she replied, and when Jasper entered the room, his face lit up with a smile.

"How you feeling?" he asked.

"To be honest, not great. I ache all over, I'm starving and why is there sand in my bed?"

Jasper's smile grew larger with each complaint, and relief swelled inside him. He knew Christine was going to be okay if she was well enough to complain.

"I'm not surprised; you haven't eaten in days."

"What... what's today?" Christine asked in disbelief.

"Sunday."

"It's Easter Sunday! I've been asleep for two days?" she asked in astonishment.

"Yes, and I was beginning to worry."

"Where are we?"

"This delightful little place is The Byron Bay Motel, in Byron Bay, of course," Jaspers replied with no attempt to mask the sarcasm in his voice. "Do you like the seventies era décor?"

"Where?" she asked, her eyebrows rising in confusion.

"It's a tiny seaside village a few hours north of Sydney."

"Why are we here?"

"We'll talk after you eat and take a shower," Jasper said as he walked from the bedroom to the small kitchen to get Christine something to eat.

The instant Jasper said 'shower,' Christine felt her skin crawl and had the urge to itch. Covered in sand and salt residue, she needed to shower above all else. Still wearing the clothes from Friday, Christine left the bedroom and raced straight to the bathroom; she was so anxious to change her clothes that she wanted to strip on the way there.

"What about your food?" Jasper asked.

"Later. I need to shower."

"I'll leave it on the table."

Standing naked in the bathroom, Christine assessed her battered image in the mirror. Like inhaling the first whiff of rotten meat, a sudden repulsion curled her upper lip. The sight of a dozen or more bright red scratches and numerous deep blue bruises was sickening. Most were on her arms and legs, but a few appeared on her swollen belly. She placed her hands on her soccer-ball-sized stomach and felt the movement inside. Christine's near-death experience had opened a door within her mind: the power of becoming a mother.

She stood in the shower with the hot water pelting her hair. Sand pooled along the sides of the old porcelain tub and formed a trail to the drain. A warm sensation permeated her body as she drew a hand cloth across her skin. It rejuvenated her, washing life back into her body. The moment she turned the taps off and stepped out of the tub, she realized she had nothing to wear.

"Jasper!" she called out loud. He didn't respond, so she called him again, but this time without using her voice.

"What is it?" Jasper responded, unable to hide the concern in his tone.

"I don't have any clothes to wear."

"Oh," he said in relief. "I got you something yesterday; it's on the dresser in your room."

"Thanks," she said, struggling to wrap the bath towel around her oversized midsection so she could walk to the bedroom.

Christine scooted as fast as possible back to her bedroom, but her self-consciousness was unwarranted, as Jasper wasn't in the room.

"Where are you?"

"Checking out," he replied.

"Already?" Christine asked, not hiding her disapproval.

"Yes, we have to."

"Why?"

"I'll explain in the car. Have you eaten yet?"

"In a minute."

"Please hurry."

Christine pulled on the board shorts and slipped into the only clothes Jasper could find on the holiday weekend. The T-shirt was so large it barley hung on her shoulders. Jasper had obviously overcompensated for her pregnancy. She peered at her reflection in the bedroom mirror before permitting a smile to form on her face. *Can't wait for the next few months*, she thought, using sarcasm to humor herself.

She sat at the small wooden table eating a muffin and a banana. Ravaged by hunger, Christine didn't care that it was convenience store food. She was thankful to have any food at all, and she was impressed by Jasper's thoughtfulness. Breakfast was going well until she reached for the cup of coffee Jasper had prepared for her. When the morning light reflected off the surface of the coffee, it triggered another memory.

She gazed at the coffee while the image of Tara and that horrific morning formed in her mind. She stopped eating and pulled her hand away from the cup. Emotions welled inside her until they formed a pool of guilt. A twisted knot formed in her stomach, replacing her hunger. The torment of emotions left her no alternative but to tell Jasper.

The motel room door opened, and Jasper stood in the doorway. Christine turned in her seat and faced him with a cold, guilt-ridden look. Weakened by the hormonal changes brought on by her pregnancy, she clenched her jaw and fought back the urge to cry.

"What's wrong?" Jasper asked, reading the expression on her face.

"Jasper, it was me," she forced the words out of her mouth and then turned to face the half-eaten muffin on the table.

"What was?"

"How they found us. It was me... I did it!" she said,

confessing her sins as she had done a hundred times before.

"Chris, don't worry about it. It's done," he said, trying to reassure her that he wasn't angry.

"But I'm responsible for that surfer's death and..."

"Chris, stop. It's over, and we're moving on," Jasper said using the tone of a father reprimanding a child.

"How can you be like that? Someone died, someone we don't even know. Think of his mom," she said, beginning to crack under the emotional strain of the memories of her mother.

"Remember what I told you. He still exists here with me," Jasper said, holding his hand to his chest and walking toward her.

Shame overpowered the guilt inside Christine, and she caught a small tear with the back of her hand before it rolled out of her eye. Never before had she been this emotional. A vortex of feelings ran through her thoughts.

"I'm so sorry."

"Please finish your breakfast so we can leave. We have a long journey ahead of us," Jasper said, now speaking in a more casual tone.

"Now where are we going?" Christine asked, shaking off her lapse of emotional composure.

"We'll talk in the car."

They left Byron Bay on the Pacific Highway north, heading for Brisbane. Jasper knew their progress would be slow, and after the recent events, he wanted to get underway as soon as possible. He was certain the VSS wouldn't be far behind. A forty-five-year-old man traveling with twenty-five-year-old pregnant woman would be easy to spot, especially with their American accents.

Progress was indeed slow, with Jasper having to make frequent stops for Christine so she could use the washroom and walk around to alleviate the swelling and cramping in her feet. Concerned about being identified, Jasper was always cautious when they stopped.

Christine squirmed in her seat, not from leg cramps or swollen feet but from the burning desire to discuss what had happened. She stared mindlessly out the window, ignoring the magnificence of the endless miles of sandy beach and turquoise ocean of the Australian Gold Coast. Jasper was first to break the uncomfortable silence.

"Have you ever wondered what you'd look like with red hair?" he asked mischievously.

"What?" Christine replied, not quite certain what he meant.

"We need to change our look; we stick out like peas in a bowl of rice."

"Oh," Christine said, realizing what he meant. "No way, not red. How about brunette?"

"Dark brown?"

"Only if you go black."

"Deal."

"Can you get me some new clothes too?" she asked while lifting the tacky oversized T-shirt back onto her shoulders.

"Sure, what do you want?"

"I'll make you a list," she replied and rummaged through the glove box for a pen and a scrap of paper.

When they reached Brisbane, Jasper found a shopping mall open on Easter Sunday and went in to purchase the items on the list. He was also able to get enough food to last for the next four days, the length of time he expected it to take to reach Katherine.

***

The first day of driving took them six hundred kilometers northeast. They had left the lush, tropical green of the Australian coast and had entered the harsh, dry, terracotta interior. Dust and heat surrounded them at every stop.

Christine had grown tired from the journey when they arrived outside of Roma, Queensland. It was just before nightfall in the small outback town. They would be easily recognized here, so Jasper pulled off the road before town and waited for the cover of darkness.

He parked the car on the street out front of the Queens Hotel and asked Christine to remain in the car until he checked in. Jasper told the clerk he would be leaving at first light and paid him for the room in advance, avoiding the need to check out in the morning. He returned to the car and handed Christine the room key while he got the groceries and hair dye. They then ate dinner and took turns dying each other's hair. Jasper went first; the black dye completely covered Father Shannon's mousey mixture of brown and grey. The new hair color took at least five years off his appearance.

"You look about thirty—he should've done this years ago," Christine said, unable to hold back her laughter.

"Really, then you're going to like this," Jasper replied. He walked to the kitchen table where he had left the shopping bag and removed a tube of hair gel.

"You're kidding!" she blurted out while shaking her head in disbelief.

Jasper squeezed a thick line of the bright pink gel into his hand and pulled it through his hair. He took the comb they used to work in the dye and parted his hair to the left.

"You look like a sleazy Wall Street banker," Christine said, erupting into laughter.

"Your turn," he said as he wiped the gel from his hands with a small towel.

The smile immediately evaporated from Christine's face. She loved her hair and took pride in its sun-bleached highlights. Like a child entering kindergarten for the first time, Christine began to lament the change before it had even happened.

Jasper pulled the box from the bag and handed it to her. She looked at the model on the outside of the box and lifted her cheeks to form a fake smile. *It's only a color change*, she thought, and handed the box back.

An hour later, Christine finished blow-drying her hair, sat on the edge of the tub and stared at herself in the mirror. *I look like a witch,* she thought. She flipped the hair off of her shoulders and began to drag a comb through it, but it was no use, nothing would fix it. She opened the bathroom door and waited for Jasper's reaction. Instead of unleashing a comment, he quietly walked back to the table and removed a shiny silver object from the bag.

"Here," he said, and handed Christine the scissors.

"No way!" she yelled emphatically.

"Think about it."

"No... I can't, I won't," she begged.

"You must. We can't be recognized. Do you want a repeat of last Friday?"

"No, but..."

"Make sure you keep your birthmark covered," he said with his hand outstretched and holding the scissors.

Jasper might as well have pushed the scissors into her heart. He had no smile on his face; he meant what he said. Surprise disappeared from her face to be replaced by anguish. Torment lingered in her mind as she reached for the scissors. It wasn't Jasper's intent to hurt Christine, but he knew they had to do whatever was necessary to conceal themselves—the VSS would stop at nothing to find them.

Christine returned to the bathroom and sat back down on the edge of the tub. She stared at her image for ten minutes before lifting the scissors to her head. The first cut was the hardest. Her hands shook so hard she couldn't close the scissors completely, causing them to yank more hair out of her scalp than they cut. The subsequent cuts came easier, and she removed six inches of hair from her head. The comb moved much easier through her shorter hair as she styled it behind her ears.

"I want a ball cap," she demanded as she left the bathroom.

"Not a problem. You look like a nun from my school days," said Jasper, straining to hold back a chuckle.

"Great, I look like a pregnant nun—very nice," she snapped loudly, not trying to hide her displeasure and sending a clear message that she was unhappy.

***

The scenery from the car window didn't change over the next couple of days. Flocks of black cockatoos dotted the cloudless sky, their crimson red crests visible against the endless blue backdrop. Like the smell of cough syrup, the fragrant scent of eucalyptus trees filled the car. The constant pungent odor was occasionally interrupted by the musty smell of the red dust flushed into the vehicle by a passing road train. As each kilometer passed, the need to know swelled inside Christine, increasing like magma beneath a volcano. She finally erupted on the morning of their fourth day.

"Jasper, how'd they do it?"

"Do what?"

"Find me so easily."

"The VSS have unbelievable resources at their disposal. They're better equipped than most governments. Just think about how prolific the Catholic empire is. The VSS have operatives everywhere."

"Empire?" Christine asked, her tone indicating that she took offence at the term.

"Yes, it's an empire. The Church you know is not the one I'm talking about. The one you know truly benefits mankind. The Church I'm speaking of does not."

"What exactly is the VSS?"

"The Vatican Secret Service has existed in some form for thousands of years. They've worked within the Catholic Church as a clandestine group of individuals focused on one goal—expanding their empire. They're hidden behind the Pope and the good work the Church does, and this has allowed them to function undetected for millennia. The Catholic Church to this day remains the most powerful empire that has ever existed. And now, to make matters worse, the Vacare control it and the VSS."

"The Vacare will stop at nothing to find and destroy you, and they have unlimited resources to do it."

"Oh great, if they've got that much power, how do you ever expect us to survive?" she asked.

"You have me," Jasper replied with a smile, but Christine didn't share his sentiment.

"So how'd they find me in Sydney?"

"Did you check an old email account?"

"Yes, but it's my Internet account. They can't..."

"I told you, they have unlimited resources. Access to technology we haven't even heard of. They probably have your computer and complete access to everything."

"You've got to be joking! Everything?" Christine asked in disbelief.

"Everything."

"Wait till Jess finds out," Christine moaned.

"Who?" Jasper asked, uncertain he had heard her correctly.

"Jess... you know, Jesse Struger, the guy I dated for fifteen years," she responded sarcastically.

"It never occurred to me... you don't know," Jasper said sadly.

"Know what?" Christine asked, uncomfortable with his change of tone.

"This is going to upset you... Jesse is dead."

"What? How? When?" she shouted as tears welled in her eyes.

Christine's heart ripped open, the last bit of emotion spilling from it. The last person on earth she had loved was dead. Gone was every important person in her life. Even though her feelings for him were forever changed the moment he had murdered Jasper, part of her never completely erased the ten years of childhood love she carried for him. Her emotions began to spin out of control like a summer whirlwind twisting the inside of her mind. Shock, anger, sadness and grief all swirled together to leave her numb.

"The VSS killed him right after he killed Jasper. They tossed his body into the sea."

Christine didn't care anymore, nothing stirred inside her. She sat frozen in her seat. As if looking down the shaft of a bottomless pit, the hollow darkness created by the news of another death kept her mind locked in thought. Her skin grew limp and pale knowing her childhood companion was gone.

"Chris, you okay? Do you want me to stop for some fresh air?" Jasper asked, concerned by the obvious symptoms of shock flooding through her body.

Still consumed by her memories, Christine didn't hear him. Jasper tried again, but this time he didn't use his voice.

"Chris, do you need some air?" he asked in a forceful tone in an attempt to snap her from the mental shock.

Christine turned her head and looked at him, but she paused before replying. Jasper's forceful words inside her mind had broken the hold her memories had over her.

"What?"

"I'm going to stop and let you get some air."

"No, I don't want to stop, just keep going."

"Are you sure? You look pale to me. I think some fresh air will do you some good," he said as he pulled the car off the road.

The vast emptiness of the Australian outback surrounded them. Ten-foot-high termite mounds covered the landscape like miniature skyscrapers, baked by the relentless sun. The Stuart Highway stretched north and south as far as they could see and disappeared into quivering heat waves where the pavement met the horizon. Christine's first deep breath was filled with the aroma of Eucalyptus; it tickled her sinuses and soothed her dry throat. Christine walked between the tufts of bunch grass, poking through the red earth; her movement startled a frilled lizard and sent it scurrying on its hind legs across the sand.

"Thanks, Jasper. You're right, I needed to walk."

"Don't spend too much time in this heat," Jasper commanded. Even though it was early morning, the sun singed their exposed skin.

"Nope, I'm good. We can get going," Christine replied, walking back to the car.

"You sure?"

"Yes. Where we going anyway?" she asked, finally realizing she had never asked.

"I was wondering when you were going to ask," Jasper said over the roof of the car as they both opened their doors to get in. "We're on our way to Katherine."

"Katherine? What's there?"

"We're meeting some friends there; they're going to help us leave Australia."

"Friends? You mean some more of your so-called volunteers or whatever you call them, right?" Christine asked, not wanting to condone the action.

"Yes."

"Wonderful. So someone else I don't know can die."

"No one else is going to die. He's a pilot, and she's a flying doctor—Dr. Melissa Fairbanks."

"A what?"

"She's part of the Royal Flying Doctor Service. They're doctors who fly to remote places throughout the Australian outback to help people who otherwise wouldn't see a doctor."

"Really?" she replied in disbelief, never having heard of the service.

"They're stationed in Darwin."

"So let me guess, they'll give me a check-up and fly me to safety. How convenient," she snapped, unable to hold back her sarcasm. Jasper refused to respond but cast a smirk toward her.

***

They arrived at the Katherine Tindal Civilian Airport fifteen minutes before noon and waited in the small lobby. It was an unmanned airport monitored remotely from Darwin and used mainly by private aircraft owners, a few local charter companies and the Royal Flying Doctor Service.

"We're landing," said a woman's voice inside Christine's mind.

"We're in the lobby," Jasper responded.

"Who's that?" Christine asked aloud.

"It's Simone," Jasper replied with a grin.

"What's so funny? It's weird for me to hear another woman's voice inside my head," Christine said, feeling slightly embarrassed by the look on Jasper's face.

"I'm pleased you can hear Simone. She and Luca are still quite a distance from us taxiing up the runway right now. You've grown much stronger over the past week."

A few minutes later, a tall and slender thirty-year-old woman carrying a leather case appeared from a secure steel door in the lobby. Her blue eyes radiated through a pair of funky-looking black horn-rimmed eyeglasses. She wore her long brown hair exactly as Christine did, pulled through the back of a navy blue ball cap that was embroidered with 'RFDS' in bright yellow stitching. She walked directly to Christine and held out her hand.

"Hi, Chris, I'm Simone," she said without speaking, while holding out Dr. Fairbanks's hand.

"Hi," Christine replied, uncomfortable communicating without speaking with someone other than Jasper.

"Shall we get going?" Simone asked.

"I'll wait here," replied Jasper.

"What, you're not coming?" Christine seemed alarmed by

his response.

"Of course not. Simone is going to give you a quick check-up in the restroom if that's okay with you."

"Oh, yah," she said in relief, but even the deep honey-brown tan on her face wasn't enough to cover the redness invading her cheeks. Her moment of insecurity triggered her heart to race, and warmth to spread throughout her body.

"Come on, it'll only take a minute," Simone said, and they walked off toward the restroom.

Jasper sat on the end of a row of bench seats and waited as the two women disappeared into the restroom.

Simone removed a stethoscope and sphygmomanometer from her leather case while Christine leaned against the small sink and pushed the sleeve of her shirt to her shoulder in preparation for the inflation cuff to be strapped on.

"How is it you can do this?" Christine asked as Simone worked the pump.

"Hold on a second, let me get this reading," Simone replied.

Christine withheld her questioning until the pressure released around her upper arm and she heard the air rush out of the cuff.

"Do what?" Simone asked as she lifted the front of Christine's shirt and moved the end of the stethoscope across her stomach.

"Be Simone and Dr. Fairbanks at the same time?"

"As Animus already explained, Dr. Fairbanks is just as much me as I am her. We share consciousness, and everything she knows, I know..."

"This is all too freaky for me," Christine interrupted. "And why do you call Jasper 'Animus?'"

"Jasper and Animus are the same. One day you'll understand," Simone said while placing the equipment back into her leather case.

"She's fine, Animus, her blood pressure was a bit elevated, but considering everything that's happened over the last week, it's nothing to be concerned about," Simone explained.

"Good. Luca, can we leave? I want to get moving before we lose anymore daylight," Jasper replied.

"Yes, Animus. I've just finished fueling. I'll bring the aircraft to the front," Luca replied.

The twin-engine white Cessna with red and blue stripes flanking the fuselage rolled up in front of the terminal. Simone lifted the security card hanging from a lanyard around her neck and swiped it through the receiver next to the metal door she had arrived through. They left the cool cover of the terminal into the midday heat of the Northern Territory sun. Exhaust fumes from the aviation fuel lingered in the air as they approached the aircraft. Both Christine and Simone held their hats while approaching the steps.

"Where we going?" Christine asked.

"Another place to hide," answered Jasper.

"Is there any place we can hide?"

CHAPTER 16

ABIGAIL MOYLE

The small Irish community of Rush sparkled under the early June sunshine. The northern Dublin suburb was tranquil and awash with color from the spring blossoms. Flowers filled the boxes and beds along the walkway to the entrance of St. Joseph's Convent nursing home. Father Black walked with confidence, certain the last few months of searching for leads had finally paid off. He entered the grounds of the convent and was greeted at the door by a nun, the wimple of her traditional white habit barely reaching his shoulders. Mother Superior Ryan, the head of the Franciscan Missionary Sisters of Mary, appeared to be as wide as she was tall. Her perfectly round face was covered with wrinkles and seemed to burst out of her habit when she smiled.

"Top of the mornin', Father. You're early this mornin'," the mother superior said with a strong Irish accent.

"Good morning, Mother," Father Black replied, and he greeted her with the sign of the cross before extending his hand.

"I don't know why you'd want to see her, the dementia is in the final stages, and she hasn't long before joinin' our Lord."

"It's very important to me. I'm trying to find my parents," replied Father Black without hesitation.

"How wonderful that one of her children took the callin'. I

don't think you'll have much luck getting' anythin' out of her. She hasn't been lucid in months," the mother superior said while leading Father Black down the hall.

They arrived in front of a small wooden door and the mother superior stopped and turned to face Father Black.

"I think you're wastin' yer time, Father, she won't even know you're here."

"Thank you, Mother, but I must try."

She opened the door and directed Father Black into the bright, sunlight-filled room. An empty bed was positioned against the wall to the right, and a pale blue curtain surrounded a second bed on the left. A mixture of antiseptic and urine filled the air when the mother superior pulled open the curtains.

"Sister Moyle, you've a special visitor," the mother superior yelled. She then walked over to the large window in the centre of the back wall and opened it. "A little fresh spring air won't hurt."

The frail remnants of a woman lay motionless in the bed. Sister Moyle's eyelids were vibrating but remained shut and her mouth and nose were obscured by an oxygen mask. Her boney legs were the thickness of a broom handle and lay slightly elevated on a pillow at the foot of the bed. Sister Moyle's breathing was barely audible from under the mask and sounded like air leaking from a child's balloon.

"May I speak with her?" Father Black asked.

"Of course, but don't expect much, and you'll have to shout if you want her to have a chance of hearin' you. I'll leave you to chat," said the mother superior, and she left the room, closing the door behind her.

"Sister Moyle, can you hear me?" Father Black asked, but she didn't respond.

"Sister Moyle, I'd like to ask you a few questions. Do you understand?" he said, much louder than the first time, but he still received no acknowledgment.

"I'm Andrew Shannon. Do you remember me?" Father

Black said, knowing she wouldn't be able to recognize him.

Sister Moyle's eyes flipped open abruptly and rolled toward the priest.

"Do you remember me? I'm trying to find information about my parents," he said while forcing a smile to his lips.

Sister Moyle stared into the void of Father Black's lifeless eyes and slowly shook her head back and forth. She knew the eyes staring at her couldn't be those of the wonderful six-year-old boy she had given to a young Swiss couple for adoption forty years before.

"Please, Sister, I need to know where my records are," Father Black asked, losing control of his anger.

Sister Moyle closed her eyes and a faint smile formed under the mask. Father Black slipped the oxygen mask from her face, placing it beside her head. He removed the pillow from below her feet and placed it on her face. It only took a moment for the frail nun to stop breathing. He replaced the pillow and drew the curtain around her bed before leaving the room.

The mother superior was speaking to a nun in the hallway by the entrance to the convent. She interrupted her discussion and called to him.

"How'd it go, Father?"

"Exactly as you said. She fell back to sleep, so I closed the curtain and left her in peace.

"Might there be somethin' I can do for you, Father Black?"

"Not unless you worked in the orphanage with Sister Moyle," Father Black said out of desperation.

"As a matter of fact, Father, that was my first assignment. I was only eighteen," replied the mother superior, laughing at the coincidence.

"You're not pulling my leg now, are you, Mother?" asked Father Black with a hint of a grin forming at the corner of his mouth.

"Before I went to Africa, I worked for Sister Moyle, right here when this was St. Joseph's orphanage. But, Father, that were a long time ago, and I was just a lass."

"Do you still have the records?" Father Black asked, trying to control the excitement building in anticipation of finally finding the information he was searching for.

"Unfortunately, they were lost in a fire back in '81. What are you looking for?" she asked, surprised by the sudden look of disappointment on the priest's face.

"I've been searching for information about my father; he was adopted from St. Joseph's in 1970."

"Sorry, Father, I don't recall any children named Black. I'm afraid my memory is becomin' more like Sister Moyle's as time passes.

"No, the name was Shannon—Andrew Shannon. He was adopted by a wealthy family," Father Black replied, and he removed the planner from his pocket, pulling the newspaper clipping from between the pages. He handed it to the mother superior, hoping it would trigger her memory.

The mother superior put on her reading glasses, which were hanging around her neck, and read the faded writing. She looked up and paused, continuing to gaze blankly into the air as she recollected. Her left eyebrow suddenly went up, lifting her wimple in the process. It was clear from her expression that a memory had returned and astonishment covered her face.

"Father, I think I do recall this boy. If this is the child I'm thinkin' of, everythin' changed right after his adoption."

"What changed?" Father Black asked, thinking he would finally get the information he wanted.

"The incredible donation that came from his family; it changed everythin' for the other children. We went on a shopping spree, and we bought new clothes, food and school supplies for the whole school," she said with a large smile.

"What was their name? Where were they from?"

"No, that's the strange thing about that adoption. Nobody knows except Sister Moyle. I know this for certain because the boy was picked up in a huge car, and the parents didn't even come. That was very odd, and there was plenty of gossip about it. I even heard that the donation came through a Swiss bank account. You can only imagine the rumors at the time; I think that's why it made the paper because normally an adoption wasn't news at all."

Anger returned to Father Black's face. He now knew that the secret he desperately craved for would never be told. This further increased the frustration building inside him. The blackness in his eyes was like a shadow over the mother superior when he looked down at her.

"Thank you for your time, Mother Superior," he said and stormed out of the convent without offering her the traditional sign of the cross and blessing.

***

A perfect image of the three men was reflected on the top of the solid oak boardroom table. Original oil paintings hung on three of the wood-paneled walls in the executive boardroom. The New York skyline glowed in the early morning sunlight flooding into the room from the floor to ceiling windows comprising one entire wall of the large room.

Tonino sat opposite two executives of the pharmaceutical company, but he focused his conversation on Phil Whitfield, the CEO, while occasionally glancing at Darren Howe, the vice president responsible for production. Tonino's tone shifted and became increasingly terse when Whitfield rescinded his support, suggesting the Church's effort was unethical.

"I'm sorry, Mr. Fabro, I don't think we'll be able to support your efforts after all," Whitfield said with finality.

"I'm so sorry to hear that. I was counting on your support," Tonino as he stood up from his seat and cast his eyes down on Howe.

Howe remained silent while he stared at Tonino then turned his eyes to Phil. Neither man rose from their seat as Tonino left the boardroom without offering a good-bye.

Tonino rode the elevator to street level and removed his phone from his pocket.

***

Father Black's phone rang as he read a newspaper in an executive lounge in London's Heathrow Airport, where he was waiting for his afternoon flight to Sydney. He glanced at the call display and answered the call.

"Hello."

"There's been a change of plans. I need your expertise here in New York," Tonino said.

"What about Shannon and the girl?"

"They can wait. Get here as soon as possible. Meet me at the Trump Hotel."

"Yes, sir," Father Black replied. He looked at his watch then the departures board.

"It's urgent. I want you here immediately," Tonino demanded.

"There's an evening flight. I'll do my best to get on it."

"Good. I'll see you tonight."

Father Black walked to the concierge desk at the entrance to the executive lounge and asked the attendant to cancel his ticket to Sydney and book him on the six o'clock flight to New York.

"Can you confirm my baggage will make the flight?" he asked the attendant as she handed him a boarding card.

"I'll call down and see," she said, picking up the radio from the desk.

She repeated the numbers displayed on the computer screen into the radio and waited for a response.

"I can't guarantee it, but we'll do our best," said the man's voice over the radio.

"They're doing their best, but..."

"I heard," snapped Father Black before she could finish.

Father Black's face crumpled with disappointment as he

turned to leave the lounge.

"Mr. Black, check at the gate before you board; they'll be able to tell you for certain," said the attendant as Father Black walked away.

He walked directly to his departure gate and approached the check-in desk. Without hesitation, Father Black interrupted the conversation between the two flight attendants seated behind the desk.

"Can you tell me if my bags will make this flight?" demanded Father Black as he offered his boarding card to the attendant to his right.

The attendant slowly reached for his boarding card while casting him an unpleasant glare. She picked up the telephone from the desk, pressed a single button on the keypad and read the details on the card into the telephone.

"I'm sorry, Mr. Black, but it hasn't arrived."

"I need my bag to make this flight."

"I'm sorry; we've done everything we can. It'll be on the eight o'clock flight. We'll send it on to you. Where will you be staying while in New York?"

"The Trump International Hotel," Father Black said, and he pulled his boarding card from the attendant's hand before storming away from the desk.

***

The Statue of Liberty glimmered in the city lights reflecting off the water as the British Airways flight approached JFK. Father Black powered on his phone and called Tonino while the aircraft taxied to the terminal.

"Welcome to New York, the local time is twenty minutes after nine p.m.," the flight attendant announced.

"We've just arrived," said Father Black.

"Good, I'll be in the hotel restaurant. Make it here before eleven," Tonino ordered.

"I'm on my way."

The traditional New York yellow cab arrived at the Trump Hotel twenty-five minutes after ten. Father Black gave the driver a hefty tip for making it across town in such good time. He checked in at the front desk then went directly to the restaurant, where he found Tonino sitting by himself at a table next to the window.

"Have a seat, Father Black," Tonino said.

As he sat in the chair opposite Tonino, the waiter walked toward the table, but Tonino waved him off. Without any pleasantries, Tonino began to speak.

"I've run into a problem that requires your immediate attention."

"How can I help?" Father Black replied, his boyish face showing signs of jet lag.

"One of my contacts has had a change of mind, and he no longer wishes to support our effort. It's a problem and must be dealt with at once," Tonino said while lifting his cup of tea to his lips.

"You'd like a permanent solution to this problem?" Father Black asked.

"Of course," Tonino stated before taking a sip and then placing his teacup back on the saucer.

"Who?"

"Phil Whitfield. He's the CEO of a large pharmaceutical company."

"When?"

"Immediately. He flew in for our meeting today, and I understand he's staying at the Four Seasons. It's not far from here."

"That could be difficult, as my tools didn't make the flight," said Father Black, displaying a disgruntled look on his face.

"I'm certain you can be creative. It would please me if this problem disappeared tonight," Tonino said as he lifted his arm to signal the waiter.

"I'll do my best," Father Black replied.

"Unlike the others, you've never disappointed me," said Tonino, signing the bill and handing it back to the waiter. He stood up from the table and began to walk away when he suddenly stopped and turned back to face Father Black.

"One more thing."

"What's that?"

"Make it immaculate."

"Always."

CHAPTER 17

PHIL WHITFIELD'S MESSAGE

I t was a three-hour flight from Katherine to East Timor, where Luca and Simone left Jasper and Christine. The humidity in Dili was stifling and was in sharp contrast to the dry heat of the Australian outback. The heavy air was suffocating, and Christine labored with every breath while waiting in the crowded immigration office. The officials cleared their documents, and they proceeded to the check-in counters to arrange the next leg of their journey.

"Where are we going?" asked Christine, showing signs of exhaustion from the traveling and the extra weight she was carrying.

"Somewhere they can't find us," Jasper replied.

"That's not an answer," Christine snapped back, further showing her reduced tolerance with the traveling.

"Brazil, they've—"

"Brazil? Are you kidding me? Why?" she asked, feeling dejected from the thought of traveling all the way to South America.

"As I was about to say, Brazil has well trained doctors and it'll be easy to blend in."

"Blend in?"

"Yes, we'll be able to disappear into the population. It's relatively easy to obtain the necessary documents we'll need to become established without bureaucracy getting in the way," Jasper said with a smile.

"You mean bribe them?"

"Don't think of it as bribes… but donations. This is how much of the world continues to function."

Jasper approached the airline representative and arranged two tickets to Rio de Janeiro. The trip would take nearly thirty-six hours and route them through Singapore, Tokyo and New York before finally arriving in Rio. Jasper paid for the tickets and broke the news to Christine.

"It's going to be a long journey," he said, flashing a fake smile.

"How long?" she asked, shrugging her shoulders.

"A day and a half."

"Really… look at me, I look like crap, and I feel like it too," she protested, disgusted with herself and the news that they would be traveling for two more days.

"You can shop in Singapore, Tokyo or New York—all three if you want, the airports have fantastic shopping," said Jasper in an upbeat tone, hoping it would lift her spirits.

The idea of shopping in those cities sparked Christine's interest, but only until another thought crossed her mind, something she should have thought about months ago: *How's he paying for all this? The cruise, the house and car in Sydney, these flights?*

"Jasper, where are you getting the money to pay for all this? This has gotta be costing a fortune."

"Don't worry. I have rich relatives," he said, smiling at her.

"They sure must like you," she replied, not certain if he meant it or not.

It was early evening when they arrived in Singapore, two hours late because of the delayed arrival of their aircraft in Dili. This left them only twenty minutes to make their connection to Tokyo. Christine's already foul mood turned to nasty, and her patience evaporated from the lack of food and her need for a shower.

Her unpleasantness subsided slightly on the flight to

Tokyo, the business-class seats and ample food making her comfortable enough to sleep on the seven-hour flight.

Tokyo Narita International Airport had all the amenities Christine could hope for. Desperate to shower, she found the first clothing boutique in the shopping area and purchased a full change of clothes before making her way to the shower facilities. The water revitalized her body and washed the nastiness from her attitude.

The freedom to walk around the terminal made their three-hour layover pass quicker. The reality of her situation returned the instant she heard a deep voice inside her mind.

"I've found you a house," he said, but Christine responded before Jasper.

"Who was that?" she asked, not knowing whose voice she had heard.

"Animus, she can hear me," Matteo said with the unmistakable sound of amazement in his tone.

"Jasper, what's wrong?" Christine asked, concerned by Matteo's tone.

"Nothing's wrong," Jasper said, also unable to mask the excitement in his tone.

"I know that voice," she said, trying to remember where she had heard it before.

"It's Matteo," Jasper said. "He helped you in Sydney."

"The turtle," she said, finally recognizing the voice.

"Hello, Christine. I apologize for not introducing myself but I didn't realize—"

"That's okay," Christine interrupted. "I'm still not used to voices popping into my head."

"I understand," Matteo replied, still sounding surprised.

"Chris, this is wonderful!" Jasper said.

"What is?"

"You can communicate with Matteo."

"We already have, in Sydney," she replied, sounding confused by Jasper's excitement.

"Chris, do you have any idea where Matteo is?"

"With you."

"No," Jasper said, unable to contain his exuberance.

"Where?"

"Brazil."

"What...? Brazil? How can that be?" Christine asked, overwhelmed by her ability to communicate with someone on the other side of the planet.

"It must be the child. The energy within you grows stronger as the child grows," Jasper explained.

"I don't feel any different—other than fatter."

"You're different from other humans; the energy within your DNA grows stronger as you get older. It increased until you were twenty-five; that's how you can communicate with us. It was the same for your mother and Jasper's father. Because you're pregnant, the child's energy and yours have combined to make you even stronger."

"Animus, I'll pick you up at the airport," Matteo said.

"Okay," Jasper replied.

Exhausted from walking, it was welcomed relief to Christine when they arrived at the departure gate. Christine's feet ached from the swelling, and she was looking forward to sleeping on the twelve-hour flight to New York.

Jasper and Christine sat next to a young mother with a crying infant and a rambunctious toddler. Christine was mesmerized by the mother's ability to handle the two children seemingly with ease.

The insecurity of a first-time mother welled inside Christine, and she began to question her ability to become a parent. She watched the woman with intent and wondered what she would do if it were her. Driven by fear, Christine's heart raced inside her chest and triggered an uncomfortable restlessness. Filled with anxiety by her unexpected loss of confidence, Christine pushed herself out of the seat.

"I'm going to the restroom," she told Jasper as she walked away.

"Better hurry, we'll be boarding in a couple of minutes,"

Jasper replied.

"I will," she said, leaving the waiting area.

Christine returned just as the ground staff began the pre-boarding announcement. With her composure restored, Christine smiled and waved at the small boy as he walked by, his mother holding his hand while expertly guiding a stroller with the other.

Business-class travelers were called next, so Christine and Jasper entered the aircraft and settled into their seats. The sun had disappeared below the horizon, leaving the sky a pallet of silver and grey. Christine gazed out the window as the massive 747 taxied toward the runway, and she subconsciously counted the painted numbers and the multicolored runway lights lining the edge of the pavement.

Her seat began to vibrate a few seconds before she heard the low rumble of the jet engines as the aircraft began to accelerate down the runway. Christine kicked her shoes off and counted down the minutes in anticipation of the pilot turning off the seatbelt indicator. She was desperate to recline her seat, hoping it would reduce the swelling in her feet. When she heard the now-familiar 'ding' sound, she reclined her seat and exhaled a long breath through her pursed lips.

Christine skipped the in-flight meal and tried to get some sleep. She knew that would give her much-needed relief from the aches and pains scattered throughout her body. She closed the window shutter and called the attendant to get a blanket and pillow.

The nightmare began the instant she fell asleep. She was lying on her back; the ground was uneven beneath her, and it was shaking like an earthquake. A deep rumbling sound echoed inside her ears while hot, stagnant air filled her lungs. Her eyes were open, and they burned from the sweat rolling into them. Christine was blind, the blackness surrounding her absolute.

A constant, dull pressure formed inside her, originating

from her lower back and radiating through her torso. The heavy sensation of pressure transformed into a needle-like pulsating pain. Like a snake plunging its fangs deep inside her, the pain grew more intense with every pulse. The throbbing grew stronger and more rapid with each successive jolt until the agony became continuous. Christine screwed her eyes shut and screamed. Her screams echoed like those of a prisoner being tortured deep within a dungeon. A minute amount of relief followed each outburst, but the sensation was fleeting.

"Jasper, where are you?" she screamed, but total silence filled her mind. *"Where are you?"* she repeated, but there was still no reply. When the pain reached its climax, it erupted inside her like a fiery explosion. But just as fast as it arrived, it suddenly vanished. Without explanation, the ground stopped shaking and complete silence enveloped her. Like a starless night, nothing was discernible in the total darkness.

***

The city lights reflected off a thick layer of clouds, which rendered the New York sky starless. Father Black left the taxi in front of the Four Seasons Hotel and entered the lobby, where he proceeded directly to the row of house telephones hanging along the wall next to the elevators. Father Black picked up the receiver of one of the phones and pretended to use it while positioning himself so he could watch the front desk.

Moments later, a taxi driver entered the hotel lobby carrying an urgent message for Mr. P. Whitfield. As instructed, he took the small white envelope to the front desk and told the clerk it had to be hand-delivered immediately. The clerk looked up Whitfield's room number in the computer and called a bellboy to deliver the envelope.

Father Black followed the bellboy into the elevator and began to fumble for his wallet in the breast pocket of his suit.

The air in the elevator was filled with the stench of alcohol, which emanated from the gin-soaked handkerchief stuffed inside the right pocket of Father Black's suit. The bellboy began to inhale through his mouth, and he inched his body into the opposite corner of the elevator to avoid the drunken businessman he was forced to ride with. He pressed the number twelve and looked over at Father Black.

"Your floor, sir?" asked the bellboy as the elevator began to rise.

Father Black ignored the question and continued to fumble in his suit pocket while sneaking a glance at the illuminated number on the panel.

"What floor, sir?" the bellboy repeated.

Father Black looked at the eighteen-year-old and squinted like he was trying to focus.

"Twelve," he said with a noticeable slur.

"Great," the bellboy whispered under his breath.

When the elevator door opened, the boy gestured with his hands for Father Black to exit first.

"After you, I insist," Father Black said in a drunken slur.

The bellboy left the elevator and turned right, trying to put some distance between himself and the drunk.

Halfway down the hall, the bellboy stopped in front of a room and knocked on the door.

Father Black looked up and quickly counted the number of doors from where he stood in front of the elevator then dropped his head and continued his stagger down the hall.

After the third knock, Phil Whitfield opened the door and the bellboy handed him the letter. Father Black could hear the nasty tone in Whitfield's voice while he scolded the bellboy for waking him. Whitfield closed the door without offering a tip. The disgruntled bellboy walked up to Father Black and reluctantly offered his assistance.

"Can I show you to your room, sir?"

"That's very kind of you, young man, but I'm fine," Father Black replied, slurring his words.

"Have a good night, sir," said the bellboy, and he left as fast as he could.

The instant the elevator door closed, Father Black regained his composure and approached Whitfield's door. He only needed to knock once before the door began to open.

"What is it now?" Whitfield snapped, thinking the bellboy had returned.

Father Black shoved the door open with so much force it knocked Whitfield to the floor. Stunned by the intrusion, he remained on the floor looking at his invader.

Father Black pulled a three-foot-long section of extension cord from his left pocket and wrapped it around Whitfield's neck. There was no chance for the man to yell for help. He tried in vain to get his fingers under the cord, but Father Black cinched it tighter.

Whitfield's body went limp, and with his face devoid of blood, it quickly turned pale blue. Father Black ripped the cord from the floor lamp in the corner of the room and fashioned it into a noose, which he wrapped around Whitfield's neck. He dragged his body into the washroom and hung it from the shower nozzle. Leaving nothing to chance, Father Black removed the alcohol-soaked handkerchief from his pocket and wiped down everything he had touched. Not wanting to be seen leaving the hotel, the priest sat in the armchair next to the window and waited for the light of dawn before he left the room.

CHAPTER 18

SHEER UNLIKELINESS

Rain covered the windshield as the taxi made its way around Central Park. The morning rush was in full swing, which made the trip back to the Trump Hotel slow and agonizing. The constant honking of horns echoing off the storefronts reminded Father Black of the streets of Rome. He removed the phone from his pocket and called Tonino.

"Good morning," Father Black said.

"How was your night?" Tonino asked.

"Problem is solved."

"I knew I could count on you," Tonino replied, having difficulty restraining his enthusiasm.

"Shall I make my way to Sydney?"

"Yes, and while you're there, make certain you give my regards to Derksen."

Father Black paused before replying, "As you wish." He was momentarily confused but not surprised by Tonino's request.

"Make certain it's immaculate," Tonino said and hung up the phone immediately.

***

Rain poured off the green awning covering the restaurant

window. The torrent of water bounced off the soil in a small flower box next to the window, speckling the glass with earth. Nearly every table in the restaurant was occupied by a businessman so that their dark suits stood out like flakes of ground pepper against the white tablecloths.

Tonino sipped a latte while he read the headline of the New York Times: *"China Follows India's Lead: Complete Ban On Abortions."* The waitress approached his booth accompanied by a well-dressed middle-aged man.

"Have a seat, Darren," Tonino said with a smirk.

"Thank you, Mr. Fabro," replied Darren Howe, his eyes shifting away from Tonino's.

"Please, call me Toni; after all... we'll be working together for a very long time."

"I'm sorry, Toni, Phil just isn't as committed as I am," Darren said, desperately trying to distance himself from his boss's refusal to help Tonino.

"Not to worry. I understand completely."

"I know he agreed to help but he seems to have had a change of mind; there was nothing I could do."

"Not to worry," Tonino repeated.

"But there's nothing I can do now; he'll be watching me. In fact, I'm pretty certain he's going to fire me over this," Darren said, the concern spilling from his voice.

"Like I said, don't worry. In fact, I'm willing to bet there's a promotion in your future," Tonino said with a whisper of a laugh.

"Not likely. Now, what can I do?" Darren asked.

"Exactly as we had discussed..."

"I told you, there's nothing I can do. Phil will be all over me, and I need this job," Darren interrupted, frustrated with Tonino's lack of understanding.

"Phil won't be a problem anymore," Tonino said, the humor gone from his tone.

Darren's face lost all expression and turned whiter than the tablecloth. Horror flooded his mind when he realized what Tonino meant. Fear ripped through every fiber of his body as he looked into the emptiness of Tonino's eyes.

"I... see," said Darren, only able to think of his children at that moment.

"When can you get started?" Tonino asked.

"I can adjust the formulation next week."

"I knew you could help."

"I just want to be clear; you want the efficacy reduced and the Clomiphene added?"

"Yes."

"At all of our plants?"

"Of course, you'll be well taken care of."

The waitress arrived at the booth to take Darren's order, but he declined and left the restaurant. Tonino ordered another cup of coffee and resumed reading the paper.

Fifteen minutes later Gino walked up to Tonino's booth.

"Well?" Tonino asked without looking up.

"Both major soft drink companies and the top three breweries are on board. The bottled water industry is owned by the same soft drink companies, so everything is covered," Gino said, proud to report his accomplishments.

"Unfortunately, I ran into a small problem. One of our contacts changed his mind. I had Father Black take care of the problem."

"What about the abortion lobbyists? Do you really think they'll have a chance?" Gino asked, not convinced they could change the law.

"Anything is possible with the right amount of incentive."

"What about Father Derksen?" Gino asked next.

"Black's on his way to clean up another mess for me," Tonino said with disdain.

Gino shifted his eyes away from Tonino's; he was unable to sustain more than a brief glance into their icy cold darkness. It was Father Derksen who had hired him, and they had worked together for more years, but there was no misunderstanding Tonino's words. Gino sat at the table riddled with sadness and fear. He recited a small prayer in his mind.

"Gino, you have family in Canada, yes?" Tonino asked, with no attempt to hide the grin on his face.

"Yes, sir. My fiancée is there now; we're from the same hometown," replied Gino sheepishly, unsure where Tonino was going with his questions.

"I didn't know you were getting married. In fact, I didn't realize you were even dating," Tonino said with surprise. "But anyway," he continued and forced a larger smile to his lips. "How wonderful, congratulations," he said, but the insincerity in his tone was even more evident in his eyes.

"Thank you, it's rather sudden and somewhat necessary," replied Gino, his face struggling to show some happiness. "We're old family friends. But I love her," he followed up quickly so as not to give the wrong impression.

Tonino ignored Gino's moment of discomfort and continued.

"How would you like to join them?"

"That would be wonderful," Gino replied, confused by the unexpected offer.

"While you're there, why don't you visit our contacts in Ottawa?" Tonino suggested, and he flagged the waitress to get his bill.

Gino now understood the true motivation behind Tonino's unusually considerate suggestion.

"Thanks, it'll be a nice surprise for them. I'll fly to Ottawa after visiting my family."

Tonino glanced at his phone to get the time as the waitress arrived and placed a black leather bill folder on the table.

"It's time I prepare for my meeting this afternoon," said Tonino. He then signed the bill and left the table.

Gino pulled out the gold crucifix hanging around his neck and held it in his hands. He recited a short prayer to himself while he stared at the rain bouncing off the cobblestone patio outside the restaurant window. The scene reminded him of his office at the Vatican and the years he had spent working with Father Derksen. Nausea grew inside him, spawned by thoughts of the methods Tonino used to deal with his problems. Gino sat and wondered what Father Derksen would do when Father Black arrived.

***

A sequence of high-pitched beeps woke Father Black at exactly three o'clock that afternoon. He touched the screen of his phone to cancel the alarm and opened the curtains before getting dressed. Droplets of water snaked down the window as sheets of rain pounded the glass. The weather made the afternoon traffic worse than the morning's, so the taxi ride to JFK Airport was exceptionally long.

Father Black entered the main terminal and found a departures monitor. He scanned through the flights listed in search of the first leaving for Sydney. There were no flights that evening; the next departure would be in the morning. Father Black decided to get help, and so he made his way to the Qantas Airlines ticketing booth.

"May I help you?" asked the ticketing agent.

"I need to get to Sydney as soon as possible. When is the next flight?"

"Our next flight doesn't leave until late tomorrow morning. Would you like me to check with one of our partner airlines?"

"Please."

The agent typed into the computer for what seemed like a half-hour to Father Black before she found an earlier departure.

"I can't guarantee I can get you on the flight, but there's a Japan Airlines flight leaving at five thirty for Tokyo and you can connect there with our Qantas flight into Sydney. It leaves in less than an hour, and like I said, there's no guarantee you'll get on the flight."

"Please do your best. I've got nothing to lose," he said.

"You'll need to clear security and go straight to the check-in desk at the gate. Tell the staff there, and they'll be able to confirm you a seat if one becomes available. I'll take your bag and send it directly to screening. That will better the chances of it making the flight, but you've got to hurry and get through security."

Father Black rushed to the security-screening checkpoint and called one of the guards. He showed his ticket to the security officer, who escorted him past the endless line of travelers to a separate line. Father Black cleared security and raced to the gate desk.

"Can I help you?" asked the young female airline attendant with a strong Japanese accent.

"Can I make this flight?" asked Father Black.

"May I have your ticket? The flight is full, sir, but I will check for a no-show," the attendant replied.

"Thank you."

"Please, Mr. Black, have a seat, and I'll call you if something opens up."

"When will you know?" Father Black asked, unable to contain his impatience.

"The flight is late arriving and three passengers haven't checked in yet. I don't expect it to take long."

***

Bright rays of sunlight squeezed through the bottom edge of the plastic shutter, and the warm rays woke Christine from her nightmare. Her eyelids snapped open, and she gulped air into her lungs. Her heart struggled to slow as she absorbed her surroundings. She had forgotten the intensity of the nightmare and its effect on her. She looked at Jasper and felt relieved that he remained asleep, negating the need to explain her condition.

The kicking between her ribs grew intense as the fetus

struggled to find room inside her small frame. It pressed down on her bladder and forced her to make a trip to the toilet every couple of hours. Christine quietly left her seat so as not to disturb Jasper and enjoyed the walk to the washroom, the short stroll relieving some of the strain from her lower back. The flight attendant took notice and approached Christine.

"Is there anything I can get you, dear?" the woman asked with a genuine smile as she glanced at Christine's stomach.

"No thanks," Christine replied as she pushed open the washroom door.

With the pressure lifted off her bladder, Christine felt the return of her hunger pangs. She left the washroom and walked up to the small galley near the front of the cabin.

Finding the flight attendant she had just spoken to, she said, "Actually, I could use something to eat."

"Of course, dear. You were asleep during the meal service, and I didn't want to wake you. I'll bring it right over. Would you like chicken or beef?"

"Chicken please."

Christine returned to her seat to find Jasper awake.

"How's it going?" he asked.

"Good, I'm a bit hungry so I asked for a meal. What time is it?"

"It's almost five. We'll land in an hour."

"Great."

"You must've been having quite a dream," Jasper said.

"Why?" Christine asked self-consciously.

"You were jumping around in your seat; I thought you might fall out."

"It was nothing... same old dream I always have," Christine replied, downplaying the havoc the nightmare continued to wreak on her.

The last hour of the flight dragged on, and it finally arrived at JFK late. Christine fought the urge to flee like an escaped prisoner, growing tired of being cooped up. She waited impatiently in her seat while the other passengers filed out of the aircraft; she knew this was less stressful than trying to fight the crowd. Jasper gathered their documents and parcels of clothing and waited in the aisle.

"Go ahead, I'll meet you inside the terminal," she said, detecting his impatience.

"You sure?"

"Yup, I'll wait till it clears out a bit more," she replied, and Jasper walked down the aisle to leave the aircraft.

With the majority of the passengers off the plane, Christine made her way to the exit. She walked up the long tunnel ramp to the terminal behind the young woman and her two children she had watched in the Narita terminal. The woman cradled her sleeping infant over her right shoulder with one arm and pushed her stroller with the other. The toddler walked along holding the stroller in one hand and a toy airplane in the other.

The quiet of the dimly lit tunnel suddenly gave way to the clamor and bright lights of the terminal. The massive building was filled with noise, the echoing of the public address system and the many voices of the crowd of travelers. Overwhelmed by the unexpected change of surroundings, the toddler tripped over one of the stroller wheels and fell to the floor. Startled but unhurt, he began to cry.

Christine scooped the boy into her arms, holding him so close their noses touched. She looked over to his mother, who had stopped walking to see why her son was crying. Christine received an unmistakable look of gratitude. It then became apparent why the boy was crying. The impact of his tumble had caused his toy airplane to take flight. It had glided for a few feet and landed on the carpet at the foot of the check-in desk.

A man bent down and picked up the toy, holding it out as he walked to the crying toddler. For an instant, Father Black's eyes met Christine's before the boy leaned out of her arms for the toy, the boy's movement covering Christine's face.

Like the distant memory of a high-school friend, the glimpse of her face triggered Father Black's memory, but her shortened black hair and swollen face, combined with the unlikeliness of meeting her at that moment provided sufficient disguise.

"Here you go, son," said Father Black, and he handed the toy to the boy.

"Thanks," said Christine from behind the boy's body, and she walked toward his mother, taking no notice of Father Black.

Father Black returned to the check-in desk and continued his discussion.

Jasper met Christine and the boy as they approached his mother, who had stopped to put her infant into the stroller.

The woman reached over and took her son from Christine's arms. "Thanks so much," she said.

"It was no trouble at all," Christine said.

"This your first?" asked the woman, looking at Christine's stomach.

"Yes."

"Enjoy it..." the woman said, and she smiled at her sleeping infant in the stroller.

"I will," Christine replied.

CHAPTER 19

FATHER BLACK COLORS

Father Black left the check-in desk with a smile pasted across his face; he had been given confirmation that he had a seat on the flight. But not all the news was good. The flight was delayed on arrival and wouldn't depart for three hours. The waiting area erupted in groans from the disgruntled travelers. The noise of the crowd combined with the lack of comfortable seating caused Father Black to leave the waiting area for the business-class lounge.

Large photographs depicting historical airplanes covered the twelve-foot walls of the lounge. Colored lights reflected off the massive windows as a nonstop stream of aircraft taxied past the windows. Pods of black leather chairs were neatly arranged around the glass coffee tables scattered through the open area of the room, and the lounge air was filled with the aroma of fresh brewed coffee. A faint voice could be heard coming from the flat screen TV hanging from the far wall. Father Black walked across the room and entered one of the small business cubicles, removing his phone to call Father Derksen.

"Hello," Father Derksen answered.

"How's it going?" Father Black asked.

"Good," Father Derksen replied, not surprised to hear from him.

"I hear it didn't go so well in Sydney."

"Those idiots couldn't even follow her until I arrived," he

replied with contempt.

"Yes, how unfortunate," said Father Black disingenuously. "I'd like to meet with you to pick up the trail. I'll be in Sydney late tomorrow."

"I'm not in Sydney anymore. I finished my meetings yesterday; I'm on my way back to the Vatican. In fact, I'm just about to board my flight now."

"Where are you?" asked Father Black, concerned he would not be able to complete his work.

"I'm in LA. Why?"

"I'd like to be briefed on all the details, and any other information you have that may help me find them."

"I can forward you the surveillance photos I have of the girl taken from a security camera, but I've got nothing for Shannon. I'll call you once I'm on the flight."

"Good, when do you arrive in Rome?"

"I've got a connection in New York so I should—"

"New York?" interrupted Father Black.

"Yes, why?"

"I'm in New York. So is Tonino. Did you let him know?"

"No, I thought he was in Rome. I was going to set up a meeting with him tomorrow," Father Derksen said, concerned with his lack of information about the current plans.

"I'm waiting for my flight to Sydney. I'll be here for the next couple of hours. You may want to contact Tonino and let him know you'll be flying via New York."

"Certainly, we're boarding now. You should receive the photos in a minute. I'll forward them when I get to my seat."

"Thanks," Father Black said, hanging up the phone.

Father Black immediately called Tonino.

"Derksen's left Sydney. He's boarding a flight to New York on his way to Rome. What would you like to me to do?"

"Find them. I'll deal with Derksen myself," Tonino said, and he hung up.

Father Black left the cubical and picked up a cup of coffee

and some biscuits from the buffet of food along the back wall of the lounge. He felt his phone vibrate, so he pulled it from his pocket and confirmed it was the incoming photos from Father Derksen. He closed the device and returned it to his jacket to finish his food.

After finishing his meal and reading the newspaper, Father Black opened the email containing the photos. The first one he opened was a poor-quality image and was no use for identification purposes. The second photo he opened was significantly better and contained two figures. He could see the back of one person, which seemed to be a waitress; she was standing in front of Christine. Christine's face was clearly visible in this photo, but Father Black's attempt to zoom in decreased the resolution on the small screen of his phone. Now frustrated, Father Black forwarded the photos to his Internet account so he could print them in the business centre of the lounge.

He logged into his email account using the business computer provided in the cubical and sent the photos directly to the printer without opening them. After the first image began to print on the color printer next to the computer, Father Black opened the first file. As was the case on his phone, the first image was too poor, and it was of little use. He minimized the first image and then opened the second as the printer slid out the printed first image.

Father Black's face compressed as if he had taken a bite of a lemon when the image filled the screen. A large lump filled his throat while he stared at the screen. He directed the mouse to highlight Christine's face. He enlarged it even more to see the details of her eyes. As if he had been hit by a bolt of lightning, his heart skipped a beat.

Unaccustomed to the anxiety rushing through his veins, he sprang from his seat and rushed to the printer. His mind was rattled with disbelief; he had to see a printed version to be certain.

He returned to the computer desk and spread the three

printed photos across the top. He tossed the first one aside and focused on the second image, the one that remained on the screen. Father Black took the pencil off the pad sitting on the desk and began to color over the woman's hair. He pressed hard to make certain his sketching was as dark as possible. A knot formed in his stomach as the blood rushed to his extremities. With Christine's hair colored black, he was now certain. Father Black pulled the phone out of his pocket and called Tonino.

"She's here!" he shouted into the phone.

"Where?" replied Tonino, confused by his statement.

"New York!"

"How do you know?"

"I saw her, an hour ago, here in the airport," he replied, continuing to shout and unable to contain his shock.

"Are you certain?"

"Yes. She got off a Japan Airlines flight. She has a child with her."

"What, she couldn't?" Tonino yelled back.

"Yes, she was carrying a young child. He dropped a toy, and I handed it to him. She was holding him in her arms."

"It's not possible. She couldn't have a toddler," Tonino said, confused by Father Black's description.

"It was a toddler, but I didn't see Shannon."

"Get to security while I call Gino. I want the airport surveillance video. No screw-ups!" Tonino barked.

"I'll go there now."

"And call Derksen. Tell him to join us: he may prove useful after all," Tonino said.

***

Gino kept looking at his watch as the small aircraft arrived at Toronto's Pearson Airport thirty minutes late. He was certain he was going to miss his connecting flight to Windsor. Gino's phone vibrated in his breast pocket. He remained in his seat and answered the call while the other passengers stood to leave the aircraft.

"Hello."

"Black spotted her in JFK. Get here at once!" Tonino demanded.

"I'll be on the next available flight," Gino replied.

"Call our people. I want access to JFK security video, and get the passenger list for all the Japan Airlines flights arriving at JFK today. I want the name of every twenty-five-year-old female passenger, as well as anyone travelling with children."

"Children?" Gino asked, not understanding the reason for Tonino's request.

"Yes, Black saw her with a toddler. It might be a cover, but I don't want any mistakes this time—understand?"

"Yes" said Gino.

***

Jasper and Christine waited at gate B1 for their 7:40 p.m. flight to Rio de Janeiro. The TAM Airlines flight would stop in Sao Paulo before arriving in Rio de Janeiro at ten thirty the next morning. Christine hated the thought of another ten hours trapped inside an aircraft, so when she heard the pre-boarding announcement for business-class travelers, she looked at Jasper and shook her head, indicating that she didn't want to board early; she relished every moment in the terminal.

The waiting area was empty as the flight staff made the final boarding announcement for TAM Flight 8081. Christine and Jasper approached the attendant at the gate and handed her their identification and tickets. The attendant escorted them to the aircraft since they were the last to board the flight. Jasper shut off his phone and placed it in his jacket breast pocket. He folded the brown envelope containing their travel documents and placed it in the side pocket of his jacket before putting it in the overhead bin.

Christine smiled when she sat down; their seats were in the front row of the business-class cabin, which had extra legroom, as there was an emergency door to the right of their seats. Christine didn't even have enough time to buckle her seatbelt when a young woman with almond-brown skin and long black hair approached her. The flight attendant noticed her obvious pregnancy and introduced herself.

"Hello, I'm Renata. Can I get you anything?" she asked Christine with a Portuguese accent.

"No thanks. I'm fine," Christine replied.

"Please don't hesitate to call me if there is anything I can do to make your flight more comfortable," said the attendant.

"I don't think there's much you can do for me now," Christine replied with a hint of sarcasm. She peered over to Jasper and smiled as he took his seat next to her.

***

Father Black stood outside the door to the main office of the Transportation Security Administration at JFK International Airport. He held his phone and stared at the time. At twenty-three minutes after seven, Gino's name appeared in the caller ID window.

"You got me a contact?" asked Father Black.

"Yes, Sergeant Gordon McNaughton. He's expecting you."

"What name is she using?"

"No name yet. Try McNaughton; it may be quicker," Gino replied.

"I'll try."

"The next flight from here is eight o'clock, so I'll be offline for about an hour and a half."

"Good luck," Father Black said, and he pulled open the door to the JFK security office.

The inside of the security office resembled a bank because of the long counter that separated the reception area from the security staff. Down the centre of the counter was a two-foot-high, mirrored glass wall allowing staff to see the entrance while preventing the public from viewing the offices. Positioned in the middle of the counter was a flip-up opening where an extremely overweight male security officer stood with his hands resting on the counter. His face was so large his glasses formed the shape of a wedge as they approached his nose and rested on his cheeks. His eyes peered over the top of his glasses to see Father Black.

"How can I help you?" asked the officer, his New York accent so thick Father Black couldn't understand him.

"Pardon me?"

"What can I do for you?" the officer asked as he raised his hand from the counter to push his glasses onto his nose.

"I'm expected," replied Father Black.

"By who?"

"Sergeant McNaughton."

"And you are?"

"Sean Black, Vatican Security."

"One moment," said the officer, and he dialed the phone sitting on the counter next to him.

Before the man had time to place the phone back on the receiver, a tall, middle-aged African-American man appeared from behind a small door to the right of the counter. He was dressed in an impeccable business suit, which hung off his immense shoulders. He extended his hand to Father Black while brandishing a smile.

"Sean Black."

"Yes."

"Sergeant Gord McNaughton."

"Thank you for helping us."

"You people move faster than a New Yorker talks," said Sergeant McNaughton, holding the small door open and signaling Father Black to come in.

"This matter is of extreme importance to us," replied Father Black, following Sergeant McNaughton through the maze of desks to the back of the security room.

They entered a room that was so dark it took Father Black's eyes a moment to adjust before he could see the entire room. The room was the size of a large movie theatre and was filled with people and security equipment. There were twenty monitoring stations evenly spaced throughout the room, each with a security officer seated in front of a bank of computer screens. Each screen was split into four sections and monitored a different location in the airport.

"Follow me and watch your step," said Sergeant McNaughton, pointing to a couple of steps.

He led Father Black into a small room near the back of the monitoring area. A woman security officer sat at a desk in front of a row of three large LCD monitors.

"Corporal Higgins, this is Sean Black. He's from Vatican Security, and they're looking for a woman who arrived this evening from Tokyo on Japan Airlines flight 087. Do what you can to help him."

"Yes, sir," said Corporal Higgins.

"I've got some work on the go in my office, but I'll check in a bit later," said Sergeant McNaughton, and he began walking back to the door.

"Sergeant McNaughton, one more thing."

"Yes?"

"Do you have access to the passenger list for that flight?"

"I'll make a call and get it sent over. It will take some time though."

"Thank you very much for your assistance," Father Black replied with a smile.

The priest returned his attention to Corporal Higgins. She had already retrieved the file containing the arrival of flight 087 and was loading it into the software.

"I understand you're looking for a female, correct?" she asked.

"Yes, Caucasian, female, twenty-five, black hair, carrying a toddler. When you locate me at the check-in desk at the gate, that's where we can begin. Once I pick up a toy and hand it to the boy, the target will appear."

Corporal Higgins worked the computer, speeding up the video until they both saw the action as Father Black described it. She stopped the video after the point where Christine handed the toddler back to his mother and Jasper and her left. It was a clear shot of them both.

"Please, can you enlarge her face as much as possible?" Father Black requested.

The screen filled with Christine's face, her blue eyes sparkling on the high-definition screen. Father Black pulled out the photo he had printed of Christine and unfolded it. He had no doubt; it was her.

"Can you enlarge and frame this woman and this man?" he asked while pointing to Christine and Father Shannon on the monitor.

"Sure," she said and filled the screen with the two people.

"She's pregnant!" he shouted.

"Apparently," she replied, startled by Father Black's outburst.

"Print them for me?" asked Father Black. recognizing their attempt to disguise themselves.

Corporal Higgins clicked the mouse a couple of times and waited for the printer to complete the task.

"It'll take a minute," she said.

"Thanks. Can we track them?"

"I'll run the program but depending on how far they have gone through the airport, it could take a while."

Corporal Higgins enlarged the image of Christine and Father Shannon. She then initiated the facial tracking software. The right screen filled with a slow-motion video sequence of Christine and Father Shannon's image walking through the terminal.

Father Black's phone rang after ten minutes of tracking. He answered Gino's call at the same instant that the video showed Christine and Father Shannon's arrival at Gate B1.

"Hello," said Father Black, walking away from Corporal

Higgins to gain some privacy but still watching the screen.

"I've got it; they're travelling as Andrew and Christine Yandel," Gino said.

"They're going to Brazil," they said in unison as Father Black saw the flight information appear on the screen.

CHAPTER 20

FATHER SHANNON

Father Black flipped his phone closed and walked back to Corporal Higgins. His pupils were dilated and blood raced through his veins while every muscle in his body tensed like a cat poised to pounce. He fought back the urge to sprint to Gate B1. He knew the security camera would get him the information he required. Father Black watched as Christine walked around the waiting area, and Father Shannon sat patiently reading a newspaper. Father Black looked at the time in the bottom right corner of the tracking video the moment Christine and Father Shannon disappeared into the tunnel to board their flight.

"Is this the current time?" he asked, pointing to the 19/06/2011 - 19:29:43 displayed in the corner of the screen.

"No, that's the time of recording."

Father Black looked out the window of the room and read the bright red 19:57:22 on the digital clock hanging from the wall in the monitoring room.

"Show me Gate B1," asked Father Black, trying not to sound demanding.

The far left screen displayed Gate B1. Father Black could see there were two members of the flight staff standing behind the check-in desk, and the tunnel door was closed.

"Call the gate," Father Black demanded.

He watched the screen as Corporal Higgins dialed the gate. One of the flight staff answered the phone immediately.

"This is Corporal Higgins with security, I'm going to pass you to..." she looked at Father Black for guidance.

"Sean Black," he said as he reached for the telephone.

"Sean Black, Vatican Security," she said.

"Hello. Has the flight left the gate?" he asked.

"Yes, twenty minutes ago. Is there a problem?" asked the attendant.

"No, I need confirmation if two passengers boarded that flight."

"Can I have their names please?"

"Andrew and Christine Yandel."

"One moment while I search for their names."

Father Black watched the attendant on the screen as she scrolled through a hard copy of the passenger list.

"Yes, both passengers boarded the flight."

"Is it a direct flight to Rio?" asked Father Black.

"No, it stops in Sao Paulo first."

"What is the exact itinerary of the flight?" Father Black demanded.

"Depart JFK 19:40 arriving Sao Paulo 06:40 June 20, depart Sao Paulo 09:40, arrive Rio de Janeiro 10:41."

"There are no other stops?"

"No."

"Thank you," said Father Black, and he handed the phone back to Corporal Higgins. "Thank you for your assistance, Corporal Higgins. Please extend my gratitude to Sergeant McNaughton. I'll find my own way out."

Anger rolled up and down Father Black's every thought for having been so close yet failing. *If I had only looked at the photos sooner, I would've got them*, he thought. *Tonino won't be pleased.* He left the security office and located a private corner to call Tonino.

"Good news I hope?" Tonino asked.

"Yes, they're on a flight to Rio," Father Black replied.

"When did it leave?"

"Thirty minutes ago. Declare an emergency and get the

flight turned back?" Father Black asked.

"No, there's no guarantee it'll land here, and if it doesn't, they'll know we've found them. We must get to Rio first. Notify our pilots and have them ready to depart by ten. I'm on my way to the airport now."

"We've got time; the flight makes a three-hour stop in Sao Paulo before Rio."

"Then we can't be certain they're going to Rio," Tonino said with anger in his voice.

"They're ticketed to Rio," Father Black replied, in an attempt to quell Tonino's anger.

"That means nothing. We must have a plan in place for Sao Paulo. They could get off there. I want this done right," Tonino said with no attempt to hide his anger.

"Yes, sir."

"That reminds me, has Derksen arrived yet?" asked Tonino, changing to a slightly more acidic but softer tone.

"Not till ten."

"Have you heard from Gino?"

"He'll arrive at nine thirty."

"Good. Derksen can assist in coordinating the back-up in Rio, and Gino can take care of Sao Paulo. I want to deal with her myself, so let's hope they continue to Rio."

"I'm certain they will," Father Black said.

"We've got twelve hours to get this right," Tonino snapped.

***

Both Jasper and Christine declined their dinner and decided to sleep, hoping the rest would counter the jet lag certain to plague them in Brazil. Christine dozed off first. Exhausted from the travelling, they remained asleep until Renata accidently woke Jasper when she hit his shoulder with the breakfast trolley.

"I'm so sorry, sir," she said.

"I'm fine," he replied with a smile.

Christine was awakened by the conversation and slid up the shade of her window. She stared out the window into the darkness, watching the light reflect off the tiny ice crystals that formed between the two panes of the window. A cold chill settled over her heart when she saw her reflection in the window. Christine caught a brief image of her face distorted by the plastic, and it reminded her of her mother. She placed her hands on her stomach and felt the new life moving inside. A hollow sadness gripped her thoughts, and the power of the memory unleashed a small tear from the corner of her eye.

Christine struggled with the memory of her childhood, growing up without family other than her mother. It had never bothered her until now. *You too will have no one, no father, no grandmother or grandfather... just me,* she thought, and a second, larger tear streamed down her cheek.

Jasper saw her wipe the evidence from her face, but the sadness lingered in her eyes. He paused for a moment.

"Why are you crying?"

"I don't know," she responded.

"Are you in pain?"

"No."

"Another nightmare?"

"No, it's nothing, really," she pleaded, embarrassed by her display of emotion.

"You're sad."

"No, I'm fine, Jasper. Forget about it," she begged, not wanting to talk about it.

"Tell me. I can help?"

"It's stupid," she said, this time using her voice.

"Don't worry about it, tell me," Jasper insisted.

"I started thinking about my mom when I was little, how hard it must have been for her not having any help, and then I started to feel sorry for myself, not knowing my father or any other family. I told you, it's silly," she said, feeling embarrassed.

"Chris, that's not silly. I think it's time you know," said Jasper and he stood up, opening the overhead bin to retrieve his wallet from his jacket.

"Know what?" Christine asked, her sadness disappearing to be replaced by curiosity.

Jasper opened his wallet and pulled out an old tattered photograph of Father Shannon with his arm around the shoulders of a young woman. Christine recognized the location the instant she saw the photo.

"That's St. Michael's!" she said.

"Take a close look. Who's next to Father Shannon?" Jasper asked as he handed the photo to her.

Christine turned on the overhead light and moved the photo closer to her face. For a brief second, she thought the woman was her but realized it was her mother and she was pregnant.

"When was this taken?"

"A little over twenty-five years ago. Chris, do you know what your middle name is?"

"Of course, I hate it. I never let Mom use it."

"What is it?" Jasper asked, not showing any emotion.

"Sandra."

"Nope," Jasper said, expecting that response.

"I think I know my own name."

"Do you?"

"Okay, what is it?"

"Shannon," Jasper said, waiting for a reaction.

"No, it's not. It's Sandra," Christine said, refusing to believe Jasper.

Jasper opened his wallet again, pulled a folded piece of paper from it and handed it to Christine. She carefully unfolded the paper, as it appeared delicate. She read the top of the document out loud.

"'State of Hawaii Certificate of Live Birth – 1986— Christine Shannon Anderson.' I don't believe it, why did she tell me it was Sandra?" Christine asked, clearly confused.

She looked at him, but Jasper didn't answer and waited for Christine to read the rest of the document. He knew Sandra had never given Christine a copy of her birth certificate, and this was the first time she would see it. Christine continued to read out loud, skipping most of the details until she approached the section titled *'Full Name of Father'*.

"Andrew Iain Shannon," she said and stopped reading.

Her breathing halted as the pressure increased in her chest until she felt as though she was buried alive. She couldn't pull her eyes off the paper. She read the words over and over in her mind, as if they would magically change. Question after question raced in her head, but not one could escape the grip the shock held over her. Emotions welled inside her; she was furious with her mother for lying to her while at the same time disappointed for never having the chance to talk to her about it. Christine's eyes finally left the page and focused on Jasper. Confusion filled her thoughts, but anger fueled her questions.

"Why didn't you tell me?" she asked without using her voice, but the anger was unmistakable.

"Do you mean me or Father Shannon?" Jasper replied.

Christine was caught off guard by Jasper's response, forgetting that Jasper had only recently found out himself.

"You, him... I don't know—both," she said, trying to process the magnitude of the information she had just found out about herself and her mother.

"I couldn't tell you until now. Too much has happened in the last seven months. I didn't think it wise to add this on top of everything else. But when you told me how you were feeling, I thought this was probably as good a time as any. As for Father Shannon and your mother, it's complicated."

"I've got nothing but time," Christine said, and she slid to the back of her seat, staring at the writing on the birth certificate.

"Andrew's parents couldn't conceive, so they adopted him

at the age of five. His adopted father is from Switzerland's wealthiest banking family, and his mother from a prestigious New York family. While on vacation with his parents in Hawaii, Andrew met your mother. He was eighteen and finishing his last year at Trinity School, a private school in New York. Your mother had finished high school, and they fell in love.

"For as long as he could remember, Andrew wanted to be a priest. He told your mother this, but she wouldn't accept it. She tried for years to convince him to marry her and move to Hawaii. Andrew studied at the Vatican and would visit your mother as often as he could. It was during his last visit, before he took the oath of celibacy, that we allowed her to conceive you."

"What do you mean '*we allowed her*'?" Christine asked.

"Remember, like you, your mother was a Vector, but critical mass hadn't been attained so her DNA had to be passed on. Jasper Stewart and you were conceived at precisely the same moment in time, linking your DNA."

"Why didn't she tell me?"

"Your mother loved Andrew too much to take away his passion to serve God. She promised never to identify who the father was if he promised to stay in Hawaii. Andrew never told his parents about you. He insisted he wanted to fulfill his calling at St. Michael's, so his father made a large donation to the church and…"

"The rest is history," Christine said sarcastically.

"Think back to your childhood, and you'll find your father was always there for you."

A wave of warmth filled Christine's heart as the memories of her childhood flooded her mind. Father Shannon was always there—he never missed a holiday or a birthday. Her anger evaporated like the white clouds outside the aircraft window. The morning sunlight caressed her skin, bathing her in contentment and washing her sorrow away. Christine folded the birth certificate back to its original size and handed it to Jasper.

"You keep it," he said.

"No, it belongs to Father Shannon. He's kept it this long, I'm not about to take it now," she insisted.

Jasper put the paper back into the wallet, placed it in his jacket and returned it to the overhead bin. When Jasper sat in his seat, a flight attendant approached them holding a sheet of paper.

"Are you Andrew and Christine Yandel?" asked the male flight attendant with a forced a smile.

"Yes, why?" Jasper asked.

"You ordered a special meal," said the attendant, looking at the paper.

"No, I don't think we did," Jasper replied.

"Oh I'm sorry, we have you here as ordering a vegetarian meal. Sorry to bother you," said the flight attendant and he rolled up the paper as he walked to the front of the cabin. There he immediately picked up the phone hanging from the wall and made a call.

At first Jasper thought nothing of it, but then he realized they had already served a meal and they should have asked them sooner. Jasper began watching the flight crew intently, observing their actions as they moved about the cabin. It was evident some of the crew were monitoring Christine when she got up to use the bathroom. As if suddenly startled, two of the cabin attendants locked their eyes on Christine's as she made her trip to the front of the cabin. A few minutes after Christine returned to her seat, the pilot announced they were beginning their final approach to Sao Paulo Airport.

"I can't wait to get out of this thing," Christine said, stretching her legs and rubbing them at the same time.

Jasper was so engrossed with watching the flight staff that he didn't hear her.

"Jasper, what's wrong?"

"What? Oh sorry, nothing's wrong," he said unconvincingly.

"You seem a little preoccupied."

"I'm okay; we've got a few hours to stretch our legs in Sao Paulo."

Jasper continued to watch the flight staff while the other passengers deplaned. The male flight attendant stared at Christine while talking on the aircraft telephone. Jasper removed his jacket from the overhead bin and followed Christine off the aircraft.

They walked side by side without speaking through the noisy and crowded terminal. They strolled around for two hours, passing time window-shopping. At times, the crowd of travelers was so thick Christine had to turn sideways to fit her oversized body between the pushcarts and luggage on wheels. She quietly dwelled on the news Jasper had told her on the aircraft. Like watching a rewinding video, her mind filled with random scenes from the past. Jasper and Father Shannon shared consciousness; they were her priest and now her father. Christine's stomach swirled inside her as she wondered what embarrassing secrets she had revealed over the past twenty years.

Jasper was preoccupied with recalling the actions of the flight staff while he scanned the terminal for the VSS and didn't notice her discomfort. Christine arched her back as they walked through the crowd in the international terminal shopping mall. Her unborn child also welcomed the movement; it kicked and poked the inside of Christine, putting pressure on her bladder.

"Jasper, I need to use the restroom."

"Okay."

They walked to the restrooms at the far end of the terminal, and Jasper took a seat on the bench out front while Christine went in. While he waited, Jasper scanned the people in the vicinity. That's when he noticed a man and woman standing in front of the large window at the entrance of a small shop to the right of the washroom entrance.

They stood facing the shop window but took turns glancing at him. In the bright light coming from the shop,

Jasper could see the faint discoloration of a small earpiece hanging over the top of each of their left ears. Jasper reacted swiftly to determine if they were security officers assigned to follow him and Christine. He moved out of his seat and walked briskly back in the direction of their gate.

"Chris, I'm going to get a coffee. Do you want anything?" he asked while Christine remained in the washroom.

"No thanks," Christine replied.

"Okay, as soon as you're finished, start walking back to our gate. I'll catch up with you."

Jasper stopped at a small coffee bar located in the middle of the open terminal two hundred yards from the washroom. He waited in line to order and began searching the area for the security personnel. It wasn't until he paid for his coffee and turned around to leave that he spotted the male security officer standing near a shop fifty yards behind him.

"Chris, you okay?" he asked.

"Fine. Why?"

Not certain if he should tell her, Jasper didn't answer immediately.

"Are you almost done because they've announced our flight," Jasper replied, looking back toward the washrooms.

"I'm right here," her voice giggled as she appeared to his right.

"I don't want to miss our flight, and it's a long walk to our gate," Jasper said, and he spotted the female security guard meeting with her male counterpart.

"Matteo, get to the Rio airport," Jasper demanded.

"I'll leave at once," Matteo replied.

"Let me know when you're there."

"It'll take a while, traffic is extremely bad today," Matteo replied.

"As soon as you can."

"What's wrong, Jasper?" Christine asked.

"Nothing."

Jasper had Christine wait until the very last second to

board the aircraft. He told her he was tired of flying and wanted to spend the least amount of time possible on the plane. Jasper used the extra time to watch the two security officers; he had to make a decision to re-board the flight where they would be trapped, or to try and leave the airport. Being under such close surveillance left him no choice, and they boarded the flight. They walked down the tunnel to the aircraft and took their seats.

The moment they returned to their seats, the male flight attendant made a call. The business-class seating was half empty since most passengers had left the flight in Sao Paulo. Jasper left his jacket on and took his seat for the short flight to Rio.

"Welcome back," said Renata, as she strapped into her seat that folded down directly in front of Jasper's.

"Thanks," Jasper said.

Christine flipped through the pages of a magazine she had purchased in Sao Paulo while Jasper monitored the flight staff.

When the flight was nearing an end, Matteo still hadn't arrived at the airport.

They were twenty minutes from landing when the pilot made an announcement, "We're expecting strong turbulence on final approach. Please remain seated."

Following the announcement, the pilot came out of the cockpit and spoke to the male flight attendant while looking directly at Jasper and Christine. Jasper knew something wasn't right and never took his eyes off the flight attendant. A female attendant joined the conversation with the pilot, and a moment later, they all nodded. The pilot then returned to the cockpit while the attendants returned to their seats.

Renata hadn't been part of the discussion and took her seat.

Christine could see the anxiety on Jasper's face and demanded, "What's going on?"

"Something's not right," he replied without speaking.

"What?" asked Christine, looking around the cabin but unable to see anything out of the ordinary.

"Matteo, are you there yet?" Jasper asked, the desperation mounting in his tone.

"I'm parking now," Matteo replied.

"Get in the terminal and check it out. Something's not right here."

Jasper watched Renata patiently as the aircraft flew closer to Rio. The long-haul flight had taken its toll on her, and her eyes began to droop, opening and closing like a child's. She struggled to stay awake but her eyes finally shut for the last few minutes of the flight. The massive jet bounced once on the runway, causing Renata to open her now sky-blue eyes.

"What's going on?" Jasper asked.

"I don't know," Simone responded.

"Where's Simone?" interrupted Christine, looking at Jasper.

"They haven't informed me."

"Can you find out?"

"They'll suspect something."

"What's going on?" demanded Christine, now aware something was not right.

"I'll call before they raise the cabin lights. I don't want to startle them," Simone replied.

Christine gasped when she saw the unnaturally bright blue of Renata's normally dark brown eyes. It would equally unsettle her co-workers.

"That doesn't give me much time," Jasper replied.

"For what? What's going on, Jasper?" asked Christine, not hiding her concern.

"They've found us."

CHAPTER 21

TRAIN CRASH

The Vatican jet touched down at the Rio de Janeiro-Galeão International Airport in bright fall sunshine, and the sleek white aircraft taxied directly to a private hangar next to the main terminal. Two airport police SUVs were parked inside the building awaiting their arrival. The constant roar of jet engines echoed through the open wall of the hangar, and the pungent odor of unspent aviation fuel hung in the air. Heat waves already danced across the airfield from the early morning sunshine.

Tonino left the aircraft first, followed closely by Father Black, Gino and Father Derksen. The men rushed to the SUVs and were greeted by an officer. With a fake smile on his face, Tonino lifted his right hand and introduced himself.

"I'm Tonino Fabro."

"Captain Garcia," responded to the officer, his English distorted by a Portuguese accent.

"Have they landed?" Tonino asked.

"Final approach," Captain Garcia told him.

"Is the area secured?"

"Yes. We'll follow the aircraft to the gate and access it from outside the terminal bridge. The pilot will move the aircraft to the last gate near the end of the terminal. It's the most isolated from inside the terminal as well as outside. There's nothing past the gate but baggage handling and courier services."

"I want the girl..." Tonino began but his sentence was interrupted by Captain Garcia's radio.

"They've landed. We must go now. Two with me and two in the other vehicle," commanded the captain, motioning to the other SUV.

Tonino pointed to Father Black to get in the same SUV with him. Gino and Father Derksen got in the other. The squeal of the police vehicles' tires was deafening inside the hangar. They caught up with the TAM flight on the far side of the airport and took position behind the jet, invisible to the passengers inside.

***

Simone unbuckled her seatbelt and approached the male flight attendant seated directly behind the cockpit. Speaking in Portuguese, she kept her head down so as not to make eye contact with the man, who was clearly surprised by her unexpected movement from her seat. They spoke for only a few brief seconds before Matteo's words could be heard.

"Animus, they're following your aircraft. There's police vehicles directly behind it!" he yelled.

"There are police at the gate too," Simone said as she turned toward Jasper and Christine.

"What are we going to do?" Christine asked, unable to hold back the fear in her tone.

"Chris, listen to me carefully, we're going to move fast, and you've got to do exactly what I say."

The words made Christine think of the marina and the last time Jasper had said that to her. The pounding of her heart began to synchronize with the clicking sound of the aircraft tires as they skipped over the expansion gaps in the concrete. A stabbing pain shot through her insides like a red-hot needle. The jolt of pain was so great Christine gripped the armrests to keep from screaming. Adrenalin saturated her blood, making her acutely aware of every sound and movement around her.

"Slowly and quietly unbuckle your seatbelt. They're watching us," Jasper commanded.

"Who?" Christine asked, looking around.

"The flight staff."

Christine slowly reached down and unlatched the seatbelt buckle under her stomach. Jasper did the same.

"Animus, they're taking you to a different gate," Matteo said as the aircraft slowed.

"Find out where they're taking us," Jasper demanded at once.

"It looks like you're going to the far end of the terminal, but I can't see you anymore," Matteo said, desperately trying to follow the aircraft out of the terminal window.

Christine peered out the window to look for the police vehicles but only saw a container loader rolling a large steel container into the side of a cargo jet. When their aircraft slowed to a crawl, Christine heard Jasper yell inside her head.

"Now!" he shouted, and many things happened at once.

Jasper grabbed Christine's wrist with his right hand and pulled so hard it lifted her out of her seat. Simone leaped to the emergency exit and disarmed the door. The second Simone ripped the inside panel off the door, the male flight attendant jumped from his seat to intercept her. Surprised by the alarm signaling loudly in the cockpit, the pilot slammed on the aircraft's brakes.

The massive jet stopped instantly and lurched forward, knocking the male flight attendant to the floor. Their ears rang from the crack of thunder as the slide inflated. Like a roller coaster full of teenage girls, the unsuspecting passengers filled the cabin with screams.

Jasper and Christine jumped out the door onto the bright yellow evacuation slide. Their twenty-foot ride was over in an instant, leaving them dazed and on their backsides on the tarmac. The jet engine bellowed in their ears, frightening Christine. Jasper lifted her to her feet as Simone landed at the bottom of the slide.

Tonino and Captain Garcia arrived first but were forced to drive around the wing, giving the three time to run toward the terminal. Christine suddenly heard the crack of gunfire over the roar of the engine, but her pregnant body would not permit her to run as fast as she wanted as Jasper pulled her toward the terminal.

"Stay behind her!" shouted Jasper to Simone as they sprinted for the cover of the terminal.

"But they're gaining on us," Simone replied.

The sound of gunfire grew louder as the noise of the jet engines faded in the distance. Pieces of concrete exploded from the ground to the left and right of them as they approached the terminal. With thirty yards to go, Christine heard a low grunt followed quickly by a muffled thud. She tried to look back, but Jasper pulled her even harder.

"Keep running!" he shouted as he yanked her forward.

Sickness welled from deep inside her. *No one else was supposed to die. I can't do this anymore,* she thought as the grief consumed her.

"Jasper, I can't..."

"You have to!" he demanded as he tightened his grip even further.

The random sound of gunfire was interrupted by the steady beeping of a reversing warning indicator, and a flashing amber light to the right caught the corner of Jasper's eye. He turned and saw the warning light atop a small tractor pulling a luggage train. As the train snaked down the terminal access road, the driver couldn't hear the gunfire through his ear protection. He continued to drive the train completely unaware of what was unfolding in front of him.

Jasper and Christine leaped in front of the tractor, which provided a shield from the hail of bullets. The driver, startled by their unexpected presence on the tarmac, pulled the tractor steering wheeled hard to the right in order to avoid hitting them. The maneuver, however, sent the luggage train out of control, and the carts swung violently left and right like a snake with its head cut off before it overturned directly in the path of Tonino and the others.

Christine and Jasper entered the loading bay of the cargo terminal and found it void of workers, as they were on the tarmac loading the cargo aircraft. Jasper unlatched the door to one of the giant steel shipping containers, and he and Christine stepped inside. He pulled the door shut, latching it. They stood in absolute darkness trying desperately to catch their breath.

"Find them!" they heard Tonino scream as he ran past the container.

"We'll go left, you go right!" another voice shouted.

"Seal the terminal!" Tonino shouted, and they heard the sound of boots running away on the tarmac.

The voices of two men could be heard laughing loudly in the bay. The workers were returning for the last container and it seemed they were quite amused by the train wreck outside. They continued to laugh, presumably at the driver, completely unaware of the events that had led to the accident.

Jasper heard the sound of the door latch click as one of the workers ensured it was secure. Low rumblings filled the darkness as the movement of the container loader vibrated through the steel floor. Disoriented by the darkness and the back and forth jerking motion of the container, Christine fell. She remained on her hands and knees on the floor of the container, hoping it would soon stop moving.

"Jasper, where do you think we're going?"

"On that cargo jet and out of here."

"Jasper, I can't do this anymore. I want it to end," she pleaded.

"I don't know how they found us."

"I don't care, I just want it to stop," Christine demanded.

"I'm sorry, Chris, they're everywhere. The VSS have unlimited resources. I've badly underestimated their resourcefulness."

The container began to shake violently as it rolled down the metal rollers of the conveyer belt and onto the deck of the cargo jet. The workers twisted and turned the container until they had positioned it correctly in the aircraft and secured it to the deck.

Jasper felt his way back to the door of the container and listened for the sound of the aircraft's cargo door closing. A moment later, he heard the high-pitched sound of the hydraulic motors closing the doors. He waited for the jet to begin moving before unlatching the container door. Trying to open it, he was disappointed to find the door had been locked from the outside.

Christine was sickened by the loss of Renata, the blackness that filled her eyes pouring into her heart. *Was she a mother?* she wondered. *Did she have kids waiting for her at home?* Her emotions ran rampant; they pulled at every corner of her mind, leaving her overflowing with sorrow. Crippled emotionally, Christine struggled to hold back her tears.

Jasper began to feel around the container to get some indication of what was packed with them. The door was located in the center of the container. Cardboard boxes were packed floor to ceiling on both sides of them. A net held them in place, so Jasper reached through the mesh and felt the cartons stacked on the other side. They were packed so tightly he couldn't find an edge to pull one open. He felt his way around the container until he stumbled over Christine's feet. Unaware that she wasn't standing, he immediately became concerned.

"Are you okay?"

"I don't know," Christine replied.

"What do mean? Were you shot?" Jasper asked, panic in his voice.

Trying to catch her breath, Christine had slid across the floor backwards until she felt the wall against her back. She sat on the corrugated steel floor of the container fighting the burning pain radiating from below her ribs. When she moved her hands over the area in an attempt to alleviate the pain, she felt the warm sensation of a liquid dribbling down the inside of her left thigh.

CHAPTER 22

IT BROKE

S mall blue lights flashed throughout the airport as security personnel locked down the terminal. Police were stationed at every exit, and long lines formed as angry travelers shouted at the police while waiting to have their identification confirmed before leaving the airport. Checkpoints were erected at all roads leading from the airport. Chaos rapidly ensued as angry travelers were left uninformed of the reason for the lockdown. All departing flights were delayed until they were physically searched.

"Animus, they've locked down the airport and they're searching all flights before they depart," Matteo said.

"We've left the terminal in a cargo jet."

Christine let out an uncontrollable wail and reached down to her left leg, where a rush of warm liquid streamed over her skin.

Jasper heard her moan and scrambled in the darkness to get closer to her.

"What's wrong?" he asked while crawling next to her.

"It's my ribs. I think I'm bleeding."

"Where?" Jasper asked, trying to control the concern in his tone.

"I can feel it running down my leg."

The heat inside the container was suffocating, and it caused beads of sweat to roll off of Jasper's forehead.

Frustrated by his blindness and growing more agitated by the second, Jasper pulled his jacket off and threw it down. It made a loud thud when it hit the metal floor. A smile filled his face, and he patted the floor, searching for his jacket. When he located it, he removed his phone from the breast pocket. He powered the phone on and used the light from the screen to survey Christine's injuries.

"Great idea!" Christine said.

"I didn't really think of it; I heard it when I threw my jacket on the floor."

"So?" Christine asked, wanting to get feedback on the extent of her injury.

"Put your hand where you feel the pain."

"It doesn't hurt anymore, but it was right about here," Christine said as she moved her hand below her ribcage and made a small circle in the area of her stomach.

"Oh," Jasper responded and positioned the phone so the light illuminated Christine's left thigh.

"What's wrong? Is it bad?"

"Well, there's good news and bad news," he replied while laughing.

"What's going on?" Christine demanded, not seeing the humor in the situation.

"The good news is that it's not blood."

"Not blood?" she repeated with astonishment.

"Nope."

"Then what is it?" she demanded.

"That's the bad news: unless you've peed yourself, I think it broke," Jasper said, making his best attempt to show no concern.

"What broke?"

"Your water."

"You're joking!" Christine begged.

"Wish I was, but that would explain why the pain has subsided for now."

"Contractions? I'm only seven months," replied Christine,

realizing they had begun on the flight to Rio.

"I don't have much battery left, so we'll need to use this sparingly."

"What are we going to do?"

"I need you to stay as calm as possible while I look for anything to help."

"Help what? Deliver a baby? Are you nuts? I'm not having my baby in here. We've got to get out!" Christine shouted, shocked that Jasper would consider delivering a baby inside the container.

"Let's see what we've got inside our container," Jasper said, and he used the light from his cell phone to look at the writing on the boxes behind the mesh.

The entire container shook like an earthquake as the aircraft suddenly accelerated down the runway. Jasper sat down on the floor next to Christine to ride out the take off. Their situation now presented new challenges, like avoiding being thrown to the roof of the container or getting crushed by shifting cargo. But their biggest obstacle was the ear-piercing noise from the roar of the engines, which now forced them to communicate without speaking.

***

Tonino marched through the terminal with Captain Garcia and Father Black. The blackness in his eyes glistened from the fire burning behind them. He clenched his teeth in anger and forced a rare smile to his lips. Twenty minutes had passed since they had last seen Christine and Father Shannon, and now Tonino was growing ever more intolerant with the failed search.

"I want to see video for the area," he demanded.

"Follow me," Garcia replied.

They made their way to the security centre, and Garcia ordered one of the video monitoring staff to locate all the video of the inside corridors connected to the loading bay doors. The security officer directed them to the two screens directly in front of him. Each screen showed different angles of the doors entering the terminal from the cargo bay.

"Tell him to speed it up; this is taking too long," Tonino barked.

Garcia spoke in Portuguese to the officer, who then clicked the mouse a couple of times to increase the playback speed. No one entered or left the two doors before Tonino saw himself and the other police officers walk through.

"Impossible!" snapped Father Black.

"Show me the video outside the bay," Tonino ordered.

Garcia relayed the request to the security officer and the point of view changed to above the tarmac looking from the terminal toward the runway. The security officer froze the screen with the image of Father Shannon and Christine sitting on the ground at the bottom of the evacuation slide. The two police SUVs appeared at the top of the screen between the wings of the jet and the cargo aircraft.

"Yes, start it from here," Tonino demanded.

They watched the events unfold on the screen.

"Stop it here," Tonino said.

The video stopped at the point where the images of Christine and Father Shannon disappeared into the cargo bay.

"There!" he shouted. "The cargo bay—show me the video in that bay."

Garcia communicated with the security officer again, and the man picked up the telephone on his desk.

"Is there coverage?" asked Tonino, his patience growing shorter.

"It's not part of our system, but the cargo company will have their own security system. He's calling them to check," Garcia replied.

The officer hung up the phone without speaking and spoke to Garcia.

"It went to voicemail; they're probably at lunch," Garcia

explained.

"Call off the lockdown, Captain. Have your men meet us in that cargo bay," Tonino said.

"Father Black, call Gino and have him ready the jet. We'll be leaving soon."

"Yes, sir," said Father Black, and he removed his phone from his pocket as he followed Tonino and Garcia out of the security office.

Gino and Father Derksen were waiting in the cargo bay when Tonino, Father Black and Garcia arrived. Garcia walked outside the bay door and located the workers talking to some other ground staff. The group of men were standing by the overturned luggage train, staring at the horrific scene.

They were no longer amused by the accident when they realized a body lay on the concrete covered with a plastic sheet. A multitude of emergency personnel and vehicles had converged on the area. One of the workers rushed into the bay ahead of Captain Garcia and unlocked a small office door.

"They have video," said Garcia as he approached the office.

"Tell him to give Gino access to the file. He'll do the rest," Tonino told him.

Gino and Garcia entered the small office, as there wasn't enough room for all four men. The others waited at the door. After the cargo worker left, Tonino entered the office and Gino played the video in fast-forward. It didn't take long for them to see the footage of Father Shannon and Christine entering the shipping container.

"Delete it," Tonino ordered.

Gino clicked the mouse a few times and the computer screen indicated a full hard-drive re-format.

Tonino turned to Garcia with a crooked grin on his face. "Ask them where that flight is going."

Garcia left the office to locate the workers.

"Did you contact our pilots?" Tonino asked.

"They're ready," Gino replied.

"Good, let's see where our friends are off to now," said Tonino, and he left the office to find Garcia.

He found the captain speaking to a cargo worker in the middle of the bay.

"Where?" Tonino interrupted.

"The first stop is Cologne," Garcia replied.

"Direct?"

Garcia turned back to the worker and asked. The worker nodded.

"Yes," said Garcia looking over at Tonino.

"Sir, we have to declare an emergency; it will bring them back," said Father Black, certain Tonino would agree this time.

"No, I told you, Father, air traffic control won't take orders from anyone. There's no way we can guarantee the flight will return here. It's too risky. Right now, we know exactly where they are, and even better, where they're going. As long as we have that in our favor, I feel it best to prepare for their arrival there. Let's try and welcome them to Germany," Tonino said, raising his eyebrow and sporting a brilliant smile.

"We thought we had them this time," Father Black said, questioning Tonino's decision.

Both Gino and Father Derksen looked away, knowing what was coming.

Tonino's eyes widened and he cast a bone-chilling glare at Father Black. His stare was so intense that it superseded any need for words. Tonino turned away after a moment and faced Garcia.

"Captain, return us to the Vatican aircraft at once. We must be on our way."

***

Sunlight blazed through the cockpit window of the cargo jet as it broke through a thick layer of clouds on its way to cruising altitude. The two seasoned pilots set the aircraft on autopilot and settled in for their long flight, unaware of the hidden cargo they carried.

***

Jasper unhooked the mesh securing the cardboard boxes inside the container and pulled one of them to the floor. He tore open the top of the box and stuck the phone inside to view the contents. It was filled with tourist T-shirts destined for France. He had begun to pull another box from the pile when he heard Christine groan in pain.

"Chris, you all right?" he asked and turned the phone screen toward her.

"Another contraction."

"I'm trying to find something to make you more comfortable. I've found some shirts; we can put them on the floor and get you off this metal. Here, I'll roll some up to make you a pillow," Jasper said as he gave one of the shirts to Christine.

"Do you honestly think I'm going to give birth in here?" asked Christine, fighting back the pain of the contraction.

"That really depends on you, the baby and where these T-shirts are headed," Jasper said, already aware that the flight was headed to Europe and they would be stuck inside the container for a long time.

Jasper grabbed a handful of shirts from the box and rolled them into a tight ball, stuffing them inside another shirt to form a pillow. He slid it behind Christine's head then returned to the box for some more, putting them underneath her.

"Try your best to get some sleep. I'm going to rummage through the other boxes."

***

Tonino met briefly with the pilots before returning to the

cabin of the Vatican jet. His instructions to them were clear: he wanted to be waiting on the runway in Cologne when the cargo flight arrived. The pilots assured Tonino this was possible since they were traveling in a faster aircraft, not carrying a load, and were less than an hour behind them. The Vatican jet left the hangar moments after Tonino took his seat.

"Gino, find a way to track that flight. I want to know exactly where they are at every second," Tonino commanded.

"Derksen, assist Black in making all the necessary arrangements to secure the aircraft the moment it lands. Send anyone you can to meet that flight."

"Yes, sir," replied Father Black, but Father Derksen only nodded.

Father Derksen completely understood the meaning of Tonino's request, and a sickening feeling filled his stomach. He had been demoted and was no longer head of the VSS. He knew better than anyone that leaders of the VSS were never demoted—they were disposed of. Looking at the young Father Black sent a chill up his spine. It was clear to Father Derksen why Father Black had wanted to meet him in Sydney.

Father Derksen followed Father Black to the back of the cabin and began making calls from the aircraft telephones. Gino typed furiously on his tablet, searching for a way to track the cargo flight in real time. Tonino lifted the telephone on the small desk in front of him and spoke to the pilot.

"When do we arrive?"

"Based on the last weather report, we'll be in Cologne at two thirty-five a.m. local time," the pilot replied.

Tonino hung up without a word and looked across the cabin to where Gino was now talking on the telephone.

"We arrive at two thirty in the morning. When will they arrive?"

Gino covered the mouthpiece of the telephone with his hand and answered, "I'm working on it," while continuing his conversation on the telephone.

A moment later, he completed his call and faced Tonino. "Their flight is scheduled to arrive in Cologne at twelve minutes past three a.m."

CHAPTER 23

MORTO DERKSEN

A war raged inside Christine's body, and she battled the pain with determination. Contractions attacked her willpower at random, giving her no warning of the burning sensation they unleashed in her womb. She clung to the last remnants of her faith with each bout of agony, and in a failed attempt to distract herself, she began to recite the Hail Mary in her mind.

Lying on the steel floor, she was incapable of finding a comfortable position and struggled to reposition her body every few minutes. Her ears rang from the constant noise of the engines. Irritated by her predicament, Christine attempted to stand but quickly gave up the instant a jarring pain flashed through her body. She resigned herself to the floor and tried to fill her thoughts with happy memories from her childhood. Christine's mind teeter-tottered between sleep and awareness, but a prolonged sleep escaped her. Hours passed like days; she felt trapped in darkness like a convalescent waiting to die.

"How long has it been?" she asked.

Jasper reluctantly tapped the buttons on his phone to wake the screen and read the time. He knew the remaining power would soon be needed.

"A little more than nine hours."

The faint blue light of the phone caused Christine to squint, having not seen any light for hours. During the

209

moment Jasper illuminated the area, she could see a half dozen opened boxes scattered around the small space they occupied.

"Find anything interesting?" she asked.

"Two boxes of terra cotta plant pots and more shirts," he said unenthusiastically.

"I was hoping for bottled water, juice or maybe some chocolate ice cream," Christine said, trying to sound cheerful.

"Ice cream? Not a chance. I stopped looking to save my phone battery just in case I..." Jasper stopped speaking midsentence, realizing his words would upset Christine.

"In case what? You have to deliver a baby?" Christine said, finishing his sentence for him.

"Animus, we're going to land soon," said Luca as he prepared the aircraft to begin its descent.

"Where is he?" asked Christine, surprised to hear Luca's voice.

"Luca and Matteo are in the cockpit," Jasper responded.

"How?" asked Christine.

"They shared consciousness with the pilots when they were sleeping. The crew always finds time to take a nap on these long-haul flights, and that's when Luca and Matteo joined us. The co-pilot took the first shift while the pilot slept, and now they've switched. It's easiest for us to share consciousness with humans when they sleep."

"Why?"

"Because they're essentially unconscious."

"I guess that makes sense," Christine responded without giving it much thought, as her mind was preoccupied with their final destination.

"Where we going?" she asked, the excitement in her tone unmistakable because she was certain they would soon be leaving the steel prison cell.

"We were scheduled to land in Cologne in less than two hours, but that's about to change," Luca answered.

***

The small red light flashed on the aircraft telephone in front of Tonino. He lifted the handset and spoke to the pilot.

"We're twenty minutes from landing."

"Good," replied Tonino. He replaced the handset and turned his attention to Gino.

"Where are they?"

Gino tapped the screen of his tablet and waited for it to display the cargo jet's location.

"They're over Barcelona, an hour behind us."

"Wonderful," Tonino said with confidence.

"When do we arrive?" Gino asked.

Tonino ignored Gino's question and called Father Black and Father Derksen to the front of the cabin.

"Is everything ready?" he asked Father Black.

"Yes."

"Have your people arrived?"

"They're waiting for us in the cargo hangar," answered Father Black with a large grin.

"We won't fail this time," Father Derksen interjected, aware of Tonino's blatant attempt to exclude him.

Tonino's look blasted through Father Derksen like a bullet from a rifle. His upper lip curled and his eyebrows touched as the words left his lips.

"You better pray we don't."

Father Black and Gino sank into their seats while Father Derksen stared back at Tonino. Neither man broke their glare until the pilot called again. Tonino answered the telephone, and Father Derksen turned his face toward the window to view the city lights below.

"We're on final approach," Tonino said, and he hung up the phone. "Gino?"

"They're over southern France," Gino replied, and he put the tablet in its case.

***

"Animus, I've notified Lyon air traffic control that we have a fuel shortage. They've given us first priority at St. Exupéry Airport. We'll touch down in a little over an hour," Matteo said.

"Fantastic, we'll be out of here," Christine chimed in.

She heard only the sound of the engines changing speed. The silence inside her mind was obvious.

"Jasper, we're getting out of here, right?" Christine asked, her tone filled with concern.

"Yes, but it's risky. I'm certain the VSS have figured out how we escaped and are tracking us right now. We'll only have a few minutes to get away from the airport," replied Jasper, the hesitation overflowing in his tone.

"No, I'm getting out, ohhh..." began Christine, but her angered response was interrupted by the most severe contraction yet.

"Chris, how bad?" Jasper asked as he activated his phone to see her.

Christine's face mirrored the pain ripping through her body. The severity of the contraction sucked the breath from her lungs, leaving her panting like a dog. Jasper lifted her hand from the floor and allowed her to squeeze it as the pain dissipated. She quickly regained her composure and continued her protest.

"I can't spend another second in this crate!" she shouted, her voice loud enough for Jasper to hear her over the screaming engines.

"I promise you, it won't be much longer. Simone is already waiting for us. After that, it's a short drive to safety."

"But we're getting out of here, right?" she begged in a fading tone.

"The moment they know where we are, they'll have people there in minutes. It's critical we disappear before they realize it," Jasper replied, hoping she would understand and avoid an argument.

"Luca, I'm in a catering truck waiting at the terminal," said Simone, who had found the young driver sound asleep in the cab of his scissor truck.

"After landing, air traffic control has requested we hold at the far end of the runway until a fuel truck can be dispatched," Luca replied.

"How long?" Simone asked.

"Air traffic replied 'unknown.' They're waiting for a fuel provider to respond. All existing trucks are scheduled for other flights. We've been ordered to hold until one becomes available."

***

The four men entered the main cargo hangar at Cologne-Bonn Airport and were greeted by six VSS operatives. Tonino spoke to the men, the authority in his voice evident. The men left the hangar and disappeared into the darkness outside. Tonino walked back to Gino, Father Black and Father Derksen.

"How much longer?"

Gino removed his tablet and launched the tracking software. It took a few seconds before the program opened and the information registered in his mind. He lost all expression. His face resembled a blank sheet of paper when he looked at Tonino, and the words couldn't leave his lips. The fear of speaking them overwhelmed him. Tonino witnessed the transformation and walked directly to him, pulling the tablet from his hands.

"Ahhhh!" screamed Tonino. "How did they know?" he shouted and tossed the tablet across the hangar like a Frisbee, smashing it against the wall.

"They must have been warned," he spit before turning to face Father Derksen.

"Sir, I didn't..." pleaded Father Derksen as Tonino's

lifeless black eyes approached him.

Father Derksen didn't have time to move. Tonino pulled his gun from his jacket and fired a single bullet into Father Derksen's temple. The sound of the gunfire reverberated through the massive hangar while Father Derksen's large body collapsed to the floor. Tonino put the gun back in his jacket and turned around to find Gino staring in disbelief.

"It wasn't immaculate," Tonino said with a smile.

Father Black remained silent as Tonino walked toward the hangar door. With his back to both of them, he continued to speak as he walked away.

"We've got work to do. Inform security at Lyon," Tonino commanded.

"Yes, sir," replied both Father Black and Gino in unison.

"Gino, call the pilots and tell them we're not finished," said Tonino with what sounded like humor.

"Right away," Gino replied as he pulled his phone from his pocket.

Back in the aircraft, Father Black and Gino went directly to their seats and began calling Lyon airport security while Tonino went directly to the cockpit.

"How long to Lyon?"

"An hour," replied the pilot.

"Get us there," Tonino said, and he left the cockpit for his seat.

***

The back of the jet shook violently when the aircraft hit the runway. Open boxes crashed onto the floor, sending shards of terra cotta scattering across the container. The sound of breaking pottery was audible over the roar of the engines, and it startled Jasper and Christine. Jasper recognized the source of the crash the moment he opened his phone.

"You okay?" he asked.

"Yah, what a mess," Christine replied.

"Chris, do you think you can stand?"

"If it means I'm getting out of here, I'll fly if I have to," she said, trying to pull herself up using the mesh netting hanging next to her. Pain flashed up her stiff legs like an electric shock. Her belly burned and she groaned in agony.

Jasper slapped his phone shut so he could help her and they plunged back into darkness. He felt his way to Christine's side and put one of his arms under hers in preparation to lift her.

"On three, Chris—one, two, three," he said and lifted Christine to her feet.

She wailed from the maneuver. The sudden position change immediately triggered a contraction, and her knees buckled from the pain.

"Chris…"

"I'm okay. That was a bit of a shock. My back is killing me. I think I was sitting too long," she responded while trying to catch her breath.

Jasper continued to hold Christine with one arm while steadying himself against the door of the container with his other. The motion of the jet rolling down the runway made it difficult to stand, like walking on the deck of a boat. The taxi to the end of the terminal was short, and the aircraft stopped after a minute.

Silence permeated the container, but it went unnoticed by Christine and Jasper as their ears continued to ring. Christine was consumed with anticipation as she waited in the darkness. She could smell freedom from the other side of the door.

Jasper grew impatient as their wait grew longer than thirty minutes.

"What's our status?" he asked, trying to hide the urgency in his tone.

"Luca's on the radio trying to get clearance to move to the terminal," Matteo replied.

"Animus! They're coming," Matteo shouted so loud Christine twitched. Still monitoring the radio, Matteo heard the pilot from the Vatican jet request final clearance from Lyon air traffic control.

"Jasper, how, how can they...?" Christine asked.

"How close?" asked Jasper, ignoring Christine.

"They've requested final approach, so no more than ten minutes," replied Matteo.

"Simone, now!" demanded Jasper.

"On my way."

From the cockpit of the cargo jet, the vehicle looked like a toy. The darkness made it easy for Luca to spot the flashing amber light atop the catering truck. Simone pulled the vehicle next to the jet and raised the box to the height of the cargo hatch. She opened the cargo door and unlatched the container, releasing Jasper and Christine from their prison cell.

Pain speared through the back of Christine's eyes from the intensity of the flashing amber light on the cab of the truck. Cool morning air soothed their lungs when they inhaled their first deep breath from outside the container. Simone took the other side of Christine and helped Jasper walk her to the box of the truck. Realization flooded Christine when she stepped off the jet and into the dark truck box.

"Of course, you knew," she said, turning her head to look at Jasper as he closed the door and returned them to darkness.

"We've got to keep you hidden. And in your state you can't exactly sit up front, can you?"

***

Tonino stared into the darkness through the small window to his left. The blue and green runway lights blurred as the Vatican jet floated a few feet over the runway. As the wheels touched the concrete runway, bright amber light from a catering truck drew Tonino's eyes to the distinctive brown tail of the cargo jet that flashed by the window. Tonino ripped the telephone off the desk in front of him.

"Take us to the end of the runway now! Get us to that jet!" he screamed at the pilot. He slammed the telephone down. "Where's security?" he yelled at Father Black and Gino.

"They said they'd handle it," Gino replied, now fearing for his life.

"There's nobody there! Get them!" yelled Tonino so infuriated that a small white ball of saliva formed in the corner of his mouth.

Gino pulled the phone and notepad from his pocket to retrieve the phone number. He called Lyon airport security.

"Allo?"

"Where are your people? Why isn't anyone at the jet?"

"No English," the officer replied.

"He doesn't speak English," Gino said to Tonino.

"Give me the phone," snapped Tonino, as he took the phone from Gino.

"Get someone there now, or you'll not see the morning light!" Tonino said, his anger unmistakable to Gino and Father Black even though he was speaking in perfect French.

The catering truck passed the terminal building and disappeared from view when the Vatican jet engines began to power down. A police car's flashing blue light reflected off the side of the Vatican jet as it pulled alongside the cargo aircraft. The small white police car parked in the exact spot the catering truck had vacated a moment earlier. Tonino skipped the top two steps when he sprang out the aircraft door, followed closely by Father Black and Gino. All three men raced to a second police vehicle and got in.

"Find that truck!" Tonino demanded.

"I'll call the service road gate. The guard will stop them before they can leave the grounds," replied the police officer, the smugness evident in his French, and he picked up his cell phone from between the front seats.

"Stop them!" Tonino replied.

***

The constant beeping of the telephone couldn't compete with the elderly guard's snoring or the announcer calling the late night rebroadcast of the soccer match when Luca arrived. The volume on the small TV was set so high it could be heard outside the glass security hut. A pair of crystal-blue eyes reflected off the glass window of the hut when Luca answered the telephone.

Simone arrived at the security gate while Luca was on the telephone. The flashing blue light from atop the police car bounced off the driver's side mirror as she slowed the truck to a crawl. Luca waved out the open door of the hut for her to drive through the gate. He hung up the telephone and pressed the button to drop the wheel knives and lift the arm blocking the exit. Simone drove the truck outside the airport security fence and stopped. Luca re-engaged the wheel knives and dropped the gate before yanking the control wires from the panel. He left the hut and jumped in the passenger seat of the catering truck.

"Animus, they're right behind us," Luca reported.

"Did we make it?" Jasper asked.

"We've got to get moving. The gate won't hold them for long."

CHAPTER 24

THE CUBE VAN

The eastern horizon swallowed the starlight as a blue-white hue brightened the morning sky. Rue Goyeau was deserted, like every other suburban neighborhood street in Lyon at five o'clock in the morning. A calico cat froze on the sidewalk, its blue eyes made brilliant by the headlights of the approaching vehicle. Startled by the low rumbling of the cube van's diesel engine, the cat darted across the narrow street before disappearing behind the juniper bushes next to a building.

Middle-aged and balding, the driver parked the van in front of the old stone apartment building where the cat had vanished. The driver glanced in the rearview mirror and tousled what little hair he had left in a vain attempt to make it appear fuller. He took a drink of his water bottle and returned the glass bottle to its holder before popping a breath mint into his mouth.

The driver tossed the wad of keys in his hand into the air, catching them as he walked up the three marble steps of the apartment building. He unlocked the front door and made his way down the poorly lit hallway to the last door on the right. A few faint rays of light squeezed into the hallway from behind the partially opened door. The driver pushed the door open and quietly entered the apartment, leaving his shoes on.

He removed his uniform jacket, hung it on the back of the kitchen chair and gently placed his keys on the table, careful not to make a sound. He then entered the second bedroom door, where his mistress waited for him.

"Gerry, please let Maurice in. You know I don't like an audience," whispered the woman while pointing to the calico cat sitting on the ledge outside the window.

"Of course, Mia," Gerry replied, and he walked to the window, lifting the old wooden sash to let the cat in.

The cat dashed across the bedroom and began meowing loudly at the closed bedroom door.

"Quickly, Gerry, I don't want him to wake Alan," Mia said, concerned the cat's request to exit the room would wake her twenty-year-old son asleep in the next bedroom.

"We must hurry, my love. I've got to finish my deliveries," Gerry said as he twisted the door handle. The cat pushed the door open before Gerry had fully opened it and sprinted into Alan's bedroom.

Mia and Gerry were completely involved when Alan awoke and put his clothes on. A moment later, he left his room and grabbed the wad of keys from the kitchen table on his way out the front door.

"Matteo, how much longer?" Jasper asked.

"About five minutes—no more," Matteo replied.

"What is it?" Jasper asked.

"A cube van," replied Matteo.

"Good. meet us at the A.432–A.43 interchange," said Simone.

***

"*Merde*!" yelled the police officer as he slammed on the brakes of the car. Tonino slapped his hands onto the dashboard to brace himself as the vehicle screeched to a halt in front of the security gate. The officer ran to the empty glass hut and pressed the button to drop the tire knives and open the gate. After his third failed attempt, he inspected the control panel and saw the hanging wires.

The catering truck accelerated as it drove out of sight.

"What's the matter? Open the gate!" Tonino yelled from the window of the car.

"*C'est impossible*," replied the officer, walking slowly back to the car.

Tonino got out of the car and walked over to the tire knives to see if there was anything he could do to get the car outside the airport fence. Tonino's thoughts immediately became toxic.

Gino and Father Black remained in the car, listening to him yell at the officer. The officer pulled the radio from his belt and spoke into the microphone while they returned to the vehicle. Father Black and Gino expected Tonino to dispose of the officer at any moment, but to their surprise, they all drove back to the terminal.

The four men rushed to the security headquarters once back at the terminal. Gino and Father Black held their silence as they followed Tonino into the police officer's small office. The officer sat behind his desk and placed a call on his telephone while Tonino took a seat across from him. The other two men stood in the corner of the office, the concern on their faces clearly visible by the light filtering through the large window behind the officer's desk.

"Our friend radioed a description of the truck to the *Police Nationale* while we were on the tarmac. He's now arranging a helicopter for us," Tonino said in a cold robotic voice.

The officer hung up the phone and spoke to Tonino. He turned in his chair and pointed out the window to the helicopter hangar on the other side of the runway. The hangar disappeared from sight momentarily as an early morning Air France jet raced down the runway. Tonino made no attempt to acknowledge the officer, and he had just stood up to leave when the officer's cell phone rang.

Tonino paused for a moment then turned and faced the officer. The man waved his hand at the men, indicating that they shouldn't leave. He lifted a pen from his desk and scribbled on a pad atop his desk.

"They were spotted heading east near the A.432—A.43 interchange," said the officer to Tonino.

"Are your people following them?" asked Tonino.

"Non, this was a report from an officer who saw the truck pass him travelling in the opposite direction," replied the officer.

"So, we still haven't got an idea where they are?" Tonino snapped.

"We know which way they're heading," the officer replied.

***

Christine and Jasper sat on the floor of the catering truck holding on to the metal braces used to secure the steel food trolleys to the box of the truck. The trolleys rocked back and forth with each turn, causing a high-pitched screech like the sound of fingernails dragged across a chalkboard. Christine's legs began to feel numb from the vibration and bouncing of the vehicle as it sped down the highway.

"This is worse than the aircraft container," she complained.

"It shouldn't be much longer," Jasper replied.

Every time she inhaled, the back of her throat burned with dryness from not having anything to drink. Her cheeks stuck to her gums, and it became harder to swallow with each attempt. The discomfort of her thirst was soon forgotten. Pain rippled up and down Christine's body as the contractions continued to intensify. She didn't want Jasper to know, so she bit her bottom lip, trying to suppress the moan begging to leave her mouth. Christine's body strained under the stress, and a small quiver escaped her lips just loud enough for Jasper to hear over the noise in the truck.

"Another?" he asked.

"Yes," she replied, feeling ashamed that Jasper had heard her.

"They're coming closer now. We need to hurry," Jasper responded.

"Where are we going?"

"To a place I know is safe…" Jasper replied, but he was interrupted by Simone.

"I don't think there's time," she said, spotting a police car driving in the opposite direction on the divided highway.

"Stop the truck!" Jasper commanded.

Simone obeyed his command and positioned the truck on the shoulder of the road under an overpass. Luca raced to the back of the truck and opened the door, allowing the first daylight to reach Christine and Jasper's eyes in more than twenty-four hours. Warm amber rays of early morning sunlight brought strength, and Christine's spirits were immediately lifted when she saw the new spring growth glistening in multiple shades of green. Jagged white peaks interrupted the marbled blue and grey horizon from the bright light reflecting off the snow-capped Alps just visible to the west.

For a brief moment, Christine found an escape from the anxiety coursing through her veins. Her thoughts drifted back to Hawaii and the countless perfect island sunrises she had watched over the Pacific Ocean.

Another contraction rocketed up Christine's spine, shocking her back to reality. This one left no room for her to suppress it, and she shouted in pain. The contractions were increasing in frequency and intensity.

Jasper looked at the time and knew it wouldn't be much longer.

"I need some water," Christine begged.

He began to help her stand up but froze the moment he spotted her face contort in pain.

"Stop, stop…" she tried to shout in protest but her words were merely a whisper from the dryness in her mouth.

"Sorry, Christine, we've got to hurry," Jasper said.

Matteo stopped the cube van in front of the catering truck

and ran to the back to assist them.

"I can't do it, I can't move, please... just get me something to drink," she pleaded.

"We haven't got time," Jasper replied.

"There's some water in the cab of my truck," Matteo said.

"Please, Jasper," Christine begged.

"Get it!" Jasper ordered, and he, Simone and Luca continued to help Christine.

Matteo ran back and handed Christine the bottle of water before closing the back of the truck, plunging Christine and Jasper back into darkness. Christine gulped the water so quickly it spilled from the sides of her mouth and covered the outside of the bottle. The sudden movement of the truck caused the wet glass to slip from her fingers, but luckily, the bottle landed on a pile of clothing next to her.

Simone accelerated the catering truck and drove as fast as possible in the opposite direction from which she originally came.

CHAPTER 25

SLIP AWAY

T he first direct rays of sunlight sparkled like crystal in the droplets of dew hanging from the tufts of grass poking through the tarmac. Their presence was a reminder of the previous night's chill. The police car arrived at the front of the helicopter hangar and dropped Tonino, Father Black and Gino off at the entrance.

The men entered the hangar to find the pilot and a technician conducting a pre-flight inspection of the aircraft, which sat on a wheeled platform in the middle of the hangar. The pilot stopped his work and approached the men.

"Mr. Fabro?" asked the pilot with a strong French accent.

"Yes," Tonino replied, and he extended his hand toward the pilot. "This is Sean and Gino," said Tonino, turning to introduce them.

"I understand you're looking for someone?" asked the pilot.

"Yes, and it's imperative we go as soon as possible," Tonino stressed.

"Of course. *Allez!*" shouted the pilot to the technician, who nodded and grabbed the rope attached to the front of the wheeled platform, pulling the aircraft out of the hangar.

The pilot opened the doors and the men boarded the helicopter. Tonino sat in the front next to the pilot while Gino and Father Black took their seats in the back. A high-pitched noise filled the cabin followed by the low rumble of the jet engine firing. The pilot instructed them to put on their headgear so they could communicate through the microphone and earpiece. Tonino placed the headset over his ears, removed his phone from his pocket and set it on vibrate.

Engine noise flooded the cabin while the vibrations from the main rotor rocked the helicopter. The pilot increased the throttle to lift off, which sent a cloud of dust swirling from under the aircraft.

"Where to?" asked the pilot, his voice sounding artificial through the communication system.

"To the A.432–A.43 interchange."

"What are we looking for?" asked the pilot.

"A scissor truck."

"An airport scissor truck?" asked the pilot in disbelief.

"Yes."

"That shouldn't be too hard to find."

"You would think not," Tonino stated.

The pilot requested permission to depart from air traffic control as he increased the throttle. Cleared to depart, the helicopter vibrated violently as it rose. They hovered for a moment while the pilot turned the helicopter and then flew straight across the runway due east. Blinding sunlight filled the cockpit, so the pilot snapped down the dark blue sun visor on his helmet, and Tonino raised his left arm to shield his eyes.

"It's just the angle; it'll get better in a second when we turn south," said the pilot, reassuring Tonino he wouldn't be blinded for much longer.

"How far is it?" asked Tonino.

"One, maybe two minutes," the pilot replied.

They approached the interchange without expecting to find the truck, but the aerial view gave Tonino the opportunity to decide which direction to proceed. The suburbs of Lyon were dotted with rust-colored tile roofs of the houses below, and the rolling hills were carved into random shapes like the pieces of a giant puzzle.

"Is this the way to Italy?" asked Tonino pointing out the front of the helicopter to the highway stretching off into the distance.

"Yes," the pilot replied.

"Follow this," Tonino commanded.

Two minutes into their flight, Tonino's phone began to vibrate. He flipped it open while he pulled the headset off his head.

"Hello," he shouted, but he couldn't hear the caller over the background noise. Tonino brought the phone down and turned the earpiece volume to maximum before trying again. "Hello."

"*Monsieur Fabro*?" asked the voice, just loud enough for Tonino to hear.

"*Oui*," Tonino yelled into the phone.

"We've located the truck," said the female officer.

"Where?" Tonino asked, his heart beginning to race at the thought of finally ending the hunt.

"Heading northwest on the A.6."

"They're on the A.6 going northwest," shouted Tonino to the pilot, but the pilot was unable to hear the directions.

"Follow them but keep your distance. We're on our way," Tonino yelled into the phone.

The pilot watched Tonino while he replaced his headset back over his ears, expecting a change of plans. Tonino smiled as he spoke.

"A.6 northwest," he said calmly into the microphone.

The helicopter dipped as the pilot turned the aircraft. With the sun at their back, the vehicles racing along the highway below became easier to see. The pilot lowered the helicopter for an even better view.

"Take us back up," Tonino requested. "I don't want to be spotted."

"Yes," the pilot replied, and the aircraft lifted so quickly their stomachs tingled with the feeling of a roller-coaster ride.

"How long?" Tonino asked.

"That depends, the A.6 goes all the way to Paris. Where were they?" the pilot asked.

"I don't know, I couldn't hear," Tonino said, losing his smile as frustration returned to his face.

"Give me the number. I'll call through the comm. system," the pilot said.

Tonino lifted his phone and pressed the call history function, handing it to the pilot. A moment later, the ringing of a phone could be heard inside their headsets. A woman's voice answered the call.

"*Allo.*"

"It's Tonino Fabro, are you still following them?"

"*Oui.*"

"Where are you?" asked Tonino.

"North of Lyon between Ecully and Champagne-au-Mont-d'Or," replied the officer.

"I'll call you when we're close. Don't do anything unless I give the order. Understood?"

"*Oui,*" said the officer, and Tonino gave the pilot the signal to end the call.

"How long until we reach them?"

"Depends how fast they're travelling. Ten minutes," the pilot said.

"Let me know the minute anyone spots the truck," Tonino commanded.

"Yes," replied Father Black and Gino in unison.

For twenty minutes, the helicopter followed the major highway around the outskirts of Lyon, twisting and turning with every bend in the road. The morning rush hour was in full swing, and traffic was heavy. Father Black was the first to see the truck from the helicopter.

"There it is!" he shouted into the headset. He said it so loud it startled the pilot, who flinched, causing the aircraft to dip.

"Call them," Tonino commanded the pilot. The rapid beeps of the re-dial could be faintly heard over the engine noise. The female officer answered again.

"We can see the truck. Where are you?" asked Tonino.

"The grey SUV, four vehicles back, the dark blue sedan and the black SUV.

"Who's driving the truck?"

"Male occupant," the officer replied.

"They're in the back."

"Unconfirmed," the woman stated.

"Get them off the highway somewhere we can land. They're armed and dangerous—understood?" Tonino added.

"*Oui.*"

The black SUV pulled directly ahead of the catering truck, followed closely by the dark blue sedan, which took position in the passing lane to the left of the truck. Simone remained unaware of the unmarked vehicles surrounding her as she drove down the highway. The female officer waited for an open stretch of road before giving the command. The black SUV slammed on its brakes only meters ahead of the catering truck.

The brilliant red taillights ahead of her caused Simone to yank the steering wheel to avoid a collision.

***

"Are you holding on?" asked Jasper as they felt the truck lurch in the darkness.

"I'm trying to, but it's like riding a boogie board at night," Christine replied.

***

Blue smoke bellowed from the truck tires as they slid sideways across the pavement. The screech sent a flock of blackbirds racing for the sky from the newly planted cornfield next to the highway. Simone pulled the steering wheel hard to the right to avoid hitting the back of the black

SUV. The truck left the highway and came to a halt in freshly sowed field. The two SUVs left the pavement and followed the truck; the black SUV stopped in front of the truck while the grey SUV went straight to the back, boxing the catering truck in.

Two officers sprang from the black SUV with their revolvers drawn as the rhythmic thumping of the helicopter grew louder. Dirt from the field lifted into the air as the downdraft from the helicopter lifted a wall of dust toward the officers. With their guns locked on Simone, they shielded their eyes with the inside of their elbows and approached the truck's cab. The female officer and her partner did the same as they neared the back door.

"*Sortez, sortez!*" shouted one of the male officers as he slowly approached the driver's side of the truck.

Simone remained absolutely still, like a mannequin in the cab of the truck, her eyes focused on the dust settling over the windshield as she looked for a way to escape.

"Animus, it's them," Simone shouted.

"Who?" asked Jasper.

"The *Police Nationale* and they're…"

Simone's discussion was cut short by the officers yelling outside her door. Their voices were distorted by the roar of the helicopter as it powered down a few feet behind the truck.

"*Sortez maintenant!*" shouted the larger of the two male officers, and he waved his free hand at Simone to get out. His partner remained steadfast, his gun pointed directly at her.

Simone lifted the door handle and slowly pushed the large door open. She slid down from the cab with her hands in the air. The roar of the aircraft quickly dissipated as the engines shut down.

"Turn around and put your hands on the truck!" the officer commanded.

Simone followed the instruction at once, making certain not to make any sudden moves. She could only hear the female officer shouting commands at the back of the truck.

"Simone, what's happening? What's going on?" asked Animus, but she ignored his demand and remained focused on the officer's orders.

"*Sortez maintenant!*"

"There's no one else," said Simone.

"*Ferme-la!*" snapped the large male officer as he patted her down.

"Unit 23, 10-20?" called the dispatcher over the police radios attached to the officers' belts. The smaller officer lifted the microphone to his mouth and relayed their status to the dispatcher when a large bang echoed through the back of the truck. The female officer hammered the back door, demanding that the occupants exit.

"Where are they?" said a voice Simone instantly recognized.

"*L'ouvrir!*" said the officer, and her male partner opened the back door of the truck.

The morning light entered the back of the truck, illuminating a scene resembling the aftermath of an explosion. The box of the truck was littered with food trays and tipped-over metal trolleys covering the entire truck bed.

"Where are they?" Tonino screamed.

Possessed with rage, he slammed the door shut with such force it shook the entire vehicle. The sight of the empty box acted like a drug circulating through his veins. *How could they get away?* He marched to the side of the truck where Simone remained handcuffed and held against the box. The large officer pressed the side of the Simone's face tightly against the metal truck facing the back. The instant she saw Tonino, Simone froze like a statue, her eyes gazing off into the distance.

"It's them!"

"Who?"

"The VSS."

"How…?" began Animus, but Simone didn't hear the rest. Tonino interrupted their conversation when he yanked

Simone by the hair to face him and began yelling in French.

"Where is she?"

"Who?"

"Don't be stupid, the girl. The pregnant girl and the priest."

"I don't know what you're talking about."

"It's only been an hour so either you have a very short memory or you're lying. For your sake, I hope it's your memory. You won't like what I do to people who lie to me," Tonino said in a vile tone.

"There's nobody, just me... ah!" yelled Simone as Tonino drove his elbow into the side of her face.

Simone fell to her knees as blood poured from her broken nose, a crimson pool forming in the dirt between her feet. Tonino cocked his leg to kick Simone when the police dispatcher's voice radiated from the police radios surrounding the truck.

"Attention all units—the van has been located, eastbound on A.41. Unit 32 is requesting backup."

Tonino turned to face the female officer. "What van?" he demanded.

"A cube van was stolen this morning."

"Where?" asked Tonino, approaching the officer.

"From outside an apartment building. Why?"

"Was it near the airport?" Tonino asked, his impatience visible on his face.

"Yes, not too far."

"Where is it now?" he asked, his voice just below a shout.

"The A.41"

"Are you certain?" Tonino demanded, his face now only inches from the officer's.

"Yes, it was spotted with a traffic camera at a toll booth. We're sending a unit to intercept..."

"No, stop them!" shouted Tonino.

The officer grabbed her microphone and radioed dispatch to stand down the units.

"Follow them until we arrive," Tonino ordered, and the female officer nodded with understanding. Tonino turned and waved his arm at Father Black and Gino. They moved quickly to the helicopter, but Father Black suddenly stopped.

"Hurry!" shouted Tonino.

"I'm going to get a radio," Father Black said.

"Good," Tonino replied.

Father Black ran back to the female officer and requested the best he could with his hands since he couldn't speak French. She understood and instructed her partner to remove his radio and hand it to him. The officer reached into his shirt pocket and gave Father Black his earpiece as well. Father Black sprinted back to the helicopter and joined the others. Once inside, he handed the radio and earpiece to Tonino.

***

Luca drove the cube van with Matteo in the passenger seat. The back of the van was lined on both sides with racks filled with clean lab coats and hospital gowns. There were bags of dirty linens piled on the floor as well, and each had an identification tag hanging from the drawstrings holding the bags closed.

Christine used her voice to communicate with Jasper, as unlike the catering truck, the cube van was exceptionally quiet. The sound of the diesel engine was muffled by the rows of clothing hanging along the walls, creating the illusion of being in a train car rather than a truck box. A moment of happiness arrived when Christine knew she could use her voice to speak, but it was quickly offset by the realization that Jasper would hear every whimper and moan she produced.

The new accommodations seemed luxurious compared to the last twelve hours, and although the bed Simone and Jasper had fashioned from the linens offered some comfort, the return to complete darkness quickly negated this momentary luxury.

Pressure gathered inside her abdomen, signaling the arrival of another contraction and she grabbed a handful of material with each hand to brace herself for the imminent pain to follow.

"How are you?" Jasper asked in a sympathetic voice.

"O... Kay..." she replied between breaths.

"It won't be long now."

"How do you know?" she said in a restrained tone.

"It's not too far from here," Jasper explained.

"Oh, I thought you meant the baby," Christine replied in a forced attempt at humor.

"Ah," Jasper chuckled.

"Where are we going? You never told me."

"Switzerland."

"Switzerland, why?" she asked, the confusion noticeable in her voice.

"You'll be safe there."

"How can you be sure?" she said and then took five short rapid breaths.

"I can't be sure of anything anymore when it comes to the Vacare and the VSS. But I do know it's a wonderful place to live and to grow up," Jasper said.

Christine could sense the enormous smile forming on his face even though she couldn't see it. "Really?"

"It's where I grew up, or rather Father Shannon," he said in a definitive tone.

"What? I thought he was from New York? You don't sound Swiss," she said in disbelief.

"Good, because I'm not. I'm Irish," Jasper boasted.

"Irish? You're joking!" demanded Christine, certain this was a tale meant to distract her from the continuous pain pulsing through her body.

"Nope. Father Shannon was born in Dublin. His parents were killed in the IRA fighting, and he was sent to a Catholic orphanage. He wasn't there long before a wealthy couple from Switzerland adopted him."

"But where's your accent?" Christine asked, trying to poke a hole in his tale.

"His father's Swiss, but his mother's American. He was sent to a private school in New York."

"So we're going to my grandparents' house…"

CHAPTER 26

A MOTHER'S LOVE

"Jasper, it's coming!" yelled Christine in the darkness of the back of the cube van.

"It's going to be okay, Chris," he said in a reassuring tone.

In their rush to get going, Jasper had forgotten to look for an interior light and was now left with a phone nearly out of power. He activated the phone and positioned himself near Christine. Jasper adjusted the sacks of laundry behind her so Christine could lay with her head elevated.

"I heard Simone. What's going to happen when they find us?"

"Don't concern yourself with that, Chris. Just focus on your child," Jasper replied, trying to keep her from worrying.

"I know but..."

Chris screamed from the pain slicing through her like a white-hot knife.

Jasper closed his phone and felt his way down the side of Christine's body, finding the waist strap of her shorts.

"Chris, we need to remove your shorts," he said, but Christine didn't answer. The sound of her short rapid breaths could be heard over the low rumble of the truck. As the pain subsided, Christine regained her composure and delivered an answer.

"Great, how embarrassing," she said half-joking but resigned to the fact that there was no other way. Jasper didn't respond. He focused his attention on planning their escape.

"We need another vehicle," he demanded.

"I'll get one," Simone replied.

"Quickly!"

***

The white BMW glided through the hairpin turns with ease as Roberto raised the silver coffee mug to his lips. His girlfriend Bianca shifted her body in the passenger seat, stretching her legs a little farther as she slept. The convertible's windshield provided little cover from the seventy-mile-an-hour wind racing over their heads, and Bianca's black hair swirled behind the seat. In typical Italian fashion, Roberto drove the road as if no one else was on it. His morning coffee finally took its toll, and he scanned the roadside for a safe place to stop. With no rest area in sight, he pulled the car onto the shoulder and left it running so as not to wake Bianca when he got out.

The sound of gravel flying from the tires stopped Roberto in the middle of closing his zipper. A smile covered his face as he raised his hands toward the rapidly departing car. This wasn't the first time Bianca had played this prank on him and he waited for the taillights to light up so he could start his jog back to the car.

Bianca's sky-blue eyes, however, barely glanced in the rearview mirror at the rapidly fading image of Roberto in the distance.

"I'm on my way."

"How long?" Jasper asked.

"Ten minutes. I'm in a white convertible."

Sunlight warmed small pockets of the mountain air, causing extreme temperature shifts on Simone's face as she raced the BMW up the road. The tires squealed through every bend as the car negotiated the winding highway.

Matteo kept driving as fast as possible, knowing that Simone would have no trouble catching up to the cube van.

***

The frequency of Christine's contractions increased, becoming continuous pain now, and the urge to bear down conquered all other feelings. Fighting back the pain was futile as an overwhelming need for release welled up from deep inside her. The total darkness acted like a blanket, shielding her from her surroundings. She lifted her legs off the floor and planted her feet flat on the bed of the van. With her legs bent, Christine grabbed her knees with her hands.

A dull, constant pressure pressed down on her chest as if someone was standing on it. It originated in her lower back and spread through her torso. The pain came in waves, filling her body like helium filling a balloon. It swelled inside her and finally exploded. It felt like a snake plunging its fangs inside her stomach, arriving in pulses, growing stronger and more rapid with each successive jolt until the agony was unbearable.

Christine welded her eyes shut and screamed with such intensity that it erupted through the steel box of the van, startling Luca and Matteo. Jasper ignored her outburst for an instant while he told Simone to position the car in front of the van.

"Jasper!" Christine screamed, but total silence filled her mind.

"Where are you?'" she repeated, but there was still no reply.

Christine's pain climaxed, erupting inside her like a fiery explosion. Suddenly, without explanation, the agony vanished and Christine felt nothing—no tingling, no pressure, no burning sensation, and like a moonless night, all that could be seen was absolute darkness.

The low rumbling of the engine combined with the

constant movement of the van resembled an earthquake. Heat from the morning sun penetrated the steel walls of the vehicle, causing sweat to roll down her forehead. The salty fluid burned her eyes as she tried to open them. She pried her left eye open and saw it, a faint blue light near her feet.

Jasper positioned his body between Christine's legs, opened his phone and positioned it on the floor to use the light. He gently held the infant's head as it emerged.

"Push, Chris, push. You're almost done," he said, trying to encourage her.

"I can't... I can't!" she cried.

"Just one more. Try."

"I can't," she said through clenched teeth and used the last bit of her strength to give birth.

Jasper placed the infant on the linens and used the last seconds of light to find the empty water bottle. He gathered some uniforms from the floor around him and wrapped the bottle to shield Christine and the infant before hammering it against the steel floor. While holding the neck of the bottle, he severed the umbilical cord with the broken glass. Jasper pulled a drawstring from one of pairs of pants and used it to tie off the cord.

Euphoria flooded Christine's mind as incredible release swept though her. The life-altering experience unleashed a torrent of uncontrollable emotions. She laughed and cried simultaneously while unstoppable joy rushed through her veins. The power of the delivery removed the last remnants of the venomous pain.

Christine watched the light fade near her feet, and for a second, darkness surrounded her again. She closed her eyes for a second, and when she re-opened them, there were two points of light. Jasper lifted the infant toward Christine and the newborn's eyes glowed iridescent blue, sparkling in the darkness like a pair of stars in a night sky.

"It's a boy!" Jasper shouted.

Christine grabbed the top of her knees, sinking her

fingernails deep into her flesh to lift herself up as the eyes came closer. The phone battery lasted just long enough for Christine to touch her son's hair, and she was captivated by his astonishing eyes.

"A boy," she cried with tears of joy and she held the infant against her chest. "Jasper, give me your phone, I want to see him."

"Sorry, Chris. There's no power left."

***

Two-foot-high amber letters scrolled across the flashing road sign, alerting the oncoming traffic of the lane closure in the Mount Sion Tunnel. Bright orange and yellow plastic road markers were placed in the center of the pavement, reducing the two-lane highway into a single lane. Simone accelerated past the van and took a position directly ahead.

"We're approaching a tunnel," Matteo said, and he slowed the van down.

"Do it inside the tunnel. Find the emergency pullout."

A line of vehicles formed behind the van as traffic slowed to thirty kilometers per hour. Matteo slowed the vehicle further as they neared the entrance to the tunnel, and the rhythmic rumbling of the van engine dissipated. The grey concrete wall of the tunnel opening formed an ominous face, complete with two massive black eyes created by the semi-circles of the entrance and exit. Like entering the mouth of an enormous monster, the cube van disappeared into the darkness.

***

"They're entering the Sion Tunnel," radioed the police officer following the cube van.

"Where's the tunnel?" Tonino shouted while glaring at the pilot.

"Right there," the pilot replied as he pointed to the

entrance ahead of them.

"Now, stop them now!" yelled Tonino into the radio, his voice cracking with urgency. He knew they were using the tunnel for cover. "Get to the other side!" he shouted at the pilot.

***

Matteo followed Simone and drove into the small bay carved into the wall of the tunnel designed as an emergency pullout.

Christine's heart began to race, and adrenalin whipped through her like a tornado, sending all her senses into action. It was apparent they were slowing to a stop, and she instinctively pressed the infant's body tighter against her chest. Jasper felt around the van until he found a pair of pants.

"Chris, give me the child. You need to get dressed," Jasper ordered as he reached into the darkness to find Christine's arm.

"No!" erupted from her gut more than her lips.

"Trust me. It's the only way."

"I can't," she cried, releasing a stream of tears down her face. Not since the death of her mother had she been filled with such emotion. Her stomach clenched at the thought of letting go of her child.

"It'll be okay. You'll see," Jasper said, and he gently tugged on her arm.

"I can't," she begged and moved slightly away from him.

"Chris, listen to me. I won't let anything happen to this child. It's hard for you to believe right now, but this child is the key to our future. One day, his words will have the power to change everything. You *have* to *trust* me!"

Christine lowered her arms from her chest and reluctantly reached out for Jasper's hand. She found his arm and followed it with her free hand so she could pass the infant to Jasper. He felt the soft skin and warmth of the tiny body touch his hand. Jasper lifted the infant to his chest and held it as he placed the pants in Christine's hands.

"Quickly. Put these on then gather some of the clothes on the floor and stuff them inside."

"What?"

"Just do it," Jasper ordered knowing the tunnel was monitored by video cameras.

Christine struggled to bend over to reach her feet so she could pull the nurses' pants on. Every inch of her body was consumed by a dull ache. Tears streamed unabated from her face, triggered by an incredible new feeling that swelled inside her like a wave. It was a powerful surge, stronger than anything she had experienced before. It emerged without warning like a tsunami, drowning all other feelings —a mother's love.

Jasper scrambled on his knees until he found a shirt. He carefully wrapped the infant inside the shirt so as not to cover the child's head and searched the floor with his free hand for one of the laundry sacks Christine had used as a pillow. Jasper removed the drawstring and pulled open the top. He then pushed the pile of laundry inside the sack to the bottom, making a small nest in the centre, and placed the infant in the depression, pulling the drawstring closed.

"Are you ready?"

"Where's my son?" Christine demanded, the tone of her voice unmistakably terse.

Jasper used the darkness to his advantage and didn't answer her question.

"Can you stand?" he asked and reached over to find Christine's arms in an attempt to lift her up.

"Jasper, where is he?" she demanded again, now aware that Jasper wasn't holding him from the muffled crying coming from behind Jasper.

"He's fine. I put him down to help you get up."

Jasper squatted on one knee and leaned over Christine to

lift her when the van accelerated. The unexpected movement sent him sliding toward the back door.

"What's happening?" Christine screamed.

CHAPTER 27

GABRIEL

A maintenance worker stood on the platform of the large telescopic lift as he drove it slowly toward the tunnel exit. The machine continued to roll methodically, lumbering like a giraffe down the road and narrowly missing the fluorescent orange cones segregating the lanes. A traffic control worker walked in front of the huge machine, holding a slow sign with her left hand and covering her ear with her right hand in order to protect it from the lift's high-pitched warning alarm. The maintenance crew entered the shadow created by the tunnel face when the ear-piercing safety alarm was overpowered by the deafening roar of the hovering helicopter.

"They're leaving," said the officer over the radio while trying to get past the line of traffic between him and the van.

"Put us down!" Tonino shouted.

The pilot held the aircraft two hundred feet over the exit of the tunnel while he searched for a safe place to land. Tonino demanded he land, but the only safe place was the road. Bending to Tonino's demand, he lowered the aircraft to a hundred feet over the road.

Stunned by the helicopter's arrival, the work crew stopped the lift at the very edge of the tunnel exit. Tonino continued to yell at the pilot to get them to the ground, but it was to no avail.

"What's happening?" Jasper asked.

"They've found us," Simone replied.

"Get us out of here!"

"Chris, do you think you can move?"

"Where's my baby?" she pleaded as she moved onto her hands and knees in a mad search to find her son. The movement of the van combined with the ball of clothing stuffed into her made it impossible to crawl.

"Jasper, where is he? Give me my baby!"

"He's fine. You've got to be ready."

The lights lining both walls of the tunnel faded into the bright sunshine as the car and van approached the end. When the police officer saw that the van had almost left the tunnel, he pulled his vehicle into the closed lane, sending orange cones flying into the air.

Matteo glanced in his mirror and saw the brightly colored cones scattering across the empty lane. The lane was blocked a few cars ahead by a generator and other maintenance equipment, forcing the officer back through the cones. He blasted his horn in a vain attempt to part the line of vehicles.

"Hold on!" shouted Matteo, hoping to give Christine and Jasper a warning.

But there wasn't enough time for them to find something to brace themselves with in the darkness. Matteo turned the van so hard to the right that two of its wheels left the pavement for an instant as it slid directly toward the lift.

The resulting screech of the tires alerted the lift operator. He stopped the machine, leaped off the platform and ran for cover while the traffic controller dropped her stop sign and leaped out of the way.

Clothing flew off the hangers in all directions, and Jasper and Christine slid across the floor of the van, landing against the wall. A loud crash and the sound of breaking glass followed when the front of the van hit the tunnel wall. The stop was instantaneous, sending them lunging forward.

The vehicle had come to an abrupt stop across the right

lane of the tunnel. Its front bumper pressed against the tunnel wall, and the back bumper was only three feet from the lift.

"The baby, where's my baby?" Christine yelled while the horror of the last few seconds consumed her every thought.

"Luca, Matteo, help!" Jasper called, looking for assistance to get Christine out of the van.

Simone watched the scene unfold in the rearview mirror but didn't stop the car until it had exited the tunnel. The downdraft of the hovering helicopter whipped her black hair into her face when she glanced upward. She put the car into reverse and backed it up to the side of the van, which partially stuck out of the tunnel opening.

With the road blocked, the pilot began his descent to the pavement. Maintenance workers began to appear around the tunnel exit, drawn by the commotion.

"They're landing," Simone reported.

"Hurry! Get her in the car," Jasper commanded.

The back door of the van burst open, and Luca and Matteo stood puzzled for an instant. There was no sign of Christine, only Jasper, who was righting himself. The daylight stung Jasper's eyes, and he squinted as he searched around the truck for Christine. A second later, a pile of clothing began to move on the floor, and Christine lifted her hand from beneath a sea of uniforms.

"Where's my baby?" she screamed.

Her plea was ignored, and the three men carried her out of the truck yelling. Anger filled her and she fought back, trying desperately to escape.

"Stop, Chris. He'll be fine. It's the only way," Jasper said.

"I want him! I want my son!" she cried.

The police car slid to a halt at the back of the van.

Carried by the three men, Christine disappeared from view. Dust stung their eyes, making it impossible to look directly at the helicopter, which was now only thirty feet from the ground. They only had a few seconds before it blocked their escape route.

"There she is!" Tonino said as he pointed out the window of the aircraft. Tonino watched as the men laid her across the back seat of the BMW and got in the car.

"Now, now! Put us down now!" Tonino shouted. He ripped his headset off and pulled the revolver from under his jacket.

"We'll land in a second," the pilot replied, but it was too late.

Simone floored the car, sending a massive cloud of dust swirling into the air carried by the downdraft. Christine continued to scream for her newborn son, but no one could hear her over the roar of the helicopter.

"Follow them!" Tonino shouted.

Unbearable noise came from the helicopter engine when the pilot started accelerating upward. In unison, the maintenance crew covered their ears with their hands and turned away from the wall of dirt flying toward them.

"Forget about the van, follow the car!" Tonino commanded over the police radio.

The police officer shouted at the bewildered work crew, desperately trying to get someone to move the lift. After a few seconds, the operator jumped back on to the platform and reversed the machine out of the way.

Luca and Matteo waited for the police vehicle to disappear from view before returning to the van. They drove it out of the tunnel, much to the delight of the line of traffic forming behind them. Matteo drove as quickly as possible from the view of any of the tunnel cameras. Once clear, they stopped the van and retrieved the infant from the back.

The BMW was no match for the helicopter. Simone drove the car like a Formula1 racing driver, but there was no way of losing the aircraft on the winding mountain highway.

Christine sat up in the back seat behind Simone. The wind slapped her hair across her face, stinging her eyes with every strike, so she gathered it in her fist. The warmth of the sunlight and the smell of fresh air wasn't enough to distract her from the pain eating away at her, but for the moment, the constant thunder of the helicopter occupied her thoughts.

Christine rested her free hand on the ball of stuffing stretching her shirt and peered up at the aircraft. At that moment it dawned on her; the reason for looking pregnant was obvious—as obvious to her as Jasper hoped it would be to them.

"We're a decoy?" she asked.

"Yes."

"Do you think it worked?"

"As long as they're following us."

"What about my son?"

"Luca and Matteo are taking good care of him."

"Will I ever see him again?"

Jasper paused.

Christine's heart slammed the inside of her chest during the silence.

"Of course you will."

"We've left the highway. We'll bring the Terminal Vector when we find a new vehicle," Luca said.

Before Jasper could respond, Christine interjected, "Don't call him that! He's not some kind of freak!"

"Sorry, Chris. Luca didn't mean to upset you. Your son's special, and he doesn't have a name."

"It's Gabriel. Gabriel Shannon Anderson," she stated emphatically.

"Then Gabriel it is."

The diversion around the infant's name was short lived when Simone spotted the fast-approaching police car in the rearview mirror. It seemed impossible that Simone could drive even faster, as they were already surpassing the hundred-mile-an-hour mark.

"They're catching up," Simone said.

Christine turned her head to see the police car only a hundred yards behind. It moved into the passing lane, and

Simone pressed the accelerator as hard as she could. The police car matched the speed and began to overtake them as the two vehicles entered a turn.

It was over in an instant.

***

Christine found herself walking down a corridor towards a bluish-white light. It was absolutely silent, and she could see nothing but light. She looked up and saw only light— everywhere only light. It was familiar and welcoming, like a morning sunrise.

Sound remained absent, gone was the roar of the car engine and the constant rush of wind past her ears. Gone too were the green hillsides and pastel blue French sky. There was only light and unexplainable peacefulness. Christine continued to walk, not knowing where she was or where she was going. Suddenly, a feeling emerged, one she couldn't explain. Christine was certain she was expected somewhere, but she had no idea where.

She walked a little farther when the image of a person appeared before her. Christine stopped but the image gestured her to come closer. She obeyed and approached until they stood face to face in silence. Christine stared at the image, desperately trying to identify it. But no matter how hard she tried, it remained out of focus. The appearance of the image unsettled her. *This can't be God*, she thought. The image awakened a fear never felt before, the fear that she had lost her faith.

Christine struggled with the fleeting images of her life as they flashed inside her mind. She saw her unwavering devotion to the Church and unquestionable faith in God crumble like a sandcastle in the wind. Unable to resist any longer, she let go of her fear—and her faith.

"Chris, what do you see?" Jasper asked.

"God."

Jasper didn't answer.

"Where am I?" she asked, never taking her eyes from the figure.

Jasper remained silent.

Doubt replaced the fear in Christine's mind, and she continued to question her faith. Standing alone with the figure she struggled to understand what was happening to her.

"Is it God?"

As if Christine were looking through the lens of a camera, the image slowly came into focus.

"Chris," whispered a familiar voice. "It's what you believe that matters."

The light surrounding Christine faded and then disappeared completely as her mother materialized in front of her.

Christine opened her eyes for the first time in her existence.

CHAPTER 28

A LOT OF MOUTHS TO FEED

A massive red and orange fireball shot into the air, obscuring the horizon as it traveled skyward. The car plowed into the back of the broken down recreation vehicle with the force of a rocket. Ignited by the impact, the propane tank exploded like dynamite, engulfing the BMW completely. Swallowed by the thick black smoke, the car disappeared into the darkness of the inferno while the police car screeched to a halt on the opposite shoulder and the helicopter hovered overhead.

"Take us closer. I want a better look," Tonino said.

The pilot lowered the aircraft toward the ground until Tonino raised his hand to indicate they were close enough.

Tonino's face glowed with satisfaction at the carnage below. Gino and Father Black leaned over so they could view the burning wreck.

"It wasn't immaculate," Tonino said, his face brimming from cheek to cheek with a smile.

"No," replied Father Black and Gino simultaneously.

"To the airport. We've got work to do," Tonino said to the pilot, and the helicopter rolled to the right, heading back to the airport.

***

Massive willow trees extended their branches over the

razor-sharp arrowheads pointing skyward from the top of the barrier. Water from the sprinklers glistened on the emerald lawn, flanking the outside of the eight-foot granite wall. The sun rose high above the Geneva skyline as the red Volvo slowly followed the contours of the wall along the private street.

Sunlight reflected off the golden manes of the two massive lion heads that faced each other on the ornate wrought-iron gates. A small camera was perched at the top of the stone pillar to the left, recording the arrival of the vehicle.

Holding his coffee in one hand and the steering wheel in the other, a tall, thin, middle-aged man turned the Volvo into the driveway just as the gates began to open. A red light flashed and a loud buzzing noise sounded when the car drove between the gates.

The medieval stone mansion was at the back of the acreage, hidden from view by the large Yew trees lining both sides of the meandering driveway. Resembling a castle more than a house, the building grew out of the manicured gardens from atop a small hill. The man parked next to the mansion and lifted the infant out of the partially opened linen sack resting on the passenger seat. He carried the child up the moss-covered stone steps leading to the front of the building.

A gently aged sixty-year-old man held the door half open, his short silver hair perfectly groomed and his kind hands expertly manicured as they pushed the door fully open. The sleeve of his business suit slid over a jewel encrusted watch when he lowered his hand to his side. A smile covered his face when he saw the infant's head poking out of the pastel green shirt wrapped around its body.

"Bring him in. She's been waiting for him."

A distinguished-looking woman rushed down the hallway, her footsteps echoing off the marble floor every time her heels made contact with it. As she ran, the movement knocked her dark brown hair out of place, covering the right side of her face and hiding the sparkle of her diamond earrings. Her normally refined demeanor was crushed by the excitement circulating through her body when she saw the tightly wrapped pale green shirt in the man's arms.

"Luca, give him to me, give me my son," Christine demanded, and she reached her hands out to take Gabriel from him.

Luca handed Gabriel to her, smiled and left the house.

Gabriel looked like a child's toy, no bigger than a doll a toddler would carry to bed at night. His skin glistened bright pink yet was wrinkled like an old man's. His hair lay matted to the top of his head but hung down from the side in curls. He looked like any other newborn child except for his eyes; they radiated light like two shimmering blue flames, casting a warm, peaceful feeling when you looked into them.

Christine supported the back of his head with her hand, letting it rest between her thumb and forefinger. She slowly lifted Gabriel to her chest, placing him just above her right breast.

Jasper smiled when he saw the two tiny birthmarks on the back of Gabriel's neck. One identical to his mother's and the other exactly like his father's; the two were joined in the middle, forming a perfect helix.

"I bet he's hungry," Jasper said, and he followed Christine down the hallway to the kitchen, stopping for moment to glance at the group of photographs hanging on the wall. Each displayed a teenaged image of Andrew Shannon, including one on a Hawaiian beach where he held a teenaged Sandra Anderson in his arms.

***

A faint clanging of church bells could be heard inside the small Vatican office. The thick Italian newspaper slammed the top of the antique wooden desk, creating a loud snap. The headline *'India Rethinking Its Ban On Abortion'* was clearly visible to Father Black and Gino.

While seated in his chair, Tonino shoved himself away from his desk. The rage was evident on his face and from his actions. He walked over to his window while holding his fingertips together and stared at the courtyard below in silence. Neither Father Black nor Gino dared let a word slip from their lips.

"That idiot—couldn't get one thing right," snapped Tonino, continuing to face the glass. "We've got to have the Indians on board. Who knows how long it'll take without them? Father Black, I'd like you to clean up Derksen's mess."

"At once," Father Black replied.

"I expect a better outcome this time."

"Of course."

Tonino moved his eyes so they locked with Gino's, who quickly directed his to the floor.

"I think it's time we put our expensive computer to work, don't you?"

"Right away... sir?"

"I want a list of the world's leading research scientists."

HUMAN

CHAPTER 1

CHANGE

L ooking into his eyes was like gazing into the abyss. Hollow and lifeless, they captured every ray of light that entered them but reflected none. Their blackness was made even darker by silvery-white eyebrows and matching brush-cut hair. His sixty-nine years were hidden in his youthful face and only evident in the color of his hair.

Tonino Fabro entered the noisy Vatican cafeteria and paused at the head of the long wooden table with a glowing white tablecloth. The clanking sound of coffee cups connecting with their saucers replaced the loud discussions that had filled the room seconds before. Tonino's gaze silenced the small room so only the snare drum tapping of rain on the terra cotta roof could be heard.

"Wonderful, everyone is here. Thank you for coming on such short notice. I trust everyone has removed their VisText and shut off their tablets?" he asked in perfect English except for a noticeable Italian accent. Tonino scanned the room and saw all but the oldest man at the far end of the table had placed a VisText in front of them. Like most people of his generation, the older man refused to use the device.

Tonino's request unleashed apprehension from all of the men except one, Father Sean Black. He was a stocky middle-aged Australian whose rapidly thinning strawberry-blonde hair gave him the appearance of a schoolteacher rather than a priest. He was the only one of the fifteen people sitting at the table who left his VisText on his ear.

"G'day, sir," Father Black replied, not attempting to hide his accent.

Tonino looked down at him, seated at the end of the table closest to him, and forced a smile to his lips, but he didn't answer. Father Black had worked at the Vatican for more than sixteen years, and he reported directly to Tonino, who controlled the Vatican Secret Service.

Tonino's reputation for intimidation was second only to Father Black's reputation for ruthlessness. The clandestine operation of the VSS had survived unchanged from the earliest days of the Church. Motivated by power, its influence remained unbound by borders or politics.

Before Tonino could continue, another voice interrupted the silence.

"Why do you bring us here again?" said an old man's voice, struggling to speak English through an Indian accent.

Tonino's eyes looked down the long table and focused on the elderly man beginning to stand with the aid of a polished walking stick. His frail body, decrepit with age, barely reached the feet of the life-sized crucifixion hanging from the wall behind him.

"I'm delighted you asked, Mr. Gill," Tonino replied lengthening the fake smile on his face. Unlike the other world religious leaders seated around the table, Mr. Gill was too old to be concerned about the price he would pay for questioning Tonino.

"We've done as you've told us for decades. Now, our people cannot feed themselves, we have nowhere to live; it only gets worse with the endless rain. Yet you demand we continue—why?" Mr. Gill complained.

Before Tonino could answer, a younger Asian man stood up and continued the dissension in a far less confrontational tone.

"The Democratic Republic of China is worse—we can't continue. I feel it is already too late; we've surpassed three billion people this year," the man said before quickly sitting down.

"Do the rest of you agree?" Tonino asked, searching the room with a menacing stare.

The room remained silent for a second, and then a short dark-skinned man stood up next to Mr. Gill. His navy blue business suit was in complete contrast to the bright orange and yellow Dhoti the man next to him wore. Speaking English with a slight accent, the man nervously addressed Tonino.

"With all due respect, Mr. Fabro, most of South America has become reliant on the handouts you provide, and I'm afraid Brazil will soon follow."

The remaining religious heads around the table nodded in agreement, and the two men took their seats.

"Don't concern yourselves; our scientists have developed new capacity in Canada, Egypt and Australia. We can now grow enough to feed double the current population."

"Are you mad?" shouted Mr. Gill. "It's not only food, there's no room! Where would thirty billion people live?"

"It's unnatural, and it's not what God intended for the earth," said the Brazilian man, shaking his head with the others in disbelief.

"I think it unwise to concern yourselves any further with this; I assure you, the Vatican will continue to provide for your people. Just as we look after you," Tonino snapped.

"Like you did for the others?" Mr. Gill replied, raising his voice and not hiding the sarcasm.

"What do you mean?" Tonino asked, casting a meaningful glare to the end of the table.

"My predecessor, those executives in the pharmaceutical companies, and all those workers in the water-bottling plants rotting away in jail—or dead."

"Ah yes, Mrs. Singh. It was unfortunate she did not agree with our ways. It saddened me to remove her from our Holy gathering. As for those others, I don't know to what you're referring. The Vatican had nothing to do with PharmaScam-2020. I can assure you, Mr. Gill, tainting the world's beverage supply with fertility drugs wouldn't be God's work, would it? It's also unnecessary since you've all dedicated your efforts to helping the Vatican complete the will of God."

Mr. Gill didn't waver in his accusations and pulled his glasses off his face, casting an equally meaningful stare back at Tonino.

"You've not answered my question. Why... Why does the Vatican, or as you say 'God,' wish it necessary to form such blight upon the earth?" Mr. Gill replied.

Tonino turned and faced Father Black, passing him a glance of indignation before addressing the table.

"Our world is on the cusp of an evolution," he said, methodically turning his eyes to meet his onlookers. "But there are those among us who wish to destroy everything. They're malicious beings, preying on the living, using them as hosts to do their bidding," he continued while pausing for the group to show reaction to his declaration.

"You can't see them... or touch them... but make no mistake, they do exist. They'll infect us without notice; taking over our minds. They communicate without speaking and move among us undetected, spreading like a virus. They're not of this earth. Only the devil could conjure something so insidious."

"This can't be so! Blasphemy!" cried the Brazilian, unable to restrain the power of his Catholic convictions.

The rest of the table erupted in jeers of confusion and disbelief.

Tonino leaned over the edge of the table, placing both hands on its surface. His movement was a signal for the group to silence their outburst so he could continue.

"Listen to me! Mankind is about to change forever, and if we don't stop them, everything will be lost."

"Who do you speak of?" asked Mr. Gill, clearly not

convinced of the satanic doom implied by Tonino.

"They call themselves 'Primoris,'" Tonino said, expecting an immediate response from the group.

The religious leaders said nothing, remaining transfixed on Tonino as if hypnotized by his words.

Surprised by their silence and lack of reaction, Tonino continued, "They spread through the universe infecting life like a disease, taking over our minds and leaving us an empty shell of who we were. There is no way of knowing where they are; who or what they'll infect next. It could be a bird outside your window, a dog running in the park or the person sitting next to you," he said, shifting his glare to Mr. Gill.

"This is nonsense... You're mad... What are you talking about...?" said multiple voices from the group, filling the room with incoherent chatter.

A loud crack startled the room into silence. Mr. Gill slammed his walking stick on the top of the table, knocking the coffee cups off their saucers on both sides of him. With the entire group's attention focused on him, he lifted the stick off the table and spoke.

"What do these Primoris want with us?"

"They require humans to make more of their kind."

"If this is true, then how do we stop them?" Mr. Gill demanded.

"Some of you may remember sixteen years ago, Mr. Gill. I'm certain you do," Tonino said, looking deep into Mr. Gill's eyes before continuing.

"The young couple we scoured the earth to find. They were Vectors created by the Primoris. The Primoris planted a genetic seed inside their DNA. That is how they infect us. If we hadn't found them and destroyed them, they would have spread their infection, causing an unstoppable pandemic."

"But you found these Vectors—so this threat is no more. What's the reason for drastically increasing the earth's population?" the Brazilian asked.

"I'd expect you to know better than any of the others. It's

God's will: '*Be fruitful and increase in number; fill the earth and subdue it,*'" Tonino said, quoting the Bible and parting his lips to form a smile.

"No, I don't understand," replied the Brazilian, shaking his head.

"The Primoris will return; it's just a matter of time. Mankind's only chance of surviving the pandemic is by '*increasing our numbers.*' The more humans there are, the greater the likelihood God will give us immunity."

"You mean a mutation," Mr. Gill said.

"This isn't the time to discuss whether it's Creationism or Evolution."

"How do we know who is infected, one of these Primoris?" the Brazilian asked.

"You will see it in their eyes. All those infected by the Primoris will have crystal-blue eyes."

"How will we know when they have returned?" Mr. Gill asked.

"Leave that to me."

This agitated the Indian. The wrinkles surrounding his eyes disappeared and his eyes exploded with anger.

"I don't believe any of this nonsense!" he said, slamming his stick on the table again. "It is rubbish! The Vatican wants all of us to believe this so they can continue increasing their numbers and coffers. I think you exploded the population by adding fertility drugs to everyday products. The PharmaScam-2020 investigators were right; the Vatican did marry big business to secure the future of Catholicism. More people means more Catholics, and more mouths to feed, clothes to buy, houses to build and most of all, more profit for business. This explains the insurgence of Catholics over the last decade in India and China. Did you realize it would push our planet into an environmental death spiral? Did you care?"

Tonino fired his glare across the room like a bullet from a rifle.

"I'm disappointed to hear you no longer support our efforts. Does anyone else agree with Mr. Gill?"

Tonino stepped back from the head of the table, looked down at Father Black and curled the right side of his mouth to form half a smirk.

Father Black stood up and reached into the breast of his suit coat, removing a small shiny metallic device from his pocket resembling a child's toy gun. He adjusted the small round dial on the top of the device before pointing it toward the far end of the table.

A crimson red beam of light, the thickness of a pencil, struck Mr. Gill directly between the eyes, splitting his glasses in two before exiting the back of his head. His body folded forward, collapsing face-first onto the bleached white tablecloth. No blood spilled from the holes in his head left by the laser; the intense heat generated by the light disintegrated the flesh as it passed through. The air was filled with the putrid smell of burned hair and flesh.

The group sat stupefied by the sudden murder of one of their members.

"Thank you, Father Black," said Tonino while Father Black returned the laser to his pocket and took his seat.

"Is there's anyone else who would like to voice their concerns?" Tonino asked while scanning the room with a large smile on his face.

"Excellent, I'm pleased to know the Vatican can still count on your support."

ABOUT THE AUTHOR

 As a young boy growing up in the Okanagan Valley in beautiful British Columbia, Canada, Mark spent most of his youth roaming the surrounding hills looking for the next perfect fly-fishing opportunity. His love of nature and the outdoors influenced his education, and Mark went on to complete a Bachelor of Science degree from the University of Windsor and a graduate diploma in Environmental Toxicology from Simon Fraser University.

Now a senior scientist working for the Canadian government for more than twenty-five years, Mark conducts cutting-edge research on new and emerging environmental issues. He has traveled the globe extensively, speaking at scientific conferences and presenting his research. Mark has published many scientific papers but *The Convergence Series* represents his first work of fiction. When asked what made him want to write fiction, Mark replied, "Because my sons asked me to." Mark still resides in British Columbia with his two boys, where they enjoy trolling the waters of the Pacific Northwest in search of that elusive Tyee.

THE CONVERGENCE SERIES

Please visit www.MarkSekela.com for details about the
other books in the Convergence Series.